The
Marvelous Adventures
of
GWENDOLYN
GRAY

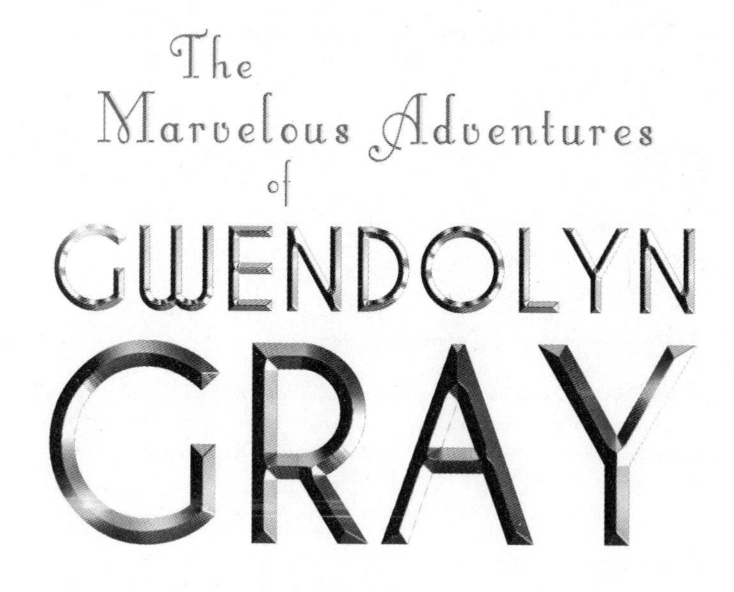

B. A. WILLIAMSON

Mendota Heights, Minnesota

First Edition
First Printing, 2018

Book design by Sarah Winkler
Cover design by Jake Nordby
Cover illustration by Sanjay Charlton

Jolly Fish Press, an imprint of North Star Editions, Inc.

Library of Congress Cataloging-in-Publication Data
Names: Williamson, B. A., author
Title: The marvelous adventures of Gwendolyn Gray / B.A. Williamson.
Description: First edition. | Mendota Heights, Minnesota : Jolly Fish Press, [2018] |
Summary: "Gwendolyn evades thought police, enters a whimsical world, befriends world-jumping explorers and ragtag airship pirates, and fights the evil threatening to erase the new world she loves and her old world that never wanted her"— Provided by publisher.
Identifiers: LCCN 2018000601 (print) | LCCN 2017055805 (ebook) | ISBN 9781631631733 (hosted e-book) | ISBN 9781631631726 (pbk. : alk. paper)
Subjects: | CYAC: Fantasy. | Imagination—Fiction. | Adventure and adventurers—Fiction.
Classification: LCC PZ7.1.W555 (print) | LCC PZ7.1.W555 Mar 2018 (ebook) | DDC [Fic] —dc23
LC record available at https://lccn.loc.gov/2018000601

Jolly Fish Press
North Star Editions, Inc.
2297 Waters Drive
Mendota Heights, MN 55120
www.jollyfishpress.com

Printed in the United States of America

For Theodore, the reason for it all.
And for the oddlings, who need it most.

A TABLE OF CONTENTS

PART ONE: GREY

PART TWO: GOLD

PART THREE: RED

PART ONE: GREY

CHAPTER ONE

Things That Begin . . .

Once upon a time, in the City of No Stories, Gwendolyn Gray ran away. Her mother yelled, "Gwendolyn, wait! Stop!" But as usual, Gwendolyn didn't listen. Her too-tight shoes pinched her feet as they slapped the pavement between identical boxy skyscrapers.

Though you may have read a story or two before, Gwendolyn had not. She had never heard any "once upon a times," nor any "dark and stormy nights" for that matter, and as for this "best of times, worst of times" business, she would say this morning was certainly one of the worst. This morning was *awful.* This morning . . . wasn't really all that different, then.

She barreled past startled pedestrians and ducked into an alley, watching as her mother sprinted past. Gwendolyn didn't know where she was running to. Not far, probably. She never ran far, and like most of you who have ever tried to run away, she always went home as soon as she got hungry.

It had started like any other morning. She'd woken up late

and begun the usual routine of not doing anything right, followed by her daily argument with her mother.

"Mother, must I go to the School today? What if I came with you? We could explore the City together!" she said. "What if we found a secret passageway and met some sort of friendly animal, like a badger—a real badger, not just the kind we see in books at the School? Oh, and what if he took us home for tea! I think it would be just wonderful to have tea with a badger. I wonder what type of tea badgers drink? Though I suppose it would be awfully hard to hold a cup with such long claws—"

"Gwendolyn, you're babbling again."

"But the School is so terribly boring, and everyone hates me," she moaned.

"Don't exaggerate. Everyone doesn't hate you."

Gwendolyn was *not* exaggerating. "Mr. Percival hates me, the students hate me, and Cecilia Forthright *completely* hates me. What if we just—"

"I don't have time for your *what-ifs* today, so come back to earth please. If we get another poor report from Mr. Percival, there will be serious consequences. Come along!"

Mr. Percival could go boil his head for all Gwendolyn cared. She did try to keep her thoughts to herself, she truly did, but it seemed that whenever she opened her mouth they all tumbled out at once.

The two of them left the house together, Mother determined to see Gwendolyn safely on the monorail to the School.

Unlike the rest of the City, Gwendolyn was a clever noticer. While the other grey-suited pedestrians trudged along with heads down and faces grim, Gwendolyn was noticing the way the clouds reflected perfectly in the mirrored skyscrapers. She was so busy noticing that she ran right into a heavyset woman waiting at the monorail station.

The woman shot her a scowl. "Watch it." Though you have never been to Gwendolyn's city, you have surely seen this type of grown-up before, the sort who believe that children should be neither seen nor heard.

Mother gave Gwendolyn a warning look.

"Sorry," mumbled Gwendolyn.

The woman took a long look at Gwendolyn's hair, like everyone else she'd ever met. It was riotous red, a massive tangle of curls. You see, in all the metal and stone of the City, Gwendolyn was the only spark of color. She stood out like a bonfire.

The woman *harrumph*ed and spun around again. Gwendolyn tried not to be bothered. She liked her hair. She liked it wild and long and didn't want the same pale-blonde or jet-black hair as everyone else in the City. But just because she liked being different didn't mean she had to like the endless taunts and teases, the stares that followed her down the street.

Eventually the train arrived, with a *screech,* then a *hiss,* then a chime. The doors slid open and the line shuffled forward, but Gwendolyn noticed something moving on the ground. A grey mouse scampered around the trampling feet. The tiny thing looked terrified to Gwendolyn's noticing eye.

And the large, unpleasant woman was about to step on it.

"Look out!" Gwendolyn shoved the woman, hard, though the only available shoving surface was the woman's rather ample backside. The woman stumbled with a bark of surprise. The mouse scuttled away and disappeared.

"Gwendolyn!" Mother hissed in horror.

The woman turned and glared at Gwendolyn with all the warmth of a glacier. "What do you think you're doing?"

"I'm sorry, miss, but you were about to–"

"Shoving old ladies at the train stop? That's what you hooligans do for fun, eh? Children these days, they aren't what they were in my time!"

Mother was aghast. "Gwendolyn, what do you have to say to her?"

"I already said I'm sorry, but there was a mouse, and she–"

"No *buts*! Just apologize."

Gwendolyn knew the routine. Grown-ups never wanted the facts, they just wanted to see you look sorry. She let her shoulders sag. "I'm sorry," she droned.

The woman wagged a finger at Gwendolyn's mother. "Keep your brat under control. And fix that hair of hers. Cover it, or cut it, or something. It's indecent."

Mother blushed. "Well, I don't know about all *that*. I mean, I did tell her to braid it this morning, Gwendolyn, didn't I? How many times have I told you not to leave it such a mess and . . . Gwendolyn, wait! Stop!"

But that had done it. Gwendolyn sprinted down the street, her face as red as her hair. She didn't stop to consider the consequences. She never had before and didn't see a reason to start.

And so she ran, hurtling down the City's walkways, pushing

past gawking grown-ups, ignoring the pointing children. She didn't care, and didn't slow down.

Gwendolyn dashed around a corner and ducked into an alley. She pressed herself against the wall and watched Mother run past, which brings us to where we entered this tale.

A few deep breaths helped loosen the knot in her chest. She sank down and sat against the wall. A flicker of movement caught her eye, and she saw the little grey mouse, snuffling around the base of the wall.

"Oh. Hello again, you little devil. This is all your fault, you know?" She loved animals, though there weren't many in the City, save for the crows and the mice and the cats that chased them.

She thought the poor thing looked rather hungry. She dug in her satchel and brought out the sandwich from her lunch, then put it on the ground. "Here you go. You need it more than I do."

The mouse darted over and started nibbling the pale, grey bread and bland, white cheese. Food in the City was none too appetizing. "You need to be more careful. People around here don't like you at all," Gwendolyn said, though she was unsure whether she was talking to the mouse or herself.

Gwendolyn glared up between the buildings at the always-cloudy sky. It reminded her of the itchy wool sweater Mother often forced her to wear. She hated that sweater, and she hated that sky. If she was going to run away, she was certainly not going to stay here in the City, under that gloomy mess.

She furrowed her brow in concentration, and beams of yellow light pierced the clouds. Grass began to grow, carpeting the walkway. Branches sprouted from the buildings. Streetlights burst into leafy saplings, telephone wires twisted themselves into ropey vines, and a passerby in a black suit burst into colorful feathers and flew away. Suddenly, she was alone in her own lush and magnificent forest.

"There," she said to the mouse. "Much better."

Though it might seem unusual to you, a forest in the middle of the City was no new thing to clever Gwendolyn. She conjured such outrageous landscapes several times a day. Unlike the rest of the City, Gwendolyn's problem was turning her imagination *off*.

She inhaled deeply, imagining how the woodland air must smell. Yes, this was exactly what she needed. She wandered through the woods, watching a rabbit chased by a bright-red fox scamper across the dirt path. The fox would never catch the rabbit of course, not here in Gwendolyn's world, but she enjoyed filling it with all the animals and things she had seen in her books.

Yes, even in the City there were books. But as anyone who has sat through a tedious mathematics lesson can tell you, *books* and *stories* are not always the closest of friends. And the City's pages were full of nothing but cold and dreary facts.

Nevertheless, Gwendolyn read everything she could plunder from the City's Hall of Records. In truth, she probably knew the City better than anyone, especially since she hardly ever saw anyone reading anything besides the City's daily newspaper. But the more she read, the more it sparked her imagination, and the more trouble she got in.

The rabbit escaped back into its hole, as it always did, leaving a disgruntled fox snuffling around the entrance.

For the first time that morning, Gwendolyn smiled, a smile that lit up the whole forest.

And she continued her run, but now with much less *away*. She sprinted along the leafy ground, hair blazing out behind her. She turned a cartwheel. She jumped and grabbed a branch, just to feel the bark under her palms and hear the leaves rustle. Yes, this would certainly be worth any trouble she might suffer when she went back.

A ripple of laughter reached her ears. Surprised, she dropped from the branch and spun around.

A pair of brown eyes peered at her through the leaves.

There was another giggle and a flash of yellow cloth, and the eyes disappeared with a rustle of leaves and a snapping of twigs. Gwendolyn heard the voices of two children where she had certainly not meant to imagine any.

"Hello!" she shouted. "Wait! Come back!" She tried to follow, but a cluster of thorn bushes blocked her way. Gwendolyn would not let that stop her. She pushed through the bushes, heedless of their scratch and tug. There was a flicker of blue up ahead, and she glimpsed a pair of children running through the trees, children that had no business being in her private world.

Gwendolyn's green eyes widened. She plowed through the underbrush, climbing logs and ducking vines. She followed the laughter until she burst into a clearing and nearly fell headlong into a wide, roaring river. She tottered over the raging foam, her arms windmilling as she struggled not to fall. The roar of the water held her frozen to the spot.

Mother's voice broke through the spell. "Gwendolyn! Gwendolyn Alice Gray, get back, you'll be hurt!"

Names have a certain kind of power, particularly middle ones, as your parents doubtless know when they call you in from playing in the street. Hearing her own made Gwendolyn snap immediately to attention. She turned and saw Mother, running as best she could in heels. Behind her, the City rippled back into existence like a dog shaking itself of water. Gone were the trees and leaves and animals, replaced by skyscrapers, lampposts, and Cityzens. The wonder and excitement were gone, crushed under the weight of being in trouble, which pulled her stomach into her shoes.

Gwendolyn turned toward the water and stumbled backward as she saw that she was no longer standing on the banks of a mighty river, but was instead on the ledge of one of the City's monorail tracks, teetering over the gap. An automated tram hurtled toward her.

Mother pulled her to safety just as the mono sped by, the wind whipping Gwendolyn's hair into a fiery frenzy. "What do you think you are doing? The City is no place to rush around! You were nearly killed!"

But Gwendolyn was too distracted to listen. She whipped around, but there were no mysterious children in sight. She sighed and resigned herself to dull reality once more. Mother was clutching her as though she'd never let go again.

"I thought we were past all this childish behavior. You can't keep running away like that! Remember the time you ran away after you let out all of Mr. Blythe and Mr. Reginald's cats? It took hours to find you!"

There was a crack in the sidewalk that suddenly grew very interesting. Gwendolyn stared fixedly at it. At the time, she had been firmly convinced that there was an underground civilization of wild felines. But that explanation did not exactly convince the grown-ups.

At Gwendolyn's forlorn expression, Mother softened slightly. She truly loved her daughter, but poor Marie Gray was not at all certain how to handle a girl who was so . . . different. She would lie awake at night and wonder what was to be done, and scold herself for all the times she had been too harsh with Gwendolyn. Parents are worried and tired creatures, so we should not be too harsh with Marie, either.

She sighed. "An imaginary mouse is a poor excuse for getting hit by a train. You can't keep letting your imagination run away with you, or the other way around. It's time for you to act your age, you're nearly thirteen—"

"I'm *twelve*," Gwendolyn corrected. "I'm not thirteen yet." She dug her heels in at the passing of each year, as if she could slow time by sheer force of will, dreading the inevitable day when she would be forced to become a Lady, and get a Job, or worse yet, a Husband.

She shuddered at the thought. She didn't *want* to grow up. She didn't want to be a lady—ladies were boring. She much preferred running and exploring and getting dirty to whatever it was her mother did all day. "I did see a mouse."

"Fine. No more trouble today?"

Gwendolyn sighed, for she loved Mother as well, and now that she'd settled down, she knew how foolish she'd been. Not that she'd admit it. "No trouble today. I'll do my best, I swear."

"That's all I can ask. But whatever did you get yourself into?" Mother pointed to several mysterious scratches on Gwendolyn's knees and a tear in her school jacket. "And if your hair wasn't bad enough before, it's positively frightful now." She made a doomed attempt to fix the tangled mess. "What's this?" she said, pulling at something.

And from those bedraggled curls, Gwendolyn's mother plucked a single, impossible, emerald leaf.

CHAPTER TWO

The Lambent

Mother stared at the leaf in shock, having never seen such a thing before. Her mouth hung open. Then she shook her head as if clearing away a cobweb.

"Look at that. You've got litter in your hair. Come along, we'll have to walk. No time to wait for the next train. It'll be a miracle if we aren't late." She crumpled up the leaf and tossed it aside. Her heels clicked disapprovingly down the street once more, her platinum hair tight in its perfect bun.

Gwendolyn glanced back at the leaf, a fragile green speck alone in the grey. She lost sight of it under the herd of pedestrians. Finally, she turned away.

As we know, Gwendolyn was a clever noticer. But clever as she was, she did not see the two men in bowler hats. She did not see them carefully inspect the leaf. And she certainly did not see one of them crush the leaf into grey powder under his black heel.

She merely shuddered as a shadow passed over her, though the day was as overcast and shadowless as always.

~~~

Much more quickly than was fair, they reached the School. Gwendolyn was patted and preened and bid goodbye, and then she was alone on the steps of the massive building. It was more than a hundred stories high and several blocks long, pockmarked with the squinty sort of windows that seem to be trying to keep light out, rather than let it in.

Every child from all three sections of the City was required to attend. Wealthier students lived in the Central City, clustered around the domed Central Tower. The Middling formed a ring around the center, and the Outskirts was the farthest ring of all, where poorer students had to travel hours by mono just to attend. Gwendolyn was a Middling, close enough to walk, but only just.

Thousands of children swarmed around her, each in identical uniforms: grey skirt or slacks, charcoal jacket, and a pair of shiny, black shoes. Gwendolyn hated those shoes. No matter how many pairs Mother made her try on, they always pinched her toes.

As you might imagine, the School was a bit different than any school you might attend. While your school likely tries to help children think and learn, Gwendolyn's school was designed to prepare children for the boredom of adult life by stripping them of any individual ideas or creativity.

She walked through orderly corridors that smelled of floor wax, but all her thoughts were on the impossible leaf. How had
~~~

her mother seen it? To Gwendolyn's twelve-year-old mind, the answer was obvious, but completely impossible. She had *made* it real. That didn't explain the *how* of it, but her imagination had actually become solid enough for Mother to touch. If she could create things from her imagination, make them real . . .

The crowded elevator ride was as long as ever, though for once Gwendolyn didn't mind, her thoughts tied up in knots. But all too soon she found herself at room 1253. On her tiptoes, she could look through the door's narrow slit of a window, and saw the students behaving as they usually did with no teacher around: pushing, shoving, teasing. They resembled a troop of monkeys at a zoo, though Gwendolyn herself knew of no such thing.

Gwendolyn groaned. "If that is what acting your age looks like, then I don't want any part of it." Bracing herself, she entered the plain, grey room of thirty desks in perfect rows.

Cecilia Forthright's perky voice broke through the noise. "Cartblatt, are you wearing a bra? Whatever do you need one of *those* for? Is it decorative, or just wishful thinking?" A gaggle of giggles followed.

Cecilia was the richest, prettiest, most popular girl in class, and so of course she was the most awful. She smiled like a hungry lioness with a mane of perfect blonde hair. She loomed over the desk of a shabby girl from the Outskirts.

It was Missy Cartblatt, with long, pale hair, clothes two sizes too large, and a tendency to twitch. A gang of Cecilia's Central friends were clustered around, snickering.

Gwendolyn's hands clenched into fists, but she had promised Mother. No trouble today.

"Oh my god, it *is* a bra!" Cecilia hooked a finger under Missy's baggy collar and stretched out an elastic strap for all to see. Missy jerked backwards, and Cecilia let go with an audible *snap*.

This was too much. Gwendolyn reasoned that being good surely meant helping someone in trouble. "Cecilia," she called, "just because Armand goes around playing with *your* bra doesn't give you the right to mess with Missy's. And you wouldn't want to make him jealous, would you?"

"Oooooooo," said the other students, like monkeys hooting before a fight.

Cecilia blushed and exchanged an involuntary glance with the dark-skinned Armand, who stood next to her. The other students caught their guilty look and laughed.

Bull's-eye, Gwendolyn thought.

The tall, blonde bully glowered and shoved Gwendolyn. She fell, nearly splitting her head on a desk, and sprawled on the linoleum.

"Watch your step, oddling. You should, you know, pay more attention." Her pretty features twisted into a snarl, her nose so high in the air it was a wonder she could see. With a flip of her hair, she turned back to her snickering friends.

Gwendolyn flew to her feet, mouth loaded with awful words like live ammunition, but Mother's warning rang in her ears. And Father had been very clear about what would happen if she was caught using *that* sort of language again, and it would certainly involve the especially nasty-tasting soap.

So in a rare moment of self-control, she kept her mouth

shut. She stared at Cecilia, imagining what it would be like if her pretty hair suddenly caught fire, just a *little*. She tried to make it real, like the leaf from that morning. But Cecilia's head remained stubbornly not-on-fire.

Cecilia caught her glare and gave her a disgusted look. "What are you staring at, freak? Go away. I know you're like, in love with me, but control yourself."

"Yeah, oddling, just go sit back down," grumbled Missy, jumping at the chance to be predator rather than prey.

Gwendolyn stammered, "I-I was just trying to help."

Missy sniffed. "Nobody wants your help. You just make everything worse."

Gwendolyn's anger dissolved, and she trudged to the back corner of the room, struggling to block out the jeers of her classmates as she went.

"What a weirdy!"

"God, she's *so* immature."

"And she's always talking to that tree in the yard."

She slumped behind her desk and waited for the taunts to die out. "Hello, desk. Hello, chair. It's us against the world again, I suppose." She opened the desktop and stowed her bag inside. The desk gave a sympathetic creak, and the chair did its best to be supportive.

Gwendolyn hid behind her open desktop. What had she been thinking? Had she really thought she could set Cecilia's hair on fire just by wishing it?

"Maybe the leaf *was* just a bit of rubbish. Maybe Mother is right and I let my imagination run away with me," she murmured to her desk. "Though if you tell her I said that, I'll never speak to you again."

She got out her sketchbook and pencil box, her favorite possessions. The sketchbook was covered in her initials, a complicated little symbol she had created with one looping, swirling G wrapped inside another.

Her elaborate pencil box had every shade available—light grey, dark grey, medium grey, charcoal, ivory, smoke, ash, and a dozen other shades. It had taken three months of begging Father to get it, but he was soft on his daughter and always gave in eventually. She remembered how excited she'd been when he gave it to her, all wrapped in its silky, white bow, his mustache twitching with fatherly pride.

Drawing was the only thing Gwendolyn felt truly good at, and it helped calm her down and slow her thoughts to normal speed. Hiding behind the open desk, she imagined she was safe in her own little fortress.

And so a fortress appeared on her paper, with lots of towers and funny bits on the walls that looked like teeth. It was called a castle, she remembered from some obscure architecture book. A paper Gwendolyn laughed from a tower window as her sketchy classmates hurled themselves against its walls. Gwendolyn laughed along, muttering the story to herself.

"Whatcha doin', Freckles?" A pale, dirty face peeked over the top of the open desk.

Tommy Ungeroot had greasy blond hair, a bulbous nose, and teeth that were slightly too big for his head.

"I'm minding my own business is what I'm doing, and it

is ever so much fun that I suggest you try it, if you please and thank you very much." She tried to close her desktop, but he held it open.

"You were talkin' to your desk again," he jeered in his Outskirts accent. "Weirdy. Whatcha scribblin'?" He snatched the drawing up.

"It's nothing! Just a stupid doodle, give it back!" She grabbed for it, but he held it out of her reach.

"It's rubbish is what it is. Bor-ing."

"A truly clever person is never bored. They have everything they need right between their ears." She was quite proud of this saying, and had it written on the inside cover of her sketchbook.

"Oh, that's jiffy for you. There's enough empty space 'tween your ears to turn cartwheels!" He crumpled the drawing and dropped it back in her desk.

"Well, your head is far too thick for any decent ideas to fit through," she shot back. "Perhaps you'd find room for something useful if you washed out all the dirt first!"

It was at that moment that Gwendolyn noticed how quiet the room was. She looked around. Mr. Percival was standing at the head of the class, giving her that withering look only teachers and parents seem able to manage. Twenty-nine students stared at her.

The balding little man waddled to his desk. "Well, it seems we are ready to start the day. That is, unless Ms. Gray has any more enlightening comments on hygiene to share with us first?"

Gwendolyn tried to make herself small. "No, Mr. Percival."

"Good. Then let us begin."

He pulled a list from his desk, and scrunched up his pug nose as he read it aloud. “Anders?” he called.

“Present.”

“Barbington?”

“Present.”

“Cartblatt?”

“Present.”

Mr. Percival knew quite well that all the students were present, as every desk was occupied. But he was a fanatic for order and procedure.

Gwendolyn’s eyes wandered to the window. The School building was a perfect square with a small dirt courtyard in the center, which was always in shadow from the towering building. The School thought it terribly unfair that any grown-up should be forced to spend their day surrounded by grubby little children, so every day the teachers were given recess to relax in their cozy lounge, and the children were sent to the dreary schoolyard.

“Coleridge?”

“Present.”

She saw the scraggly grey tree down in the corner. A trunk and limbs had somehow clawed their way from the dirt, the tree’s branches forever bare. She sat alone under it every day, but now she tried to picture someone else sitting under it with her. Perhaps those two children she had glimpsed in the forest.

And suddenly, something moved against the glass.

There, on the tiny concrete windowsill, were two colorful birds. One was small and reddish-brown, with a yellow stripe around its throat. The other was larger and shimmering blue-green, its underside a vibrant orange. They sang in a way Gwendolyn had never heard—musical and sweet, not the harsh caw of the City's crows. She was transfixed.

"Finkmeyer?"

"Present."

They had learned all about music, of course, but only in theory. All the music in the City was such dreary droning that no one ever bothered with it. This was quite the sweetest sound she had ever heard. The melody came clearly through the glass, and as it washed over her, she forgot all about the troubles of the morning.

"Gray?"

She listened to the tune, and made up a bit of nonsense verse to go with it. She murmured quietly to herself:

"Sparrow and starling, darrow and darling,
wander along the way.
Hither and yon, but never far gone,
they always come out to play.
Hey, ho, here we go,
they always come out to play."

"Gwendolyn Gray!"

"She's miles away, Professor! Best mark her absent!"

"Her brain's certainly absent. She's all hair."

A roar of laughter brought Gwendolyn back to her senses, and she shrank lower in her seat. "Present," she mumbled. She vowed again not to draw attention to herself. Head down, nose to the grindstone, all the sayings Father liked. She looked back to the window. The two birds had vanished.

"Just imagining things again. But that doesn't mean they weren't real," she reasoned, whispering to her desk. "A leaf. A pair of birds. How terribly curious."

Gwendolyn looked up and caught Tommy staring at her. He whipped back around, blushing. Gwendolyn rolled her eyes. Sometimes that boy was even stranger than she was.

Mr. Percival finished the roll. "All right, students. Take out your Lambents," he commanded.

Gwendolyn stopped humming, and her happiness fluttered away as quick as any bird. Of all the various torments the School had to offer each day, the Lambent was the worst.

Mr. Percival flipped off the lights and the students each took a small, round bead out of their desks. Each Lambent was the size of a large marble, smooth and clear as cold water. The beads fit perfectly into an indentation at the front of their desks.

The students grew quiet, staring hungrily at their Lambents. A familiar sick feeling rose in Gwendolyn's stomach. She reluctantly took out her own Lambent but refused to look into it.

The Lambents began to shine with a cold, white light, brighter and brighter until the dark room was filled with a shimmering gleam. The glowing beads painted the children's faces with ghostly patterns. The students grew slack-jawed and glassy-eyed, drinking in the light, mesmerized.

They would sit this way for the entire morning, every child on every floor. It had long ago been decided that teaching was too important to be trusted to mere teachers, and too awful to be forced on poor adults, so the Lambents were used to transmit knowledge directly, without mucking about with all that messy learning.

None of the students knew how the Lambents worked, and of course none of the adults did either, though they would never say so out loud. It was simply the Way It Had Always Been Done, and that was as good as any law in the City. Whenever tests rolled around, the students all had the answers in their heads, so none of the children complained. The Lambents also made the students quiet and manageable, so none of the adults complained either.

Gwendolyn never looked into the glowing bead anymore. Ever since she was little, it had hurt her eyes, made them itch, and given her a vicious headache. Consequently, Gwendolyn rarely knew the answers on tests. With all her reading, she knew more things than any other child in the room, and she was really quite bright. But it never seemed to be the sorts of things the teachers wanted her to know. She got poor grades at the School, which her parents could not explain and her teachers never let her forget.

She spent most mornings with her eyes squeezed shut, blocking out both the Lambent and the eerie classroom around her. Thirty blank faces, mouths open and eyes unblinking for hours at a time, gave her the willies. If you've ever glanced around at the movie theater, you will understand the feeling. So every day Gwendolyn had long hours to fill with nothing but her imagination, and her imagination had grown quite powerful indeed.

Quietly, she stowed her Lambent back in her desk, and tried to block out the pounding in her head by drawing.

"I'm sorry I called you a stupid doodle," she whispered to it, smoothing out the crumpled paper. To make it up to the poor thing, she spent a while shading the bricks on her castle. She added an ashy grey sun to the top of her paper, but that didn't seem to fit. The clouds hadn't broken in decades, and she had never seen the sun herself, but whatever color it was, she supposed it wasn't grey. She held a rather one-sided conversation with her desk and chair.

Now, talking to objects is problematic at best. As a lonely little girl, she had begun talking to whatever would listen. She was older now, and knew it was a silly thing that made any other twelve-year-old practically allergic to her friendship, but she was stubborn, and she liked silly things, so it was worth doing.

Mr. Percival stared into his own Lambent at the front of the class. Gwendolyn liked to imagine that he was a grumpy little badger, teaching the class from atop a spotted toadstool. She had never seen a badger, of course, but they had learned about them from Lists, which they spent every afternoon memorizing.

No one understood why the children were given lists of things like animals and airplanes and oceans and were forced to memorize their names and pictures. None of those things seemed to be around anymore, and every time Gwendolyn asked what happened to them all, she was met with glazed expressions and told not to ask silly questions. The children were taught their animals like you and I are taught our fairy tales, and who's to say that dragons and witches are any less real than foxes and badgers?

The School was full of things that children Ought To Know, even if they would never need to know them. No one could say why knowing the difference between a participle and a gerund was essential to becoming an accountant or tax lawyer or button manufacturer. But again, that was The Way It Had Always Been Done.

So she imagined. She imagined Mr. Badger-val giving lectures to a class of forest animals, calling on critters who raised their paws. Gwendolyn imagined herself as a lovely red squirrel, admiring her fabulously bushy tail.

In her mind she went down the rows, turning each student into a different creature: Amy Fletcher into a deer, Cecilia Forthright into a shrew, Armand Barbington into a weasel. She took great pleasure in imagining Tommy Ungeroot as a rat with large buck teeth. Lastly, her eyes settled on Missy Cartblatt. Gwendolyn imagined her as a rabbit, with long, furry ears instead of long, pale hair.

Gwendolyn the squirrel looked over the forest schoolroom and decided that *she* should be the teacher. At once, the woodland students turned toward her. Then, just as she began a lesson on the finer points of tail grooming, she was interrupted by a horrifying scream.

The forest vanished, and she looked around. No one was watching their Lambents anymore. Missy Cartblatt leapt from her chair and was screaming fit to burst, her hands frantically beating about her head.

Then Gwendolyn saw the problem.

Growing out of Missy's head were two long, white rabbit ears, as floppy and velvety as you please.

CHAPTER THREE

Curiouser and Curiouser

Chaos erupted, as the sight of a girl with rabbit ears will easily overwhelm the fragile self-control of any child. Students around Missy leapt up and ran to the back of the room. Other children began to scream as well. A flustered Mr. Percival waddled over and tried to examine her without getting walloped as she continued to thrash, ears flopping left and right. He finally managed to get his arms around the screaming girl and escort her to the door.

"I-I-I'm taking her to the nurse. Or-or-or the headmaster," he stammered. "I-I don't know. Just, oh, class dismissed!" And he rushed her out of the room, leaving the students in turmoil.

Gwendolyn had an ever-so-slight feeling that she might be to blame.

Of course you're to blame, you stupid girl, she grew flopping rabbit ears! she scolded herself. The class lost themselves in a fog of gossip, and Gwendolyn took the opportunity to grab her satchel and rush out the door.

She was the first one to the row of elevators at the end of the hall, and once the doors of the drab metal box had closed she tried to sort her racing thoughts. Had she seen it right? Was it even possible? Was Missy okay? She was not sure what the School's nurse could do for a student who'd grown rabbit ears.

"Maybe Missy will like them," she said. "They are rather lovely ears, after all."

There are no lies quite as astounding as the ones we tell to make ourselves feel better. But deep down, Gwendolyn was racked with guilt, and her head was reeling.

She exited the elevator and walked down the silent hall. The other classes were still in session, since no one else had grown any new appendages. She emerged onto the cloudy street and hid behind the massive front doors, listening as her classmates swarmed out of the building moments later.

They were all chattering about it, but none of them could say for sure what *it* was. It had happened so fast, they said. But they had all seen something furry on Missy's head. Gwendolyn listened carefully for any mention of her name, but soon they all agreed that a rat must have fallen from the ceiling and landed in Missy's hair. Something really should be done about the state of the School, they said, it was in such terrible disrepair it might as well be in the Outskirts.

No one mentioned Gwendolyn. She was safe, she decided, and stepped forward to join the crowd. She passed some Outskirts kids who were clustered around a glowing bead and laughing. These Lambents were School property, and it was forbidden to take them from School grounds, but everyone did anyway.

Outside the School, the Lambents could produce different effects. Instead of making them calm and quiet, the Lambent could flood them with a light-headed euphoria, sending them into giggling fits as they gazed at it.

Gwendolyn walked on, her thoughts full of leaves and birds and rabbits, until she heard an unpleasantly familiar voice call her name.

"Oy, Freckl—uh, Gwendolyn. Wait up."

She turned and saw Tommy jogging to catch up with her. She hesitated. "Yes?"

He slowed. "That was somethin' wasn't it? Honkin' big rat falls right on Missy's head? Unbelievable. And we get an early day off school, how great is that?"

Gwendolyn eyed him suspiciously. "Um . . . yes. It's wonderful. Unless you're Missy Cartblatt, I suppose."

"Heh. Too right. Are you ridin' the mono today?"

Gwendolyn raised an eyebrow. "Don't you normally ride with Missy?"

Tommy looked at his shoes and shuffled his feet. "Er, yeah, I do, but you know, she won't be comin', today, so I thought—"

"Yes, I think I will," she said, sparing him further embarrassment. She was surprised at her answer, but if he was going to be nice, so would she.

"All right then!" Tommy smiled a shy smile, which was real emotional progress for him. Normally, he would have pulled her hair and run off laughing to hide any hint of bashfulness. They walked to the monorail station and up the metal staircase to the platform, where they sat on a bench together.

There were several moments of awkward silence. Not knowing what else to do, Tommy took a Lambent out of his pocket. It began to glow, and Gwendolyn turned her face away in disgust. She did her best to ignore the light, but it was already giving her a headache. Soon she heard Tommy's chuckling "hurr-hurr-hurr."

"What's so funny?" she asked.

He didn't answer.

"Tommy?" she said, but she might as well have been talking to her desk. She nudged his shoulder. "Tommy?"

Tommy's trance broke. His smile melted away and he squinted at her warily, as though she were going to take his toy away. "What do you want, Freckles?"

Gwendolyn frowned. "I just asked what you were laughing at."

"What d'you mean? It's the Lambent, innit?"

"Yes, but what do you see in the Lambent?"

"What? There's nuffink *in* here."

"Well, then what were you laughing at? What do you see?"

"I dunno. Same as you. Just light. It's all white."

"Then . . . then what are you laughing at?"

"Are you mental or something? The *light* makes you laugh. You look at it, and it makes you feel stuff. Why all the questions? Why, why, why, it's all you ever do."

She scrambled for an explanation, since any normal child would never need to ask such obvious questions. "I-I just wanted to make sure that, that it was working, you know, that what I see is the same thing you see."

Tommy frowned at this weak excuse. "No, that's not it. How

come you never look at it? You just sit there with your eyes closed. It's weird."

"I don't like it. It makes my head hurt," she admitted. "Would you mind putting yours away?"

Something white flashed behind his eyes, and Tommy's expression went sour. "Grief, if it bothers you, go talk to a chair or somethin'," he snapped.

Gwendolyn was shocked at his sudden turn. "You're the one who came up to *me,* remember? It's not my fault your girlfriend Missy can't ride home with you." Then she remembered that it was precisely her fault.

The Lambent flickered again, and Tommy looked at her in confusion. "What? Who's Missy?"

Gwendolyn rolled her eyes. "Missy Cartblatt. Rides with you every day, pale hair, long ea–" She stopped herself.

"What are you droning about? Who the blazes is Missy Cartblatt? Quit talking nonsense and leave me alone, *oddling*. Go bother your imaginary friends." He trailed off, already transfixed by his Lambent again.

Gwendolyn felt as confused as Tommy usually looked. Tommy had never been the brightest of bulbs. This was probably his stupid way of teasing her. Well, she didn't have to sit here and take it. She could walk home instead. She stormed down the steps to the street. *Some people are just not worth bothering with,* she thought.

But something did bother her. "He wasn't teasing," she said. "He really didn't remember her." Thoughts whirred, and new ideas clicked into place. "The Lambent . . . Then maybe . . ."

On a sudden impulse, she dashed back to the steps of the School, over to the group of boys who'd been sharing one, and spotted Ian Haldrake.

"Ian," she called.

One of the boys groaned. "What, Gwendolyn?"

"Umm, did you see what happened to Missy today?"

He looked at her like she was a worm that had learned to speak. "What are you talking about? Who's Missy?"

Gwendolyn was struck speechless. The boys looked at each other, rolled their eyes, and walked away, leaving Gwendolyn frozen on the sidewalk.

"They don't remember either. And they certainly weren't pretending." Everyone had just been talking about Missy—then the ones with Lambents suddenly forgot her? Couldn't be a coincidence.

"There is something wrong with the Lambents," she murmured. Something beyond the headaches they always gave her. But that left her with one question: what *had* happened to Missy Cartblatt?

She could have gone home right then. After all, Missy hadn't wanted her help that morning. But Missy certainly hadn't wanted rabbit ears either, or to be erased from the memories of her classmates. Gwendolyn couldn't just leave her to . . . whatever might be happening. She had to find her.

If Gwendolyn had turned around and boarded the monorail like a good little girl, her life would have turned out very differently. But stories are rarely told about normal, well-behaved little girls, the ones who go home and grow up into normal, well-behaved ladies. So it is fortunate for us that she did *not* go home, but went back into the School instead, though I cannot promise that it will end fortunately for Gwendolyn.

She snuck down the hallway toward the headmaster's office, hoping that Mr. Percival had taken Missy there like he'd said. The Headmaster's Hall was an excruciatingly long corridor designed to give rule-breakers plenty of time to ponder their fate. It was a walk and a feeling Gwendolyn knew well. Outside the door was a long and uncomfortable couch for the headmaster's victims, where Gwendolyn practically had reserved seating.

She crouched down and leaned against the door, just below the window that said HEADMASTER in big black letters.

She peeked through the window. She couldn't see much, but she was quite familiar with the office, and knew that to the left would be the big desk and the big chair and the big headmaster. But from the door, all she could see was a chair against the wall. Missy Cartblatt was sitting in it, sobbing quietly into her hands. The velvety rabbit ears drooped comically over her face and quivered as she cried.

Gwendolyn crouched down again. A sour feeling sank into her gut. *She'd* made Missy cry like that. Missy was such a shy, fragile girl to begin with.

Voices were coming through the door, though she couldn't make out the words. Mr. Percival's reedy hysterics clashed with the deep, calm voice of the headmaster. But there were other voices, ones Gwendolyn did not recognize.

Suddenly, there was a bright flash of light through the window, like the Lambents but far brighter. Gwendolyn whirled and had to shield her eyes, even with her back to the door. After a long moment, the light vanished. Once the spots had left her vision, Gwendolyn rose to peek through the window again.

Missy's chair was empty.

She had no time to think on it, because she heard someone walking toward the door. There was no way she could make it to the end of the hall before they came out and saw her. So she ducked behind the arm of the couch, farthest from the door, out of sight of anyone leaving. For once, she was thankful she was so small for her age.

She heard the door open, then close. Heard footsteps click on the polished floors. Watched as two gentlemen in grey suits and bowler hats walked down the hall, each step in unison. The very same two men that Gwendolyn had failed to see on the street that morning, just as they failed to see her now. But the hallway seemed colder as they passed.

Gwendolyn watched them reach the end of the hall and turn to leave. She looked back at the office, but neither Mr. Percival nor the headmaster came out. She dared to peek inside.

Mr. Percival and the headmaster were dazed, shaking their heads as though coming out of a Lambent trance. And there was no sign of Missy Cartblatt.

Gwendolyn's eyes widened. There was no other door to the office, no window, nowhere for Missy to have gone. But gone she was. The sour feeling in Gwendolyn's gut doubled. She pulled back, heart hammering, and took off down the hall.

Gwendolyn had never seen those two bowler-hat men before, but they were up to something, she was sure of it. She decided to follow them, to eavesdrop on their conversation, and find some clue as to where Missy had gone.

The men were nowhere to be seen in the entrance hall, and as she emerged onto the steps of the School, she could see no sign of them on the street either. She thought she glimpsed them turning the corner at the end of the street to her right, and bounded down the steps to follow . . .

. . . only to be frozen at the bottom of the steps by another unpleasant, and unfortunately familiar, voice.

"Oh, *Gwendolyn,*" came the sing-song sweetness of Cecilia Forthright. "Hold it right there, freak."

CHAPTER FOUR

Snip Snip

Cecilia stood at the head of her gang: Armand Barbington, Jannette Tice-Nichols, Carter Shrewsbury, and Vivian Coleridge. The three girls had perfect hair, perfect make-up, and perfect teeth behind those cocky sneers, all to make sure that despite the identical uniforms, everyone knew they were above the rest. The two boys just hit anybody who looked twice at them, which had the same effect. The Centrals were so full of themselves it was a miracle they could button their jackets.

"We've been talking, little Gwenny," Cecilia said. "You see, we know what you did to Missy."

The gut-tightening feeling of "being in trouble" was an old friend to Gwendolyn, but that didn't make it feel any better. *They haven't looked in a Lambent yet,* she realized. *They still remember. All of it.* "M-me? I don't know what you're talking about."

"Don't play dumb, you're already a professional," Jannette interrupted.

"Everyone said it was a rat—"

"It wasn't a rat. It was weird. And you're weird. And nothing weird ever happens unless *you're* around."

"Yeah, the only rat is you," Armand said.

"Don't help me, Armand," Cecilia snapped.

"I didn't do anything," Gwendolyn lied.

Vivian sneered. "See? That just proves it. You're such a terrible liar."

Cecilia put her hands on her hips. "The problem, oddling, is that your head is always full of weirdo nonsense. We finally realized that awful hair of yours must be rotting your brains. If you ever had any. So we're going to do you a favor, No-friend-o-lyn, and get rid of it. It's a fair punishment, don't you think?"

I wish I could tell you that everything would be all right. That children may tease and brag, but they are never too cruel. But I cannot, for though children like Tommy might be misunderstood, all the understanding in the world won't stop a gang of vile twelve-year-olds from being exactly as mean as they wish to be.

Armand brandished a pair of scissors, and Gwendolyn turned to flee, but chubby Carter and prissy Vivian moved behind her.

Gwendolyn was trapped, surrounded by her taller schoolmates, alone on the street. She tried to sound as cool as she knew how, which wasn't very. "Look, you don't even like Missy anyway. So why don't we all—"

"It doesn't matter," Cecilia said. "At least she was normal. You need to learn what happens to freaks like you."

Gwendolyn clenched her small fists. "I'm not scared of you," she lied again. "Lay one finger on me and you'll be in serious trouble. So don't you dare." She wanted to sound tough, but her voice squeaked at the end.

The others laughed. "Did you hear that? I think she was *daring* us," Carter said, and pushed her into Vivian.

"Ooooo, she's going to tell on us, whatever will we do?" Vivian pushed her back to Carter.

"Who's she going to tell? Her desk? That tree she talks to in the schoolyard?" taunted Jannette, peering over her stylish glasses.

Vivian chomped her gum and cocked a bleached eyebrow. "Who's going to listen to a little freak? The teachers can't stand you, and your parents would probably rather have a bald daughter than an embarrassment like you." She popped a grey bubble in Gwendolyn's face.

Armand snipped his scissors in the air, grinning like a lunatic.

Cecilia leaned in until Gwendolyn was choking on her perfume. "Let me teach you how the world works. No one likes you. No one wants you. And no one wants to deal with your weirdness, so when we're through, you just stay away. Out of sight. Alone." Her words dripped like icy venom from her perfect smile. She planted a finger on Gwendolyn's chest. "Do you understand, *freak*?" And she spit in Gwendolyn's face.

If you have ever been so unlucky as to have a horrible teenage girl spit in your face, or anyone at all for that matter, you will understand the sudden blaze of anger that flared within Gwendolyn Gray. All the problems of the day—the nagging, the taunting, the teasing, making her classmate disappear—had been shoved down deeper and deeper inside her, until the pressure of them all formed a white-hot ball. The moment that warm spittle struck her cheek, the ball exploded.

Gwendolyn let out a bellow of twelve-year-old rage, threw her hand into Cecilia's face and shoved as hard as she could, raking her nails downward.

The taller girl screeched and stumbled backwards. "Get her!" she yelled, cupping a hand to her bleeding cheek.

Armand darted in with the scissors. Gwendolyn tried to run, but Carter grabbed her, and he and Vivian pinned her arms behind her back. She struggled, but was no match for the larger students. Jannette held her head in place. There was a sickening *snip* and a lock of red hair fell to the ground.

Gwendolyn screamed and brought her heel up, striking Carter in an area that will cause male readers to wince. He clutched himself and collapsed, slamming his head into Vivian's face. She squealed and her hands flew to her nose, her prey momentarily forgotten.

And for the second time that day, Gwendolyn Gray ran away.

Jannette started after her, but she collided with Vivian, who was stumbling around clutching her nose. Jannette's glasses went flying and the two girls toppled to the ground, the others tripping over them in their haste.

Gwendolyn raced toward the monorail station. She reached the metal stairway and took the steps two at a time, bursting onto the platform. A monorail tram was just arriving. The doors opened with a chime and Gwendolyn darted inside.

There were several rows of padded seats, but no passengers.

Gwendolyn ran to the back, hurled herself to the floor and rolled under the last bench.

Feet clanged on the metal walkway outside, and she had to think quickly. Luckily, quick thinking was what Gwendolyn did best. She looked around, noticing everything she could. She noticed that the monorail seats were held up by a row of support bars, suspended about a foot above the ground. She noticed that there was a gap between the support bars and the seats. She noticed that this hollow space was just large enough for a small and imaginative child.

She squeezed into the gap, lying on the support bars among the springs and cobwebs. This hid her quite well, and if she let her head hang down she could just see a bit of the aisle.

Five pairs of shiny, black shoes stormed in, their owners all talking at once.

"Where is she?"

"Find her! She's here somewhere! Carter, hold the door, don't let it leave."

"She hurd by dose! It's bweeding!"

Jannette's black bob haircut came into view as she looked under the seats. Her glasses were cracked.

Gwendolyn jerked her own head up and out of sight. There was a chime as the doors tried to close, but then they opened again, presumably because Carter was in the way of the motion sensor.

"She's not under the seats," Jannette said.

"What do we do, Cici?" came Armand's voice. A black heel kicked someone's shin. "Ow!"

"We saw her run into this car, so she's stuck here, you idiot. Does anyone see her?"

Silence. Gwendolyn hoped they were all shaking their heads. The chiming door became more insistent, resenting being held open this long.

"Ugh," Cecilia said. "Well, I'm not riding this thing out of Central. Not even for little Miss Freak. Let's go."

"But whad aboud by dose?"

"God, shut up, Vivian, it's probably an improvement." Two pairs of feet stayed behind as the rest walked away. "Armand, I *told* you, don't call me Cici, not in front of the others." Then the last two pairs of black shoes moved to the door as well.

"Goodbye, freak!" Cecilia called. "Enjoy your last night. Because this isn't over."

Gwendolyn heard the *ding* of the doors turn into an insistent *clang* of alarm bells, the automated train insisting that it be allowed to resume its route. She heard a frighteningly familiar *snip,* a puzzling *snap,* and then the sound of the door closing. The alarm stopped, and the train began to move.

Gwendolyn crept from her hiding place, limbs cramped and tingling.

She had never been so happy to be alone. She brushed dust and cobwebs from her jacket, and wiped a bit of spit off her cheek. A screen on the wall behind her showed a map of monorail stations with a blinking light for her train. She was approaching the edge of the Central City, and soon would reach her stop in the Middling. She wanted badly to get off there, run home, and hide under the covers of her bed, pretending that this day had never happened.

But she couldn't. Her thoughts, freed from worrying about her own safety, turned back toward Missy. She had vanished, and people were forgetting she ever existed. Gwendolyn had to do *something*. At the very least, she owed it to Missy's parents to tell them what had happened and apologize. Then maybe they could start a search for her, instead of being left to sit and worry when she never came home.

Yes. That was it, then. She knew roughly where Missy lived, not far from Tommy, on the same tram line that Gwendolyn took each day but much farther out. She could get off in the Outskirts and start asking around whether anyone knew where the Cartblatts lived.

She had time. It wasn't even lunchtime, so she should still get home before Mother noticed. She relaxed cross-legged on the floor and looked out the windows at the permanent wall of clouds, trying to find shapes in the never-ending haze, trying to find a little calm. By the time her blip on the map entered the Outskirts, she was feeling a bit more like herself again.

Buildings out here were smaller, no more than a dozen stories tall. There was a general air of shabbiness—peeling paint, dirty walkways. Vagrants and beggars dotted the streets with hastily scrawled cardboard signs. Mother never let her walk out here alone.

The three sections of the City were not divided by any official borders, but the divisions between them were harsh and concrete divisions of money, class, and status. Everyone knew where the Central became the Middling, and where the Middling gave way to the Outskirts, even without any lines on maps. It was the same way at the School: everyone wore identical uniforms, yet everyone could instantly tell where you were from by your name, or accent, or the way you wore your clothes.

The tracks traveled above the buildings, and with no outbound passengers to pick up at the platforms, the automated conductor blew through every station. Eventually she saw the stop she wanted, stood up and pulled the stop-request cable.

The cable went slack in her hand, and the train kept moving. She pulled again, with the same result. The limp cable led her to the front of the car, where she noticed something that made the gut-tightening panic return in an icy rush.

The cable had been cut.

"Armand, you—" and she let loose several words that would have earned her a good mouth-soaping at home. The monorail had heard much worse in its time, and kept going.

If you've ever ridden on a train, bus, or monorail before, you will know that pulling the cable signals that a passenger wishes to get off. Without it, the monorail would not stop.

"Maybe the train will stop to let someone else on?" she wondered aloud. "No, stupid girl, no one is going to board a train going *past* the Outskirts."

She tried pulling the other end of the cable, but it was no use. She was well and truly stuck.

She pounded on the door of the train for a while, then kicked it, then screamed as long and as loud as she could, but all she got were sore hands, feet, and throat. Finally, she collapsed back onto the floor. "Now what do I do?"

The monorail ignored her, heading past the Outskirts into the unknown beyond.

CHAPTER FIVE

The Edge

It is a well-known fact that children are more adaptable than grown-ups. If, for example, you woke up one morning and were suddenly a giant cockroach, as a grown-up you might spend weeks locked in your room, agonizing over the unfairness of existence and pointlessness of life. As a child, on the other hand, you would quickly learn that being a giant cockroach is a fantastic way to frighten your sister, that no one will stop you from eating all the junk food you like, and that six arms make you a tremendous athlete.

Likewise, Gwendolyn was quickly adapting to the idea that not only could she create physical objects with her mind, but she had also accidentally given her classmate a pair of giant rabbit ears, and she was now stuck on a train to the edge of everywhere.

There was nothing to be done. The train had to turn around at some point, she reasoned.

So she sat down and crossed her arms to wait.

And wait.

Her hand kept wandering to the place where her hair had been so cruelly sheared off, the way your tongue will always find its way to the sore on the inside of your cheek.

So much for no trouble today.

After what felt to Gwendolyn's restless mind like three eternities, the train finally slowed to a stop. But the doors did not open.

That wasn't good.

Gwendolyn looked outside. She was well past the Outskirts, and there wasn't another person in sight. The buildings were all industrial facilities, with towering smoke stacks belching grey clouds. A sign read *End-of-Line Turnaround F—The Edge.*

Gwendolyn frowned in confusion. She'd never heard of the Edge before, but she had to get those doors open. Of course, wishing wasn't going to make it happen.

Or would it?

Maybe she could *imagine* her way out.

Then again, that hadn't worked out very well so far. She looked down at her hands. "Like Missy said, I just make things worse. Still, I can't be stuck out here forever. I have to try."

She looked at the doors, taking a deep breath to quiet her thoughts. She tried to picture them opening and sliding back, and imagined the sound of the *chime-hiss* they always made.

And at her command, the doors slid open.

Gwendolyn snatched up her satchel and hurled herself onto the platform before she got trapped again. The monorail suddenly reversed direction, speeding back toward the skyscrapers on the horizon, as if anxious to be away.

"Fantastic," she groaned. She'd just have to wait for the next one.

But then, as she so often did, she noticed something. On the empty street below the platform were two strange men in bowler hats. They were the only moving things she could see, besides the smoke pouring from the factories.

She knew she should stay put.

She knew she should not leave the station.

She knew she should wait right here until another mono came to take her home.

But she didn't care. She was tired of being told what she should do, how she should act, who she should be. She was tired of all the rules everyone else seemed to follow on instinct, tired of feeling like she was born with the wrong set of instincts. Those men had done something to Missy, because of Gwendolyn, and she had to find out what.

And so she hurtled down the stairs to the street.

Though Gwendolyn knew nothing about it, I can tell you that the Edge was the farthest ring of the City, past the Outskirts. It was filled with automated facilities that kept the City running. No one ever went there, and less than no one knew it existed.

People in the City did not wonder how the City worked, where they got their food, what made the lights come on. They believed that asking how things worked was the quickest way to make sure they didn't. They paid their bills and lived their lives and the Lambents kept everybody happy, dull, and away from any troublesome wonderings.

She shook off these thoughts and followed the strange men

down the deserted walkway. The street was not the smooth-poured concrete she was used to, but was instead made of old-fashioned cobblestones, wobbly and cracked. A harsh smell filled the air, the smell of burnt metal and smoking oil, like the time Mother had left a pan on the stove too long.

She stayed far back, out of sight of the two strangers, but lost them when they turned a corner. Gwendolyn followed, and as she rounded it, she found herself looking down the street at . . . nothing. A dozen blocks away, the street ran into an enormous wall of flat, featureless grey.

The size of the wall nearly knocked her on her back. It was the biggest thing she had ever seen, the biggest thing in the whole City, even taller than the Central Tower. The Wall, which was so large she couldn't help but think of it in capital letters, seemed to stretch to infinity in all directions. It was the exact color of the clouds above, and blended in so well she almost couldn't see the top.

Gwendolyn felt suddenly tiny and weak, and her knees shook a little. But as I said, children are adaptable, and Gwendolyn's curiosity could not be stopped. Like a light coming on in a dark and cobwebbed room, a thought lit up her mind.

"Outside . . . What is *outside* the City?" she mumbled. She was shocked that in all her wondering, she'd never thought this thought before, never bothered to think what might lie past the Outskirts, and none of her readings had ever come near the topic.

She did not have time to think about it now, because something moved.

Two men in dark-grey suits with black bowler hats stood at the base of the Wall. She hadn't noticed them before, as the size of the Wall pulled one's eyes up, not down. She saw them now, and she somehow felt sure that they saw her too.

A feeling of dread poured from the men like the smoke from the factories, and it made Gwendolyn's stomach churn. All her questions evaporated, and she suddenly realized the flaw in her plan, namely, that she *had* no plan, had not thought what to do once she caught the men. Now she was the one who was caught.

She ducked back around the corner and walked briskly down the street, refusing to admit how badly she wanted to run. Problems with her mother and the School seemed small, almost cozy in the face of the enormous Wall and the reek of wrongness from those men. They made Missy vanish; there was no telling what they'd do to Gwendolyn.

She tried heading back the way she'd come, toward the domed Central Tower in the distance, but was brought up short. The two men were now standing at the other end of the street, blocking her way. Which was impossible. They could not have moved fast enough to get so far ahead of her.

Slowly, they stepped toward her.

She felt another surge of dread, but felt something else as well, a pull of some kind, drawing her toward a gap between two buildings. For once, she did not ask questions, and ducked into the gap.

A dead-end. It was a small alley with grimy brick walls and a boarded-up doorway. Footsteps were approaching, rattling the wobbly cobbles. A thin, high voice crept around the corner.

"Come out, come out, little girl. We know you are there. You cannot hide."

She shuddered at the eerie voice, ran to the doorway and kicked the bottom board. It wiggled a little. She kicked again, harder. The board came loose and she crawled inside, squirming on the filthy ground. She whirled around and pulled the board back into place, hiding her escape.

Slowly, she stood up. The dust made her sneeze, but she covered her mouth and listened for more footsteps. They grew closer, then farther, then all was quiet.

She silently counted out two full minutes, the longest in her life, but heard no further sound.

"Well, I'm certainly not going out *there* anytime soon," she mumbled. Not until she was sure those men were gone. So, true to form, she decided to explore a bit. She struggled to see through the gloom. Trickles of light came through the cracks in the boards, and her eyes eventually adjusted.

This was a house. A very old house. She ran her finger through a thick layer of dust that coated the ragged, moth-eaten furniture. Gwendolyn was in someone's living room, though it had been some time since anyone had done any living in it, so it did not feel rude to intrude.

"I wonder who might have lived here?" she said in a whisper. "It's awfully small, though I suppose anyone living this far from the Center would have been very poor, indeed."

She found a room that she first took to be a large closet, but then she saw that it was actually an incredibly tiny bedroom. It held a small bed, a dresser, and an old trunk, with scarcely enough room to turn around. Shelves crowded the walls. They were packed with jars and boxes, which she immediately started to open, as Gwendolyn had more curiosity than manners.

The jars were all full of dust, and the boxes contained various stones and even a skeleton from some small animal. All were labeled, but the labels were so faded she couldn't make the words out. You might have recognized it as the remains of a child's collection, of rocks and butterflies and frogs, but Gwendolyn was not a collecting sort of child.

It was then that she noticed a dim, blue light shining through the lid of the old trunk.

Her eyes grew wide. "Why, hello . . ." She felt that pull again, and she tiptoed through the dust, dead insects, and animal droppings. She opened the trunk.

Inside, partially covered by a pile of old rags, was a glowing blue gemstone resting on an old book.

The gem was about the size of her fist, oval and slightly flattened, with glittering facets of a deep, gorgeous blue. She stared at it, having never seen such a vibrant color in her life. It glowed, but it was different than the cold light of the Lambents. It seemed warm and full and was twice the size of a Lambent. She could feel a tingling in her fingers.

And it had her initials on it. Two swirling, interlocking G's twinkled at her, etched into the crystal surface. Her special symbol. How it came to be here she didn't know, but this little bit of impossible hardly stood out against the rest of her day.

She was about to put it in her pocket when she stopped herself. "Stupid girl," she said, "you can't go around taking things that aren't yours." The gem glinted at her. "Then again . . . It isn't as though anyone is going to miss it here. Whoever owns it must be long gone, probably dead. They wouldn't want their beautiful things to stay locked inside an old trunk forever. And after all, it's got my initials on it."

Gwendolyn turned her attention to the book. She had never heard of anyone having books in their home before. All the books were kept in the City's dreary Hall of Records.

This book, however . . . This was unlike any Gwendolyn had ever seen. For starters, it was a shocking red, even brighter than her hair. The cover glittered with golden gears and sprockets stenciled around its edges, and a title in fat, gold letters:

Kolonius Thrash and the Perilous Pirates

by Stanley Kirby

She sat down on the filthy bed and rolled the jewel around in her palm, wondering what exactly a *pirate* was. She had never heard the word before, though it sounded worryingly like math. Gwendolyn had not spent the long afternoons you probably have swinging sticks in her backyard and shouting "Yarr!" until dinnertime. To her, "pirate" might as well have read "flibbersham," or "snizzlewick."

It wasn't as though she had anything better to do, she reasoned. And if she was going to be holed up here, waiting until it was safe to come out, she may as well give it a look. Turning to the first page, she began to read.

"Once upon a time," she said. Oh, she liked that. What a wonderful way to begin.

Unfortunately, nearly everything after that was more

gibberish, and she ended up so confused it made her head hurt. So she went back to admiring the beautiful cover instead.

Playfully, she put the blue gem up to her eye. Instead of turning everything blue, as she expected, the room turned stark black and white. She looked through it at the book's cover, but it was even redder than before. And when her eye came to the word "Pirates," she was nearly knocked over by the force of the images that rushed into her brain.

Her mind was suddenly full of dangerous men with pistols, swords, hooks, peg legs, eye patches, planks to walk, decks to swab, and wags to scally–whatever those were.

She dropped the gem in surprise. "That was strange," she said to herself, "even for today." Then a thought occurred to her. "I suppose it isn't much different than the Lambents. Except the Lambents are empty, while this . . . this is full."

Picking up the gem, she put it back to her eye and looked again at the cover. She opened the book and began reading again, this time through the gem's blue glass. "Once upon a time, in the land of Tohk . . ."

After that, she understood every word she read, the jewel rushing to fill any gaps in her mind. The dingy old house faded away into a sea of words and images and bright, shimmering blue. Thoughts and information poured into her mind as they never had with the Lambents. The rush was incredible! It would have been frightening, but it felt so nice. Like she'd been thirsty her whole life without realizing it, and now that thirst was quenched.

Even so, the book still puzzled her. Every book she'd ever

read was made of cold, hard facts, but how could anything in this book be real? It was impossible!

Then she realized that it could *not* be real. Things like this simply weren't possible. It must be like one of her own daydreams, full of things that had never happened and people who had never lived. None of it was real, yet here it was, all written down in front of her.

It was a story.

It hit her like the first breath of fresh air after hiding under your covers. It set her mind on fire, and she devoured it.

Kolonius Thrash turned out to be a dashing young hero who lived in the magical land of Tohk. It was a world of gears and goggles and gauges, of ropes and pulleys, dirigibles and locomotives, clockwork men and steam-powered engines.

Kolonius was seventeen, but he was already the captain of his own airship, the *Lucrative Endeavour*. He called himself a hero for hire, willing to save anyone and stop any villain if the price was right. Together with his crew, he fought for the weak and defenseless, battling sky-pirates and robber-barons with flashing swords and daring deeds. He was gruff and headstrong, but he had a deep sense of justice and a caring heart. Or at least the author, this Stanley Kirby fellow, said he did.

Gwendolyn savored every sentence. When she read things like *airship* and *automaton* and *petticoat*, the ideas would pop into her mind like so many bubbles bursting, as if she had known them all her life. The blue gem twinkled softly, silently performing its task, as the girl stretched out on the bed, reading and reading and reading.

Finally, she forced herself to stop. She had no idea what time it was. If it had been late before, it was certainly later now. She looked down and realized how absolutely filthy she was from all her fighting and crawling and hiding. The chances that the men were still out there were small, especially when compared to the chances that she would be in a tremendous pile of trouble when she got home, and every extra minute made the pile grow larger.

She crawled back through the gap in the boards, slung her bag on her shoulder, cradled her two new treasures in her arms, and dashed out of the alleyway at full speed. There was no sign of the two men, but also no sign of the monorail tracks, and no more time for the mystery of missing Missy today. Gwendolyn wandered the streets blindly, looking for some sign of the elevated tracks, some way home to her furious mother.

After three wrong turns and three more dead-ends, she had to admit it. She was lost. The Edge was eerily quiet, save for the ominous drone of the factories, and Gwendolyn realized that, for the first time in her life, she was totally and utterly alone. In the crowded City, it was impossible to be more than a few dozen feet away from some other person. And though she'd had lots of practice feeling lonely, that is different from feeling truly alone.

As black feelings crept into her heart, she muttered the nonsense song from that morning to try to drive off some of the gloom and fear.

"Sparrow and starling, darrow and darling,
winging their way in the sky.
Birds in the air, haven't a care,
oh how I'd like to try.

Hey, ho, here we go,
oh how I'd like to fly."

And it helped, a little. She sang, her voice a nervous whisper. Then she heard a fluttering above her. She looked up, and was astonished to see her two birds from that morning, back again. They dipped and twirled like sparks above a fire. Gwendolyn smiled. She sang again, a little louder, a little less scared, a little less lonely. The birds joined the song with tweets and chirps.

Gwendolyn smiled wider. But as soon as she did, they flew off.

"Hey! Wait! Come back!" she shouted. She followed the birds around one corner, then another, running to keep up . . .

. . . only to smash directly into something hard, grey, and very person-shaped in front of her. She fell to the ground, landing in a tangled and unladylike position. The jewel rolled away and her book landed on its spine, falling open at the feet of two men in black bowler hats.

CHAPTER SIX

Birds and Bowlers

Gwendolyn sprawled on the sidewalk, nose to toe with four polished, black shoes. Above the shoes were crisp grey pants, and above that were twice-buttoned jackets with black ties pinned smartly to white shirts. The men both wore black bowler hats, and they had no faces.

Let me be clear: they had noses, yes, and mouths as well. Likewise eyes and ears, all in the right place and amount.

But Gwendolyn could not have told you what they looked like.

Looking at them was like trying to picture the face of a friend you haven't seen in years. The men stood plain as day in front of her, but the faces underneath those bowler hats slipped from her mind like eels, as though her eyes saw something terrible, and refused to tell her brain what they had seen. Most people have never seen a man with no face, but let me assure you that it is a sight so unsettling that it puts goosebumps on your eyeballs.

A white-gloved hand reached down. Gwendolyn thought it meant to help her up, but it picked up the book instead. The man's eyes examined the gleaming title, and the gloved hands flipped through the colorful illustrations.

Gwendolyn snatched up the gem and snuck it in her pocket.

The man turned to his comrade. "This is a very interesting book, Mister Five," he said. His voice was a high-pitched, whining monotone, crisp and proper. The voice she'd heard in the headmaster's office.

"Very interesting indeed, Mister Six," replied the other, his voice identical to the first. He leaned in slightly, ever so slightly, to examine the book.

Gwendolyn got to her feet and put on her precious-little-girl voice, all sweetness and light, the kind you use when you want a second helping of dessert. "I'm terribly sorry, sirs. I wasn't watching my way."

Slowly, ever so slowly, the two men's eyes turned from the book toward Gwendolyn. Their heads cocked to the side and stared at her, faces instantly dissolving in her memory.

Gwendolyn shuddered. "If you will accept my polite apologies, I will take my book and be on my way. Mother will be quite cross if I am late."

The men ignored her. Carefully, ever so carefully, their hands flipped through the book as though the pages were covered in muck, and they didn't wish to dirty their white gloves.

"Where did you get this book, my dear?" said Mister Five.

"Uh," Gwendolyn stammered. "It's mine, and I would like it back now, please."

"This is a very unique book, little girl. My partner and I . . . collect . . . things such as this," said one of the men.

Gwendolyn again felt the gut-wrenching sensation of being caught, as she had felt earlier with the Centrals, but these gentlemen made Cecilia and her gang seem positively fluffy. "I'm sorry, sir, but it is mine, and it is not for sale. I must insist that you give it back. Please?"

"What do you think, Mister Five?" one of the men whined eerily.

"She has seen the book, Mister Six, and would appear to have been reading it quite intently," said the other, examining the edges of the pages. "And unless I'm very much mistaken, and I seldom am, Mister Six–"

"–No, indeed, Mister Five–"

"–this girl is not where she should be."

"Most assuredly not, Mister Five. The Edge is not permissible to the citizenry, *particularly* children. Most particularly not to children so particularly . . . strange." Gently, ever so gently, his gloved hand reached out and caressed a lock of Gwendolyn's fiery hair.

Gwendolyn flinched. The man's brief touch made her skin want to crawl off her bones, into bed, and under the blankets. She slapped his hand away, but Mister Six didn't react.

"You are correct, Mister Six," said Mister Five. "She has seen the Wall, and this book, and who knows what else. She is also certainly the one causing these unacceptable changes. No, no, no, I'm afraid we really have no choice," droned Mister Five.

Mister Six's hand reached up slowly, ever so slowly, to his black bowler hat. "I agree completely, Mister Five. These changes simply must be dealt with." His tone turned sweet, dripping more venom than honey: "Girl. Might I draw your attention here, to my lovely hat?"

He took off the hat and turned it toward her, like a magician showing that his hat is indeed empty. But instead of a rabbit, a pinpoint of light came out of the hat's black interior. Gwendolyn's gaze was locked in place.

Cold light poured out of the hat. It was just like a Lambent, but one more potent than any she had ever encountered. Her eyes burned but she could not look away. With an awful shock, she found she could no longer move. Any thoughts of running or escaping faded. She could feel her mind slipping away, drawn toward the light, drowning in it.

"Perfectly done, little girl. It doesn't hurt."

He was wrong. It did hurt. Her head felt like it would split in two. The searing pain brought her back to her senses. "No!" she shouted, and reached forward to knock the hat away.

Mister Six stepped easily out of reach. "The girl resists, Mister Five."

"Indeed she does, Mister Six. She is stronger than anticipated. Increase the power." The light doubled in brightness. She held up her hand to block it, but it didn't help.

Her hand. She could see right through it. It was vanishing before her eyes, disappearing like a puddle on a hot day. She felt disconnected from her body, her arms and legs as far away as yesterday's dream. She felt like a glass of water being poured into a swirling drain. Her thoughts, normally so fast she couldn't control them, began to slow. She felt *less*.

Mister Six's mouth curved upward slightly, ever so slightly. "Yes, this will only take a mo–"

"Look out!"

Someone collided with the faceless man, and hard. Mister Six was knocked to the street, his hat rolled away, and the book skidded down the sidewalk. Senseless Gwendolyn was grabbed by a pair of rough hands and pulled down the street like a rag doll.

"Move your feet, or I'm leaving you!" came another voice, a girl's. Gwendolyn shook her head as the volume on her senses was turned back up.

And for the third time that day, Gwendolyn Gray was running away.

She noticed several things all at once. She noticed a very peculiar-looking boy, about her own age, running beside her. She noticed a bright-red jacket and a long, yellow scarf that fluttered behind him. He grinned recklessly, holding his flat and checkered newsboy cap. He held up a red book. "Here! You dropped this. Clumsy."

Gwendolyn took it, noticing that her hand was solid and whole again. She noticed the girl pulling her other hand wore a complicated-looking set of goggles on her head, all dials and lenses. Her shimmering blouse was not quite green, not quite blue, but was somehow both at once underneath a coppery-orange vest. She looked back at Gwendolyn and gave her arm a fierce tug. "Quit staring at me and *run!*"

She did, pushing her feet as fast as they would go. They sprinted through the deserted streets. The Mister Men followed effortlessly, seeming almost to float over the ground.

After a while, Gwendolyn noticed some scattered pedestrians in shabby clothes. She and the strange children must have run all the way to the beginning of the Outskirts. People gaped at the wild children who would dare run through the City's streets, but the Mister Men passed by without so much as a glance from the Cityzens, and the sparse crowds moved mindlessly aside to let them through.

Gwendolyn turned to look behind, but the Mister Men never grew any closer or farther away. "I can't . . . keep running . . . like this!" she gasped, her satchel banging against her side with every step.

"Quick! This way!" the boy shouted.

"Sparrow, wait!" the girl said, but the boy ducked into an alleyway. The girl groaned and pulled Gwendolyn in after him.

It was a dead end.

The boy spun around. "Oh. Never mind. What now, Starling?"

"What? Not again! This was your idea!" she groaned. "Fine. Take her! I'll catch up." She pointed at something down the alley, then pushed Gwendolyn at the boy and started patting the pockets of her pants. The girl was nothing *but* pockets from the waist down. Her black trousers were covered in them, and she wore crisscrossing belts full of dangling tools and gadgets. Gwendolyn wondered if she needed all those belts to hold up such heavily laden pants.

The older girl pulled a copper sphere from a pocket on her thigh and twisted the two halves, winding it up. She leaned out of the alleyway and tossed it into the air just as the Mister Men came around the corner. The sphere whirred, clicked, and then exploded with a loud *snap!*

The alley entrance was instantly filled with orange smoke. One of the men stumbled out of the cloud, but the girl shoved him back in. She pulled her goggles down over her eyes and flipped a lens into place. "Go! I'll lead them away and circle back!" Then she plunged into the fog.

"Come on!" the boy said. He pulled Gwendolyn down the alleyway and studied the wall at the end. "Now, what was Starling pointing at?"

Gwendolyn noticed a fire escape above them, old iron ladders and walkways bolted to the side of the building. "Do you think she meant that?"

"Oh, yeah. Good call." The boy shot her a toothy grin, one that was altogether too cocky for their present situation. He jumped up and pulled the ladder down. "Ladies first."

Gwendolyn hesitated. "Uh, I'm not climbing over you in this skirt. I'll thank the gentleman to go first." It was a good excuse, but truthfully she just wanted to see if it would hold his weight.

The boy's jaw dropped, taken aback. "I didn't—that's not—I would never!"

A loud crash came from the smoke behind them.

"Just climb!" Gwendolyn shouted, though she was glad to wipe that smug smile from his face. She had the presence of mind to stick the book in her bag.

He scrambled up the ladder, but was already grinning again, and gave her a wink. "Be careful, *girlie.* Wouldn't want to tear that precious skirt of yours."

"Just worry about yourself, *little boy,* and when you fall, try and avoid my head." Teasing him was an easy way to hide how terrified she was.

The fire escape held, and they reached the roof. They crossed to the other side and looked down. The sheer drop to the street below made her eyes swirl. A twelve-story fall is not the sort of story you'll ever get to tell.

"What now? There's nowhere to go!" Gwendolyn said.

"Nowhere to go? Please. I have a plan. Well, *we* have a plan. Er, Starling will have a plan. Any trouble down there?" he asked the goggled girl, who was clambering over the edge of the roof.

"Yes. And all of it is your fault. But I bought us a few moments. Now take one of these." The girl produced a collection of objects from another one of her pockets and tossed something to each of them.

Gwendolyn caught it. It was a miniature umbrella, bright pink with purple spirals on it, not much larger than her hand. It was the same sort of umbrella your parents might put into a tropical drink on the beach when they've left you and your sister at home with relatives. Gwendolyn frowned at it, but she opened it with a crinkly *pop.*

"When I say so, jump," said the older girl, approaching the edge of the roof.

This was too much, even for Gwendolyn. "Jump? We'll be smushed!" She glanced at the pitifully small umbrella in her hand.

The boy rolled his eyes. "You wanted a plan. Maybe you

should ask *them* about it." He cocked a thumb at the Faceless Gentlemen, who had just appeared on the roof.

"This is a most inappropriate way for young children to act, Mister Five," said the man on the left, his face slipping from Gwendolyn's mind like water through her fingers.

"Most inappropriate indeed, Mister Six. They will have to be dealt with immediately. These sorts of intrusions cannot be tolerated," the other replied. They strode across the roof toward the children, each step in perfect unison.

Gwendolyn looked down at the punishingly solid sidewalk. She glanced at the boy, and got another infuriating wink. For someone saving her life, he was certainly not impressing her. "Isn't there another way?"

"Of course there is another way," droned Mister Five. His hand reached toward her in a gesture that absolutely failed to be comforting. "Come with us." His voice took on the sickly sweetness of cough syrup. "Your parents must be worried sick about you. No little girl should be out this far. Just what would your mother think?"

"What indeed, Mister Five. We will take care of you, girl, and see you home safe. We will explain everything to your parents, make all your problems disappear. We might even allow you to keep that little book. The Status Quo will be preserved. All will be well. After all, you cannot trust such *dreadful* children as these." His white-gloved hand waved toward her brightly colored companions.

You and I might be able to spot the lie these men told, but we are not the ones teetering over the edge of a fatal fall. Gwendolyn hesitated. What *would* Mother think? She would certainly not approve of any of this dashing about, nor of her two rescuers. But her parents had also never seen anything like these men, and she wasn't certain they'd approve of them, either.

The boy put a hand on her shoulder. "It's us or them. Now or never."

She took a deep breath and looked over the side. She had to do it. She couldn't turn back now. She would imagine she was brave, even if she felt like throwing up.

"Then I guess it's now," she whispered. She squeezed her eyes shut, gripped the umbrella, bent her knees . . .

"Sorry, girlie, time's up!" The boy gave her a shove, and Gwendolyn fell with a shriek. The older girl followed, leaping from the roof.

"So long, chaps!" The boy tipped his cap to the Mister Men, showed them a very impolite finger, and jumped.

CHAPTER SEVEN

The Magnificent Bathysphere

Time is a cruel thing. At those moments when we are enjoying ourselves most, it runs away as fast as it can. Yet at times of terror or pain, it delights in slowing down so that every moment stretches for an unbearable eternity.

So as Gwendolyn's eyes shot open and saw the ground so far below, she had more than enough time for a rapid barrage of thoughts. *What am I doing? I jumped off a building! This is real. Is this real? I jumped off a building! He pushed me! I'm going to die!*

Then her tiny umbrella burst open wider and expanded into a six-foot canopy of pink ruffles.

A single, surprised *Oh!* was all she could manage as time sped up again.

The giant umbrella twirled downward, and Gwendolyn clung to it in equal parts wonder and terror. Her feet dangled nervously, unsure, until at last they touched the asphalt again. She looked back up to see the Faceless Gentlemen standing on the edge of the roof.

The umbrella-parachutes shrank back to their hand-held size once more. A very surprised little boy stood nearby, his pale and dirty face gaping.

"Follow me!" the girl named Starling commanded, then dashed away.

"So long. Don't try that at home," Sparrow said, patting the open-mouthed boy on the head. He grabbed Gwendolyn's hand and pulled her along.

~~~

On top of the building, Mister Five and Mister Six watched the three children scamper around the corner. Then the two men leapt, casually plummeting to the ground with a hard *thump* that neither of them seemed to feel, as if leaping a dozen stories were no more trouble than stepping off the curb. The pale boy's eyes looked like they would fall out of their sockets if they opened any wider. He stared up at the two men, speechless.

"This is an unfortunate turn of events, Mister Six," said Mister Five. "The balance is threatened. The Status Quo must be preserved. The girl is an anomaly."

"Most definitely. This sort of infestation must be dealt with before it spreads any further, Mister Five. The girl must be erased, and the City scrubbed clean of her changes," said Mister Six.

"We must return to make our report," said Mister Five.
~~~

"Yes, but first we must cleanse the remaining contamination." Mister Six turned to the gaping boy. "Young man, might I ask you to direct your attention here, to my lovely hat?"

There was no one on the street to witness Mister Six remove his hat and shining it on the boy's dirty face. There was no one around to see the boy slowly fade, his body flickering into nothingness. And when the boy disappeared completely, there was no one who would remember that he had ever existed at all.

~~~

Several blocks away, the three children came to a stop, panting.

"Nice work with the parabrellas, Starling," said the boy.

"Are we safe?" whispered Gwendolyn after she caught her breath.

"Not likely," said Starling. "We're too exposed."

"Yeah, and we don't exactly blend in here, if you hadn't noticed." The boy gave her another maddening wink.

Gwendolyn frowned. What kind of person winked that much in casual conversation? It wasn't normal. Though nothing about this boy was. "Well, I *am* grateful to be rescued, but it's hardly a rescue at all if we haven't anywhere to go."

"The rescue isn't over yet. When you're good and rescued, you'll know it. I have a plan. I always have a plan." He paused for a moment, then turned to the older girl. "Starling, what's the plan?"

Starling scowled at him the way that only family can, and Gwendolyn realized they must be siblings. The older girl checked a screen on her complicated-looking wrist device. Then she
~~~

whipped a tool from her belt and pried open a nearby manhole cover. "Down here. Maybe we'll find a portal out of this place." She looked around at the grey buildings in disgust.

Gwendolyn bit her lip as she looked down the hole. She thought of how angry Mother would be if she knew her daughter was roaming the sewers.

The boy sidled up next to her. "What's the matter, girlie?" he whispered. "Scared of the dark?"

Starling rolled her eyes. "Shut up, Sparrow. If she won't go, just leave her."

But children will do all sorts of foolish things to prove themselves to each other. Gwendolyn strode to the hole, shot Sparrow a dirty look, and hopped in.

She fell a few feet, landed on slick stone, slipped, and fell on her face. "Ow!" she cried, then spotted the ladder she could have used. "Stupid girl."

The boy jumped in the hole and landed gracefully beside her. "Well, it's smelly. And dark. Starling, can we take care of that?"

"Maybe if you took a shower once in a while," Starling said as she climbed sensibly down the ladder. There was a *click* and the lenses of her goggles lit up, casting two yellow beams. She looked at the blinking screen on her wrist, and waved it around. "I'm getting a reading. Should be this way. Move it, munchkins." She led them down the tunnel, her goggle-lights bouncing.

Fortunately, these tunnels were not actually for sewage, but rather were maintenance corridors for the City's utilities. Gwendolyn had read all about them. The ancient grey bricks were covered in electrical wires, dripping water pipes, and the

City's network of pneumatic postal tubes. Letters and packages zoomed through the glass tubes, whooshing around the City with puffs of air.

"This appears to be safe enough," Gwendolyn said. "Would you mind telling me who you are?"

The boy tipped his flat, checkered cap. "I'm Sparrow. This cranky creature is Starling."

Starling grunted. The girl had jet-black hair, save for a lock of bright blue that had come free from her ponytail. It dangled in her face as she looked down at her equipment.

"Yes, I heard you say so," Gwendolyn said. "But where did you come from? And why did you save me?"

"We just . . . popped in," Sparrow said. "We saw a pretty redhead in trouble, and couldn't help ourselves."

"*He* couldn't help himself," Starling grumbled.

"Fine, *I* decided to help, it was all my idea. And who do I have the pleasure of saving today? And who were those creeps we were saving you from?"

"Oh! My name is Gwendolyn. I don't know, and thank you," she mumbled. "But don't think sweet words will make me forget you pushed me off a building."

"Oh, come on, girlie—"

"Not girlie, *Gwendolyn,* as I have just told you—"

"Both of you, shut up, I'm trying to work here."

"All right. Gwendolyn, yeah? I'm sorry for pushing you off a building. It worked, though, right?"

Starling swatted his head.

"Ow. I mean, I'm really very sorry for pushing you. We've never even been in your city before, but you were in trouble, so—"

"What do you mean, *my* city? It's your city too."

"Nope. We aren't exactly from here."

"Thank goodness," Starling grumbled.

"Don't be stupid, it's the City. Everyone is from here," Gwendolyn snapped. She was still a bit irritable, though after the day she'd just had, it was understandable.

"Not us. We come from somewhere, umm, outside the City," said Sparrow.

"Outside?" Gwendolyn's mind whirled back to the Wall. "You've been outside the City? What's out there?"

Sparrow grinned. "No idea. Never been there. At least not on *this* world. But there's plenty of others to choose from."

"Other what?"

"Other worlds, of course. We're travelers. Explorers, kinda."

Starling snorted.

"Explorers," Sparrow repeated, giving his sister a hard look. "We hop from place to place and have adventures, and . . . stuff."

"Adventures?" Gwendolyn's curiosity twitched. "Other worlds outside the City? How do you get there?"

Sparrow wiggled his eyebrows. "Magic."

"Magic?" She'd never heard the word before, but she liked the sound of it.

"Sparrow, don't tease the girl, it isn't magic."

"*Some* people say it's magic," he grumbled.

"No they don't, and if they do, they're idiots. We use portals." Starling tapped her beeping gauntlet.

"Portals?"

"Science-y stuff. Weak spots between the worlds. If I could get a clear signal, I'd show you, but you're giving off an insane amount of interference."

Gwendolyn was confused. "Me?"

Starling held her wrist device next to Gwendolyn and was rewarded with a loud *beep*. "Yep. The portals give off a certain energy, *not* magic, but there's not a speck of energy on this world, except for one ridiculous girl–"

"Hey!" shouted Gwendolyn.

"Yeah, you're bursting with it. I've never seen a signal that strong . . ." Starling trailed off.

"What does that mean? Is it dangerous? Am I going to explode?"

"You never knoooow . . ." Sparrow sang.

Starling rolled her eyes.

"But what does it *mean?*" Gwendolyn repeated. "What kind of signal?" She was not sure she could take much more strangeness. Instead of finding answers, each impossible thing just brought a thousand new questions. It was almost enough to make her wish to go home to her normal trouble instead. Sparrow placed a hand on her shoulder, but she shrugged it off.

"Look, Gwendolyn, we don't know much about it, but we *do* know that when there's enough of this energy in one place, weird things happen. Like holes between worlds. Weird things have been happening around you, right? Maybe you've felt out of place? Like you didn't fit in?"

Gwendolyn's shoulders slumped. "Is it that obvious? Everyone tells me I'm a freak."

"Hey, no one said you were a freak—"

"But I *am* a freak, I made a girl in my class grow rabbit ears this morning!"

"Wait, what?" Starling said.

Gwendolyn sighed. "It's a long story. I . . . imagine things. Daydreams. But today, they haven't exactly stayed inside my head. Some of them have become real."

Sparrow and Starling exchanged glances. Starling coughed. "So, you just imagine something, and it happens? Just like that?"

"No, not exactly, and saying it makes me sound deranged. I knew you wouldn't believe me. I'm not even sure *I* believe me—"

"No-no-no, we believe you," Sparrow said, a little too quickly. "It's not the weirdest thing we've heard of—"

"Yes, it is," Starling admitted.

"Quiet, sister. With all that energy, anything's possible. And you're not a freak." Sparrow looked at Gwendolyn, his brown eyes shimmering in the dancing yellow light. She scolded herself a little for noticing them in such detail.

"Trust me. Being different doesn't make you strange, Gwendolyn. It makes you special. Not everyone can, uh, do whatever you do—"

"I'd say nobody can do what she does." Starling smacked her wrist device, which gave another loud beep.

But his words rang in Gwendolyn's ears. A sense of relief flooded Gwendolyn, one she wasn't ready to trust. "What makes *me* so special?" Gwendolyn said.

Starling groaned. "Enough talk, let's just get out of this place."

Ignoring her, Sparrow rubbed his hands together and asked Gwendolyn, "How about a demonstration?"

"Sparrow, we don't have time for–"

"No, listen, I actually have a plan this time. Gwendolyn, you say your imagination has been coming to life, right?"

Gwendolyn fidgeted. "Well, yes."

"Well what if you just imagine some way to get us out of these tunnels. You know," he leaned close and whispered in her ear. "Something *magical*."

Starling elbowed him. "Stop that. No one can just imagine things out of thin air. Let her find her own way home. We'll never find *ours* if you keep picking up strays."

"But maybe she can get us out of Dullsville, and even get us home–"

"It's rude to talk about someone as if they weren't there," Gwendolyn interrupted. "And it doesn't work that way, anyway. I've never been able to do it on purpose. I can't just click my heels, blink my eyes, and poof! I'm not a *wizard*," she said, the word coming to her in a blue flash, though she wasn't entirely sure she even knew what a wizard was. "And every time it happens, I just make things worse. It's dangerous."

"Oh, we can handle danger," said Sparrow. "Just try really hard."

Gwendolyn frowned. "Brilliant plan." Imagining wasn't the problem. The problem was that it would just foul everything up if she tried. The Faceless Gentlemen would come after them again, or the tunnel would collapse. But she didn't want to risk going back above to find a monorail, either.

So she closed her eyes and gave it a try. She tried to push the thoughts out, to make something happen, but as you can understand if you've ever been forced to write something for school, the more she tried to force the ideas to come, the more her mind remained blank. Discouraged, she leaned against the damp wall.

Starling snorted in disgust. "Told you it wouldn't work."

"Shhh! Just give her a chance."

All Gwendolyn could think of was the Centrals, and the mono, and everything that had happened at the Edge. The part of her that wanted to go home was slowly winning the wrestling match with her curiosity. Like when you tell your parents you want to stay up late and do grown-up things, but are secretly very tired and would like to go to bed.

As they sat in silence, she became more aware of the noises around her. She noticed the *whoosh* of letters as they sped through the tubes. She noticed the steady drip of water. She noticed the breathing of three children, very small and very alone.

"I wish we could fly away like these letters do," she wondered aloud, the thought coming as if from nowhere.

And like a dam bursting, that thought led to a flood of others. "I wonder where all these tubes go. Are they only inside these tunnels, or do they go other places as well? What if there are more cities out there, and the tubes go between them, running through real jungles and forests and oceans? What if they were big enough to carry people? And . . ." she stopped.

"And?" Sparrow prompted.

"And, and look!"

At the end of the tunnel, there was a pinpoint of light that had certainly not been there before—a blue speck that shimmered and danced.

"Look at that!" Gwendolyn said. "Did I do that? What is it?"

"*Told* you," said Sparrow.

Starling rolled her eyes. "So she can turn on a light. Big deal."

"You can see it too?" Gwendolyn asked hopefully.

"Of course we can," Sparrow said. "Let's go see!"

He grabbed her hand and pulled her forward. Gwendolyn found that she did not resent holding his hand. It was warm, and a little rough. And he did not try to squish hers, the way other boys might. In fact, she liked it more than she'd like us to know, and would be embarrassed if she knew I told you.

Then she remembered how he'd nearly killed her, and his stupid smirk, and she pulled her hand away. Soon the blue light was bright enough to see by, and what they saw stole Gwendolyn's breath.

At the end of the tunnel was a golden sphere, large enough to hold all three of them comfortably. It had four wheels on golden tracks that reminded Gwendolyn of the monorail. It was like something out of the pages of *Kolonius Thrash*. Blue light streamed through the windows of the sphere. Gwendolyn pulled the jewel out of her skirt pocket, noticing it was the exact same blue as the light.

"Well, I think we can all agree that this must be for us." Sparrow grinned.

Gwendolyn banged on the side. "Is it real?"

"Real enough," Starling said. "Though I don't know what's harder to believe, that you imagined it out of thin air, or that one of Sparrow's plans actually worked. And I'm still not sure I believe either."

"Ouch. That hurts. Seriously." Sparrow strode up the steps, turned a crank, and the hatch swung open. He bowed. "Ladies, if you please."

Inside were three ornate golden chairs with rich red upholstery. Starling's eyes lit up when she saw the control panel covered with toggles, dials, and levers. She rushed over to it and began tinkering.

"So what exactly is this, Gwendolyn?" Sparrow asked.

"I don't know," she said. "I think it's a . . . a . . ." She glanced at the jewel in her hand, which twinkled the word into her mind. "A bathysphere!"

"It's a good transport," said Starling, emerging from under the console and stowing her tools back on her belt. "Well designed."

Gwendolyn smiled. "Thank you! But it still doesn't feel like I did anything."

"I'm not convinced you did, but it'll do." Starling sat in one of the seats and set to work, flipping toggles and pulling levers. The hatch closed behind them, and the bathysphere lit up.

Sparrow stuck his hands in his pockets and nodded. "Yeah, she'll do okay. All set, girls?"

"Ready," said Starling.

"Ready!" said Gwendolyn.

"Then let's go!" He dramatically yanked a large lever. Nothing happened. "Starling, can you tell me how this stupid contraption works?" He kicked the base of the console.

Starling glared. "No. You'll just crash it."

"But it's on rails—"

"Never stopped you before. Gwendolyn, flip that switch."

Gwendolyn did. The needles on the gauges began to creep upward. With a shudder, the sphere lurched out of the tunnel and into an enormous glass tube, a much larger version of the ones lining the tunnel walls.

Gwendolyn pressed her face to the window. The rails ran along the inside of the glass tube, and everything was surrounded by shimmering blue light. Bubbles floated just outside. "We're underwater!" she gasped.

Sparrow sat and propped his feet up on the console. "Nice job, Gwen."

"It's Gwendolyn, if you please and thank you very much. I think my name is quite lovely, and I would rather not have it abbreviated." But she couldn't help smiling while she said it.

"Starling, look," Sparrow said. Up ahead, the glass tube ended in a clear sort of door, through which they could see two sets of rails, one path heading up, the other curving downward. The bathysphere slowed.

"I see it," she replied. "An airlock. We need to make our way to the surface, figure out how this is supposed to get us out of here."

"And where's the fun in that?" asked Sparrow. "To adventure!" he yelled, lunging for the control panel and pushing all the levers down.

"Sparrow, no!" Starling said, but it was too late. The glass doors split open and water filled the tube. The bathysphere emitted a terrifying series of clunks and groans and lurched onto the lower track. The ocean outside grew darker as the rails took them out of the glass tube and into the murky depths, inky water pressing directly against the windows.

Starling whirled on her brother. "Sparrow! What have I told you? You have to control yourself or we'll *never* get home again!"

"Oh, loosen up. Have a little fun!"

"Excuse me—" Gwendolyn muttered.

"Fun? It's your *fun* that always gets us into trouble!"

"Yeah, but—"

"Hello? You might want to—" Gwendolyn tried.

"If we keep going on your little 'adventures' we're never going to find our way back!"

"This one can help us, you've seen the readings—"

"Hey! Children!" Gwendolyn shouted. "If you could stop bickering for a moment, you might want to look at that!" She pointed to a seam in the bathysphere where a thin trickle of water was coming in and puddling on the floor. "Does that look like a problem to either of you?"

Starling tapped one of the dials, then flipped a switch. Pumps activated, and the water started draining through tiny holes in the metal floor. "There. Just a little leak. Nothing to worry about."

A loud thud rocked the cabin, and something white flickered past the window.

Starling frowned. "Now that, on the other hand . . ."

CHAPTER EIGHT

The Neyora

Something slammed into the window again, rattling the bathysphere. "What is that? What have you us gotten into, Gwendolyn?" Starling accused.

"*Me*?" she roared. "You brought us underground, Sparrow hit that lever, all I—" But two more thuds cut her off.

Imagine your darkest, most slithering nightmares; the kind that make you crawl into your parents' bed, even though you are far too big for such things. Then you'll have some idea of what Gwendolyn felt when she looked out the bathysphere window.

A trio of serpentine shapes swam alongside. They had translucent, slimy bodies, thirty feet long at least. One of them darted forward and smashed its head against the glass. Gwendolyn jumped. She caught a glimpse of sightless eyes and needle teeth the size of her forearm. It hissed and swam off. A trickle of water spouted where it struck.

"Quick, Gwendolyn! Do something!" Sparrow shouted.

"Like what?" she shrieked. Another thud came from below. Water pooled on the floor.

"I don't know! Use your imagination!"

"I-I can't!"

There was another thud, and the bathysphere ground to a halt with a metallic squeal. The lights went out.

Starling's goggle lamps clicked on. Outside, there was a flash of an eel-like face, and another impact shook the bathysphere. "Gwendolyn, we need you to think of something. Literally."

"But I'll just make it worse, I told you! All it does is make things worse!"

"Use your head! You got us down here, you can get us out. Control it. What are those things out there?"

"I've never even left the City before, I don't know!"

"You *do* know, Gwendolyn, think! Take a deep breath and tell me: what are those creatures? What are they called? Anything at all."

Gwendolyn brushed her hair out of her eyes and tried to focus. "I-I think they're called . . . the Deepworms," she said, conjuring the name from thin air.

"Good. Tell me more."

Another thud, louder this time.

"Th-they live in the dark."

"And?" Starling said.

"They're fast, their teeth are sharp, they're very strong—" She was cut off by another impact.

"We've got more leaks," Sparrow groaned. The water was lapping at their ankles now.

But Starling ignored him. "Now, Gwendolyn, tell me a different story. Something else that might live down here."

"W-well . . . there are the Neyora."

"Good!" Starling said, sounding unnaturally sweet. "And what are those?"

Images filled Gwendolyn's mind. She felt the familiar rush of new ideas. She rolled the blue gem in her palm. "They're a bit like manta rays. They've got long, leathery wings, and big, swishing tails with a pointed barb for spearing fish. They don't usually come down this far."

"Starling, hurry–"

Two Deepworms slammed into the bathysphere, and the viewport splintered. The water came in even faster.

"How big are they?" Starling asked.

"Quite big, big as monorail trams. And they're . . . they're . . ." The gem flashed at her. "Bioluminescent! They glow! It attracts the fish they like."

Suddenly, six glowing shapes swooped down from above. They gleamed pink and purple and orange and flapped huge, leathery wings just as Gwendolyn described, their sleek, triangular bodies tapering to a thin tail with a pointed barb. They surrounded the monstrous serpents.

"Look at that!" shouted Sparrow.

"Quick, Gwendolyn, do they eat the Deepworms?" Starling asked.

"Oh no," Gwendolyn said softly. She felt calmer just looking at the glowing creatures. "But they don't like them. Deepworms scare off all the fish."

The Neyora paired off to circle each of the Deepworms. The monsters gnashed their hideous teeth. Then the Deepworms coiled in on themselves and dove down into the black.

"Where did they go?" asked Sparrow.

"They ran away. The light from the Neyora hurts their eyes. They're made for darkness."

The Neyora twirled and rolled, dancing around the bathysphere. A magenta one swam close to the viewport and dipped its fin in greeting. Gwendolyn waved back.

"They're beautiful," Starling said.

"See?" Sparrow said. "Magic."

Starling rolled her eyes. "Don't be so gullible. She's just accessing the ambient subconscious energy to create physical manifestations of her mental hallucinations–"

"You can't just make up words to confuse me–"

"I'm not, you twit. And don't say–"

"–maaaaaaagic."

"Shh!" Gwendolyn pointed. "They're singing!"

A wailing cry sounded through the bathysphere. It was joined by another, moaning in harmony with the first, and then there were more; a whole chorus of unearthly voices.

Sparrow grew quiet. The light and song made the three children feel warm and comforted, like when you were small and your parents would plug in the night-light and sing you softly to sleep.

"Each one has a unique song, but it blends with the other members of the herd. When they're together, the stronger glow attracts more food. They can talk to each other with the light as well, flapping their fins to create patterns. They're quite peaceful, really, living down in the depths, singing and glowing and . . ." Gwendolyn trailed off. "You haven't interrupted me."

Starling actually smiled, and shrugged. "It was interesting."

"Everyone always interrupts me."

Sparrow reached into his jacket pocket and pulled out an apple. He bit it and chewed thoughtfully. "Well, if you hadn't noticed, we're not like everyone else," he mumbled. He pulled out another and tossed it to Gwendolyn. "Kind of like you."

She felt a blush rise in her cheeks, but quickly pushed it down. Instead she looked at the apple, admiring its color. She decided it was far too pretty to eat, and put it in her bag instead.

The lights in the bathysphere came back on. Starling jumped to the controls. "Let's get out of here before these cracks get any bigger."

The pumps came back on with the rest of the power, and the water drained out. The cracks remained, and water kept trickling in, but without the Deepworms to make them worse, the pumps kept up as the bathysphere limped its way down the tracks.

The Neyora followed along, and Gwendolyn collapsed into her seat. "If I'm imagining all of this, shouldn't I know what's happening and be able to control it?"

Sparrow sat as well. "Have you ever been able to control your imagination?"

Gwendolyn frowned. "I suppose not. Maybe that's why those men are following me," she wondered.

Sparrow raised an eyebrow. "What do you mean?"

"Well, you said no one else has any of this mag–energy." She glanced at Starling. "Maybe that's what they're after."

"Wouldn't surprise me," Starling said.

Gwendolyn looked down at the jewel in her hand, the same blue as the water. Then an idea hit her like the Deepworms slamming into the bathysphere. "It's the Lambents!"

"The what?" Sparrow said.

"The Lambents! The Mister Men! They were trying to . . . to drain me, or something! That's what the Lambents are designed to do. They drain everyone of their energy. Their imagination." Something the men had said pinged in her memory. "They protect the Status Quo. Keep everything the same. If no one has any ideas, then nothing ever changes. Everyone stays empty and happy. And that's why Tommy didn't remember Missy. They drained it from him, erasing my changes. That's why no one ever wonders anything, ever thinks about what's outside the City, or goes looking for the Edge, or the Wall."

"I have absolutely no idea what you're talking about," Sparrow said.

"Quiet, I'm thinking! Everyone drained of imagination, except for me. I'm not the one who's broken. It's the City. It's the Lambents. And this." She looked down at the blue gem. "This is the opposite, somehow. It's been filling my mind with new ideas, instead of taking them out. And then the Mister Men found me. They were going to drain me dry. No . . ." She remembered her hand vanishing, just like Missy had vanished. "Not drain me. *Erase* me. They erased Missy, they wanted to erase me, too." Her thoughts went very dark then, realizing that Missy was much worse than missing.

"You *were* pretty out of it when we found you," Starling said.

"Thank you again for that. Even if your brother did push me off a building, I suppose it turned out all right."

Sparrow grinned again, all dimples and teeth.

The bathysphere slowed as the rails entered another glass tube, and a circular hatch appeared, lights ringing a door just large enough for the bathysphere.

"We're here," said Starling. "Somewhere."

Sparrow brought a pretend microphone to his mouth. "Thank you for using Imagination Underwater Railways. We hope you enjoyed your ride. Please do not leave any belongings inside the metal ball, and watch your step as you reenter the Big Boring City of Sameness. Any weirdness from here on out is your own problem. Goodbye!"

Gwendolyn groaned, but couldn't help smiling a little. The airlock admitted them and sealed itself after they passed. The tube drained of water and the battered bathysphere shuddered to a tired stop.

Starling opened the bathysphere's hatch. Outside was another underground maintenance tunnel, identical to the one they'd left. She pulled on her goggles and flipped down a lens. "I don't see anything out there. It should be safe." She stepped out.

"Why would I imagine something that wasn't safe?" asked Gwendolyn, descending the steps.

Sparrow followed. "Who knows what goes on in that head of yours, girlie."

This time, Gwendolyn did not bother to correct him.

Their wet feet squelched through the tunnel. This one was clearly newer and in better repair. Gwendolyn's mind reeled. She felt like she had been sleeping her whole life; now she was awake, and reality looked like a very different place.

"So, there are other worlds besides this one?" It was the sort of thing that sends a grown-up mind scrambling for the nearest exit. Grown-ups are so certain they know everything that they struggle when the rug of reality is pulled from under them. But children are only just beginning to understand the world at all and learn new and surprising things about it every day, so they are much less shocked to learn one or two more. Gwendolyn was taking it all in stride.

Starling's face darkened as she nodded. "Many."

"And you, what, you travel between them? Exploring?"

She grunted. "Something like that."

"So what are you doing here? There's certainly nothing interesting in the City." *And now I know why,* she thought.

Sparrow grinned. "Oh, I don't know, we haven't exactly been bored. Hopping from place to place, having grand old adventures, scraping by on the skin of our teeth. Loads of fun."

Starling mimicked Sparrow's voice perfectly. "*Loads of fun.* Idiot."

Gwendolyn's jaw dropped. "How did you do that?"

"Ignore her," Sparrow rolled his eyes. "It's just her stupid little talent."

"*And I'm just her stupid little brother,*" Starling added in Sparrow's voice again.

"Cut that out! It's creepy."

"And I'm such a scaredy-cat, what would I ever do without my big sister—"

"Quit it!"

"Do you think there are any portals around here?" Gwendolyn interrupted, preventing any arguments.

"There's a weak signal," Starling said in her own voice. "Over here."

They came to a dead end where a ladder led up to a manhole cover. Starling cranked it open. Outside, evening was just beginning to fall, but the streetlights had yet to come on. Gwendolyn clambered out of the hole, the other two following close behind. She looked around at a part of the Middling City that she knew quite well. "It worked. This is my street, that's my home."

Starling nodded. "All right. Goodbye."

Gwendolyn frowned. "Really? Just like that? You don't have to go so soon."

Sparrow shrugged. "Gotta find the next portal. Always keep moving."

"But I—" She didn't quite know what to say. It sounded childish, but she had thought she'd finally found some friends, and she wasn't ready to let them go just yet. "Maybe I could go with you! What if I'm not ready to go home?"

Starling pointed to her apartment building. "Your subconscious seems to say otherwise, since it brought us here."

Passersby were starting to stare. "Look at the state of those children," said one aghast woman.

"Awful filthy brats, scurrying around in the sewers," said a well-dressed gentleman.

"Brats? More like rats," sneered his son.

"You three need to move along, now," came a voice from behind them. It was a policeman Gwendolyn recognized, for he regularly patrolled their neighborhood. There were plenty of policemen in the City, but Gwendolyn had only ever seen them wave to the adults, shoo mischievous children along, and hustle the odd vagrant back to the Outskirts.

Mr. Nandrani from downstairs never stopped grumbling about the constant rise in crime, the hoodlums who counted as children these days, and the general decaying state of the world; but if there was any criminal activity in the City, Gwendolyn had certainly never seen it, and nothing ever really changed anyway.

"It's dinnertime. No need for you youngsters to be wanderin' about unaccompanied. Best be getting home now."

"Yes, officer." Gwendolyn forced a polite smile, which melted to a scowl the moment she'd turned away.

"And change into somethin' more respectable, right?" he called after them. "The clothes you kids wear these days."

Her face burned as she led the other two toward her building, the policeman still eyeing them warily. "See what I mean? I *hate* this place. How can I possibly go home after all this?"

Sparrow looked at her. "Yeah, but are you really ready to go dashing off to worlds unknown? You don't have any spare clothes or food or anything in that bag of yours, do you? And what about your parents?"

"My parents . . ." *That* certainly didn't make her want to stay.

She was going to be in so much trou– "Oh! My parents! I have to go, I have to make sure they're all right! What if the Faceless Gentlemen came here, what if they've done something to them?"

Starling furrowed her brow in concern. "Do those men know who you are? Do they know where you live?"

She hesitated. "No, I don't think so."

Starling nodded. "Then you should be fine. Just keep your head down."

Gwendolyn nodded, biting her lip as they crossed the street to her building. "All right. I still have to make sure. But where will you two go?"

"We'll find our way," said Sparrow.

Starling tapped her wrist. "We always do."

"Will you come back tomorrow? To . . . to help me? I have to do something about those men, and I can't do it on my own. Promise me you'll come back," Gwendolyn said.

"Of course. We promise," Sparrow said. His sister glared at him, but he ignored it.

Gwendolyn was not so gullible as to trust the rascal, but when we want something as badly as Gwendolyn did, we shout down the little voices that tell us to beware.

"Thank you. For everything," Gwendolyn said.

Sparrow threw her a jaunty salute. "You're welcome. See ya."

Gwendolyn watched them disappear into one of the alleyways that honeycombed the City, any trace of cheer gone from her heart.

She trudged to her apartment door, the one marked 6E. One

hand on the knob, the other clutching the jewel in her pocket, she took a deep breath to prepare for whatever lay inside.

The Grays lived in a spacious Middling apartment, stylishly decorated by Mother. The furnishings were elegant and modern, with lots of clean, straight lines and open space. As Gwendolyn entered the living room and set down her bag, she saw Father sitting at his desk to the side, clacking away at his typewriter. Nothing out of place at all.

She sighed in relief. The Faceless Gentlemen had not been here. Coming home seemed to put an immediate wall between her and the events of the day. Everything here was so plain, so familiar. Girls with rabbit ears and monsters with teeth seemed completely unreal, crushed by the weight of normal routine.

Father, or Danforth Gray as the rest of the world knew him, wore his usual black suit, white vest, and thin bowtie. His dark hair was swept back, not a piece out of place. His deepest pride was his mustache, which was thick and full and curled at the tips. He was one of the dreadfully nice sort of grown-ups, the ones that are a bit funny in their own way, and don't actually seem to mind the presence of children. If they had any sports in the City, he would have been the type who would drop whatever he was doing to play with you in the yard. Unfortunately, the City had no time for games, and no space for yards.

He sat in his straight-back chair, nattering at the keys of the typewriter. The writing looked awfully dull and businessy to Gwendolyn.

"Ah, Gwendolyn dear. Welcome home. I trust that you have had an enjoyable afternoon, adventuring with your chums from the School," he said, hitting the carriage return with a satisfying chime.

"Uh, not exactly," she mumbled, squirming uncomfortably.

He turned in his chair with an appraising look and a kind smile. "Hmmm. Well, you are late, and incredibly dirty, so I'm sure there's a story to be had somewhere, but I know better than to pry into the secret affairs of children. Your mother, on the other hand . . ." He lowered his voice to a whisper. "Well, she's been talking to herself in the kitchen, which means she must be rather upset indeed. Come. Best wash up a bit before she sees you."

Gwendolyn washed her hands, and she entered the kitchen with her father.

"Ah. So *there* you are," Mother said, wiping her hands on a towel. She slapped it down hard on the counter. "Now, just what do you have to say for yourself?"

CHAPTER NINE

A Rather Smashing Evening

Father gave Gwendolyn a sympathetic look, then busied himself setting the table. Gwendolyn said nothing, hanging her head and hiding her face in her hair.

"Look at me, I can't see your face when you do that," Mother scolded. "Where have you been? We get a phone call from the School saying you had been dismissed early. And then you never came home! We were worried sick! Just look at you, covered with dirt from head to foot."

Gwendolyn looked down at herself, smeared with all manner of grunge and grime. Sheepishly, she held out her freshly scrubbed palms.

Mother's eyes narrowed. "Don't get cute, Miss Gwendolyn Alice. I haven't even gotten to the worst of it yet. Cecilia Forthright's mother called. She says you attacked her daughter? Cecilia has scratches all over her face! I was horrified!"

"Mother, it wasn't like that, she–"

"I don't want to hear it! Did you scratch her?"

"Yes, but–"

"Ah-ah-ah. Yes. Or. No."

Gwendolyn sighed, trying to exhale her frustration. "Yes."

"Then that's the end of it. Your behavior was entirely unacceptable, no matter what Cecilia did. And you know better. I can't . . ." She made an exasperated noise. "I don't know what to do with you anymore. You seem determined to continue acting like a child. Now sit down for supper."

Father coughed softly, his arms full of dishes. "Well then. Now that that's all settled, let's tuck in. I'm positively famished."

They had some kind of tasteless noodle casserole with gravy, but Gwendolyn just moved the noodles around to look like she'd eaten something. She couldn't stop thinking about poor Missy. She pictured what the dinner table at Missy's house must look like, with one empty chair. Her parents would be worried sick, if they even remembered they *had* a daughter.

"Jenkins caused a bit of a kerfuffle today," Father said. He was the inter-office communications editor for a large company. "The man is completely inept. His margins were far too narrow, and his font was all wrong. Everyone knows you need to use a lighter typeface for the semi-weekly accountancy update!"

Gwendolyn didn't know what Father did, exactly, but it had something to do with answering lots of messages, sending them back, sitting through meetings, and complaining that nothing ever got done at the meetings. Personally, she didn't want any part of it, if you please, and thank you very much. The grown-up world was quite as unfathomable to her as the depths of the ocean or the beaches of Zanzibar, and much less exciting.

"I honestly don't know how the man has held onto his job as long as he has. If he weren't such a laugh to have around, he'd have been canned months ago. The other day, on a lark, he submitted a departmental memo in a serif font, instead of a sans serif! Well, I hardly need to tell you, we were in stitches!"

"May I be excused?" Gwendolyn blurted. She couldn't take any more of this normalcy.

"All right then," Mother said. "But straight to bed, no Lambent time. Lord knows I could use some, a little relaxation after the day you've put me through."

Gwendolyn froze, halfway out of her chair, plate in hand. The Lambent. Theirs was tucked away in its little drawer in the coffee table. After dinner her parents normally sat on the couch and spent an hour or so staring at the flickering light.

She took her plate to the kitchen, thoughts whirling. Maybe the Faceless Gentlemen would find her through the Lambent. Or maybe her parents' minds would be erased, just like Tommy's and Ian's, and they wouldn't even remember Gwendolyn at all. Then the men could come for her, and no one would even notice.

She couldn't let that happen.

She snuck into the living room and slid open the coffee table drawer. The little glass bead was inside. She would run to her room and hide it, just until she could sort everything out.

"Just what do you think you're doing, young lady?" Mother stood in the doorway to the dining room.

Gwendolyn froze, bent over the open drawer, caught red-handed. "I was, um—"

"Deliberately disobeying me. What part of 'no Lambent time' was unclear to you?"

Gwendolyn stood up, the Lambent behind her back. "No, you don't understand—"

"Don't tell me *no*." Mother walked over, hand outstretched. "Give me the Lambent and go to your room."

Gwendolyn moved to the opposite side of the couch. She had never so blatantly defied Mother before, and it was a whole new kind of terrifying. But she clutched the Lambent tighter. "I can't, I'm sorry."

"Gwendolyn Alice Gray!" Mother's face darkened, shocked and furious. "Come over here this instant!" She tried to come around the couch, but Gwendolyn just went around to the other side again.

"Please, you have to trust me!"

But Mother kept coming. They were running now, doing laps around the white couch.

"Stop running away! Give me that Lambent, now!" Mother started climbing over the couch to get at her but her skirt was too tight to manage it, and she fell forward, rolling onto the floor.

Gwendolyn backed away, only to bump into Father in the dining room doorway.

"Gwendolyn," he rumbled. "Give it back to her. Now." His mustache quivered with rage.

She felt like a caged animal. She couldn't let them have the Lambent, she had to protect them, but she had no way to make them understand. Father stepped forward, and Gwendolyn backed up, bumping into the desk. "I . . . I . . ."

Her parents approached, angrier than she had ever seen. Mother held out her hand. "I'm going to ask you. One. Last. Time. Hand it over, young lady."

Gwendolyn was frozen with indecision. But Mother seemed tired of waiting, and lunged forward to take it.

Quick as a wink, Gwendolyn put the Lambent on the desk, picked up Father's typewriter, and brought the heavy black thing down on the Lambent with a thud and a brief flash of light.

Mother gasped. Father's face turned an unsightly shade of purple, and he pushed Gwendolyn aside to inspect his typewriter. He lifted it, revealing a small pile of pulverized glass powder underneath.

Mother pointed at the stairs with a shaking arm. "Room. Now."

Gwendolyn didn't hesitate. She fled up the stairs into her room, and closed the door.

She took a long, deep breath and slumped against the door, catching sight of herself again in the bedroom mirror. She looked frightful. Her clothes were filthy, her hair a dreadful nest of tangles and dirt.

At least her parents were safe. There was no Lambent to tamper with anyone's mind, or bring the Faceless Gentlemen down on them. Dealing with whatever her parents could devise would be a carnival compared to Mister Five and Mister Six.

The safety of her little bedroom made all today's strangeness seem unreal and far away. Tired as she was, her mind was nowhere near calm enough to consider sleep. She thought of diving back into *Kolonius Thrash,* but as she dug through her bag, she found her picture from earlier that morning. Inspired, she got out her pencil box and sketchbook. Drawing was her usual evening habit, and it never failed to settle her thoughts.

She sighed. These colors just weren't enough anymore. Not after what she'd seen. This is a common problem for adventurers, for when the running and screaming is over, how can normal life possibly compare?

She started sketching, but she wanted to capture the glowing magenta of the Neyora, or Starling's turquoise blouse and matching streak of hair. She tried drawing Sparrow, with his red jacket and yellow scarf. Suddenly, she was startled to see that the colors in her head had found their way onto the paper after all. Reds, yellows, greens, and blues smiled up at her from the crisp, white sheets.

She smiled back, for the first time in hours, and turned to a new page. She talked to herself as the colors spread across the paper. "Once upon a time," she said, remembering *Kolonius Thrash,* "in the forests of Baroom, where the gum trees grew, there lived a furry little creature named Criminy the Falderal. Every day the other Falderals would tease Criminy, for their fur was the blackest of black, but Criminy's fur was a bright and shocking orange from head to toe." She paused to admire her work. The creature smiled up at her. Its stubby, purple antenna, flappy feet, and goofy smile made her feel much better. "Hello, Criminy."

She tore his picture out and stood on her chair to hang it

on her bulletin board. "Now, Criminy didn't like living in the forest of Baroom. One day, after a particularly nasty teasing from the others, Criminy left the forest to find somewhere he could belong. Over the hill, across the field, and up into the Cranky Mountains–"

"Meep!"

Gwendolyn froze, push pin in hand. She turned slowly. A furry, orange creature was standing in the middle of her bedroom.

"Meep!" it repeated.

"Aaaah!" Gwendolyn fell off her chair.

"Meep!" The creature waved its flipper arms and waddled in circles. Orange fuzz filled the air.

"Gwendolyn!" Mother shouted. "What the devil is that racket?"

Fear broke through the shock, and she leapt up. "Nothing, Mother!" she called, chasing the oversized puffball.

"Meeeep! Meeeep! Meeeep!" it squealed, slapping around the room.

"Criminy! Stop that! Come here!" She tackled it to the ground.

"Meeeeeeeeeeeeep!"

Over the racket, she heard Mother's footsteps on the stairs.

Thinking as quickly as anyone could who'd just conjured a monster in their bedroom, Gwendolyn stuffed the squirming Falderal into her closet. "Be quiet!" she hissed, and slid the closet closed just as Mother opened the door.

"What was all that noise?" she demanded.

"It was nothing!" Gwendolyn panted. She prayed the dark closet would keep Criminy quiet.

Mother's eyes blazed. "Don't take that tone with me. You're in enough trouble as it is." She crossed her arms and tapped her foot, beating the parental war drum.

Gwendolyn glanced around the room, searching for an excuse. "I'm sorry. I didn't mean to snap. It's only that . . . I hurt my foot!" she blurted. "Ooooo, it hurts. No, I mean, only a little, I'm fine now. I climbed on my chair to hang a picture on my bulletin board, but I fell. I'm sorry."

Mother let out a sigh and uttered a familiar catchphrase of mothers everywhere. "How many times have I told you not to climb on furniture?"

Gwendolyn thought *that* was a bit hypocritical, but this was not the time. "A thousand. I'm terribly sorry. You won't ever have to do it again, I've learned my lesson this time, you can go back downstairs with Father and everything will be all right, I promise."

Mother's eyes narrowed. "Uh-huh. Well, get changed and in bed. I better not hear another peep until I come check on you." She slammed the door and Gwendolyn heard her stomp down the stairs.

"Another *meep,* you mean." She leaned back against the closet, and sighed with relief. Then she turned and flung open the closet door, arms spread wide to catch the Falderal.

Her closet was empty, save for the heaps of clothes Mother was always begging her to hang up. She searched the room and under her bed, but Criminy seemed to have vanished like a bad dream. Even the orange fur was gone.

She looked at his picture on the bulletin board. "What else could go wrong today?"

Which, as everyone knows, is quite the worst thing to say in such a situation. But the fates had mercy on her this time.

She threw on her plain grey pajamas, pulled back her plain grey covers, and jumped into her plain grey bed just as the door opened.

"No more last-minute antics?" Mother asked.

"No, Mother," she politely replied.

"All washed and brushed? Teeth and hair?"

"Yes, Mother," she politely lied.

Which did not fool her mother in the slightest, but she sat down on the edge of Gwendolyn's bed with a long, weary sigh. "What are we going to do with you, Bless?" She used Gwendolyn's special pet name, which meant she must have calmed down considerably. "Today has been . . . difficult. And make no mistake, I am still utterly, completely furious at you. But . . ."

Gwendolyn waited though the awkward pause.

"I know I'm not entirely without blame. I never should have shamed you in front of that woman this morning. I was frustrated, and we were late, and—well, that's no excuse. It wasn't something a mother should do, and girls are terribly sensitive at your age. I can imagine it affected your behavior the rest of the day. Forgive me?"

Gwendolyn nodded. She could only hope for forgiveness in

turn if Mother ever found out what she'd *actually* done—erasing a classmate from existence was an awfully unforgivable thing.

"Mother, I—" For a moment, Gwendolyn thought of telling her everything, explaining the terrible danger they might all be in.

"Yes?"

But of course, it was simply too unbelievable. "I love you."

"I love you too, Bless. That doesn't get you off the hook for any of this madness, but I can wait until tomorrow to be angry at you. And even though you made some astonishingly bad choices today, and are in quite a lot of trouble, I *am* proud of you. I don't say it enough. You are growing up to be quite a wonderful young lady."

Gwendolyn blushed at this rare praise, but she cringed at that last bit. "Um, all right."

"Oh, and by the way, you are spectacularly grounded."

Gwendolyn nodded. "For how long?"

Mother smiled a bit. "We'll start with eternity, and then decide what to do after that." She stood up to leave, but then exclaimed, "Oh my! What is that thing?"

"What?!" Gwendolyn sat bolt upright, scanning the room for orange intruders.

Mother tapped the picture of Criminy on the wall. "That! Where on earth did you see something like that?"

"Oh. That. I didn't see it anywhere."

"What do you mean? You drew it, you must have seen it somewhere."

"No, I just made it up."

Mother gave her a quizzical look. "You made it . . ." But her eyes glazed over, and Gwendolyn thought she saw a flicker of white in Mother's pupils. "Well, it's a lovely squirrel, dear. Very vivid, somehow. That pencil box your father bought is certainly something, isn't it?"

"But it's not a sq—"

"Well, good night." She walked to the door and gave her daughter a last long look, the way mothers do before turning down the lamps and leaving their darlings for the night. Then she turned out the light and shut the door.

Gwendolyn considered the flash of white in her mother's eyes. So, the Lambent's effects ran deep. Even when you weren't looking at one, it could steer your mind away from any unpleasant ideas.

She looked out the window at the lights of the Middling. The Mister Men were out there somewhere. And Missy Cartblatt was not. And it was all Gwendolyn's fault. She would have to do something about that tomorrow. But those were dark thoughts, and in her dark room they seemed all the more terrible.

So she snuck out of bed and rustled through her things. On her nightstand, she carefully arranged *Kolonius Thrash,* the apple Sparrow had given her, and the blue gem. That was better.

The gem glowed pleasantly in her dark bedroom. Her initials twinkled on its surface. "You're very pretty," she told it. "Not like the Lambents at all. A tiny piece of . . . magic," she said, bringing out Sparrow's word and trying it on for size. "But you're really just a figment of my imagination, aren't you?" she whispered. "Yes, a little Figment." And so she named it.

She looked at the bright-red apple, lit by the glow from the

Figment. She glanced at her open closet, at her comfortable grey play dress, and wondered how it would look if it were red too.

And so the fabric rustled gently, then changed, and suddenly it was the same shade as the apple on her nightstand.

Her eyes widened, and she pulled the covers over her head. *No more trouble today.*

Eventually, she relaxed enough to find sleep. It is amazing how much less strange everything can seem at home in your own bed. All the events on one side of the day can seem just as far away as the dreams that lie on the other side of the pillow. The Figment shone on her sleeping face and filled her mind with blue dreams and stories and pictures and words.

PART TWO: GOLD

CHAPTER TEN

Not That Sort of Skipping

It was dark. The ground was rocky and hard. Flashes of lightning briefly illuminated a ruined landscape as thunder rumbled. There was nothing but bare, black rock, the ground pitted with glassy craters. The sky was a boiling, black soup.

She trembled in her pajamas. This place felt *wrong*. The air smelled burnt, and heat prickles danced across her skin, giving her a sickly feeling. In the distance, she could make out a range of broken mountains, shattered and crumbling.

A shriek ripped through the sky, a roar that chilled her bones. The clouds rumbled and began to take shape, forming an enormous pillar of blackness that stretched toward her, grabbed her, tore at her.

She tried to scream, but her throat was choked by the noxious clouds. There was a blinding explosion that seared through her eyelids, and she could feel herself burning, burning away to nothing.

Her eyes shot open. Morning had snuck up outside her window. She wiped cold sweat from her brow. *Only a nightmare,* she thought, no matter how real it might have seemed. But she secretly felt that dreams like that are never merely dreams.

She got up and shook her head, trying to clear it. Her mind felt full to bursting, thanks to the Figment. The little blue gem twinkled on her bedside table.

Gwendolyn looked at the pictures on her bulletin board. Words could not express how much she loathed the thought of going back to the School. "Must I go?" she exclaimed to her bed, rolling over to face the wall. Her bed tried to comfort her, but her window would have none of it and continued to shine cold, unforgiving light on her, forcing her to get up.

She had to go and talk to the other students, see what they remembered about Missy, try to find some clues. Maybe do something about the Lambents in class. She also had to go back to the Outskirts, find Missy's parents and explain everything to them. Not a conversation she was looking forward to, but someone had to do it.

None of which would happen if she stayed in her room all day.

Gwendolyn grabbed her treasures—the apple, the book, and the Figment—then put on her terribly uncomfortable school uniform, casting a longing eye over the apple-red dress hanging in the closet. But there was no way she'd get away with wearing *that.* She headed downstairs.

"Can you believe it, Marie? Those old duffers on the Council are at it again," Father called out. He was on the couch reading his morning paper, sipping his morning coffee, and doing his morning grumbling. "A right bunch of do-nothings. They're delaying the expansion of the new Central–Middling monorail line. It would do my commute a treat, but they can't seem to get their thick heads 'round the idea."

The City Council was a collection of the stodgiest old men you could ever hope to avoid meeting. At the Hall of Records, Gwendolyn had stumbled upon minutes of their meetings, where they did nothing but recite the minutes of the previous meetings, which was more nothing. The most they occasionally got around to was basic monorail maintenance, walkway repair, changing the bulbs on the streetlamps, and other such chores to keep things running smoothly. As far as governments went, the Council was the equivalent of brushing your teeth after every snack and always remembering to floss, and was about as interesting.

"That's nice, dear," said Mother, who had long since learned to tune out her husband's political opinions. She was busy in the kitchen cooking runny eggs. Marie Gray was not a great cook, but a determined one, and she insisted on cooking all the family's meals.

"Ah, someone's ready nice and early," Father commented over the top of his newspaper as Gwendolyn crossed to the kitchen.

Gwendolyn nibbled a piece of toast as she thought through

her plan for the day. "Mother, is it all right if I walk to the School myself today?"

Mother raised an eyebrow. "Really? No argument this morning?"

"Why, would you let me stay home if I did?"

Mother smiled and waggled a wooden spoon at her. "Smart girl. But no. You're grounded. I'm going to walk you to the mono, and then I have some errands to run. Sit down, I'm going to braid your hair."

Gwendolyn groaned inwardly, but bit her lip and sat at the table. She did not complain at all the tugging and yanking as Mother struggled to make her presentable. No sense inviting trouble early, there was plenty of chance for it later.

Eventually Mother was done. Father put down his paper. "Gwendolyn, come here for a moment." He patted the couch cushion next to him.

Mother took her cue and left to touch up her makeup. She always seemed in such a rush, though Gwendolyn never knew why. Like most women in the City, she had no job, and her only responsibilities seemed to be caring for Gwendolyn, Father, and the apartment. Which, as any grown-up knows, is a tremendous amount of work in itself, but children seldom realize this, and the City had very particular notions about which jobs were important and which people should be allowed to do them.

Besides trips to the grocery store, Gwendolyn did not know how Mother filled the time. Spending time with her friends? She must have some, though anyone who came to dinner was usually an acquaintance of Father's from work. And they didn't have any grandparents or other living family to speak of.

She sat down, preparing herself for a lecture.

"Bless, do you remember the time at the dinner party with my boss, Mr. Goldstein, when you claimed the gravy had insulted you? And it took them two weeks to get the ceiling clean?"

"Yes," she said reluctantly.

"Or when you said you could hear voices in your closet and it must be a door to a secret world? And you knocked a hole in the wall with my hammer, straight into Mr. Buloff's bathroom?"

"Yes, but I wasn't *entirely* wrong, he did sing quite loudly in the shower."

"Yes, well, he certainly doesn't anymore."

Gwendolyn thought these examples were hardly fair, since she had been much younger then. At least a year or two!

Father stroked his mustache absently. "Ahem. I guess what I'm saying, Bless, is that you must learn to control your imagination. You're growing up."

Gwendolyn groaned silently.

"And while I expect a little teenage rebellion, destroying property is more than a bit too far. New Lambents don't fall from the sky, you know. But this is the time of your life where you begin to change from the girl you were into the lady you're going to be. So you must make your choices carefully, for as they say, your choices become your habits, and your habits become your character. So let's have no more trouble of this sort, yes?"

Gwendolyn put on a sufficiently regretful expression with just the right amount of pout. "Yes, Father."

"Good. And, erm . . ." From between the couch cushions he pulled a small parcel, wrapped in black paper and a white silk ribbon. "I got this for you yesterday, but with your outburst and all, well, let's just call this a down payment on your good behavior from now on, yes?"

Gwendolyn took it and started unwrapping, too curious for words. It was a pack of white erasers and a new pencil sharpener, a very nice one, gleaming with silver and chrome. "Th-thank you, Father!" she said, and flung her arms about his neck.

"Yes, well then," he said, awkwardly patting her back. "Let's not tell your mother about it, shall we?"

~~~

Gwendolyn and her mother shared a quiet walk to the monorail. Mother kept her under a watchful eye until the last second, when the mono's doors closed. Gwendolyn had a sudden fear that they wouldn't open again, but that was silly. The mono was full of other children and commuters. She rode into the Central City, surrounded by the tallest and shiniest buildings, all clustered around the Central Tower and its mirrored dome.

Her hands went to her hair and undid her mother's hard work, but froze when she felt the piece that was shorter than the rest. Somehow, her mother had failed to notice it. But Gwendolyn was sure that Cecilia Forthright would not fail to notice *her*. She and her friends would surely be out for blood today.

The mono slowed as it approached the School. Sure enough, Cecilia and her friends lounged outside the doors. But as the
~~~

mono stopped, Gwendolyn saw something that that made a fight with Cecilia seem like a pleasant way to spend the morning.

On the steps of the School stood two Faceless Gentlemen in black bowler hats.

Gwendolyn ducked down in her seat. They were looking for her. Of *course* they were looking for her. Every child in the City would be passing through those doors in a few minutes. Where else would they look?

She blew at a lock of frizzy red hair that was already falling into her green eyes. She wouldn't exactly blend in, now would she? They would have picked her out in an instant. She couldn't go to the School now. The doors hissed shut and the mono accelerated, leaving Gwendolyn to conjure some new plan.

Now I must remind you that skipping school, no matter how awful it might be, is not acceptable. But given the dangerous circumstances she faced, I think we can excuse Gwendolyn. As her father would say, some youthful indiscretion, which is a fancy term for "being a little naughty," keeps one from growing into a stale and boring adult. Though she did feel a stab of guilt at the thought of the pencil sharpener, and how quickly she was betraying Father's trust.

She needed a plan—she needed help, that was what. Sparrow and Starling! They had promised to come back, and they knew all sorts of things she didn't. But how could she reach them?

She'd just have to find one of those portals. But how? She didn't have one of those wrist detectors like Starling, and she didn't even know what a portal looked like.

The Figment grew warm in her pocket, and she pulled it

out. It twinkled at her, as if anxious to reveal some secret. With no better idea, she held it to her eye, like she had when reading *Kolonius Thrash,* and examined the City for any hints or clues it might reveal as to where to go.

Through the blue glass, the City looked stark black and white, with even less color than usual. But out of the corner of her eye, she caught a bright flash of gold, shiny and alluring. She yanked the stop request cable, felt a surge of gratitude that it actually worked, and dashed off the train at the next stop.

She stood before the large concrete brick that was the Hall of Records, the building where all the knowledge in the City was stored. Though Gwendolyn didn't know why, since nobody ever used it.

She'd spent many a day in here, reading everything she could get her hands on, though her parents could not comprehend her interest in all those dusty old books. The building's square stone columns towered above her, with large double doors spaced between each pair.

She held the Figment to her eye again, looking for the glint of color she'd seen. The golden gleam flickered through the seams in the doors.

She dashed toward it, nearly skipping with the joy of her discovery, but quickly stopped herself, checking to see if anyone was watching. *Don't attract attention,* she thought. *You're skipping school, it's an entirely different sort of skipping. Much more quiet and sneaky.* But she saw no one, and she bolted inside.

The high ceiling flickered with cheap fluorescent lights. She was met with floor-to-ceiling rows of metal bookshelves that stretched farther than she could see. To save space, the tall, motorized shelves were pressed together like the pages of a book, with a button on each to slide them apart. There was not another living person to be seen.

No stories here, though. She held the Figment to her eye, and a golden gleam appeared in the crack between two shelves. She hit the button to separate them, they slid apart, and she followed the golden gleam down the eternally long aisle.

She passed collections of meaningless facts. Profit records from some obscure old company, data from the previous year's census, articles about tiny insects that lived in the air vents of large buildings. Every shelf on every floor of the building was virtually identical, designed in the uninspiring fashion of an oversized filing cabinet.

Finally, she reached the end of the long aisle and found herself facing nothing but a blank, grey wall. Although if she squinted, she could see a sort of quiver, like heat haze on a summer day.

She pressed the Figment to her eye. A doorway appeared on the wall. Plain, grey, and unremarkable, save for the shimmering golden light around the seams. She took the Figment away. The door disappeared. She put it back, and there it was again. She smiled.

"A portal, then. This must be what the two of them were talking about." But where did it lead? How did she find them?

"With your imagination, of course. Like with the bathysphere." She placed her hand on the doorknob. She tried to picture the two of them, standing plain as day in front of her. "Sparrow and Starling, darrow and darling . . ."

The knob began to shake under her fingers.

And then a cloud of cold crept up behind her.

"Come out, come out, dearest Gwendolyn. We know you're here somewhere, don't we Mister Five?" came that horrible voice. She could not see where it came from, but its piercing tone reached her ears perfectly.

"Most assuredly, Mister Six. We know her name, we know where she lives, and we know she is here."

Frantically, Gwendolyn pulled at the door, but it wouldn't open. Two bowler hats bobbed into view as the Faceless Gentlemen rounded the corner at the far edge of the aisle.

Terror slowed time for her again, and her first thought was, *They'll know I wasn't in school!*

No, stupid girl, she replied. *You're in a lot more trouble than truancy. How did they find me?* She looked back at the door. A portal. *Energy*. She remembered Starling's wrist gadget. *They can detect it. That's how they keep finding me. Whenever I change something.*

She put her back against the locked door. The two men began the long walk down the aisle toward her. The lights above cast no shadows, but the men had them anyway—shadows that wriggled and moved of their own accord, as if they longed to break out and take shapes of their own.

"Come, Miss Gray," said Mister Five. "You have nowhere else to run."

"These changes of hers are most upsetting, Mister Five,"

said Mister Six. "That dress she made. Completely indecent. The Collector cannot stand such things, little girl. Things are the way they are, and so they must remain. The Collector would like to see to your erasure personally. So once again, I ask that you direct your attention to my lovely hat."

He took the hat off his head, but this time no light shone forth. Instead, writhing, shadowy tentacles emerged, twisting and tangling and reaching for her, stretching and growing down the alleyway.

She tried to scream, but her throat was too dry to cooperate.

"It is fitting, is it not, Mister Six?" said Mister Five. "I believe this is what is referred to as a . . . *dead* end."

At that moment, the door behind her rattled.

Gwendolyn stepped aside, and the door flew open.

"Gwendolyn?" came Sparrow's voice. He and Starling tumbled out, bumping into shelves, knocking books to the floor in a cloud of dust. He coughed. "W-what's going on, where–Ah!" And he *did* scream, a high-pitched squeak, as he saw the shadow tentacles reaching for them.

"What the . . ." Starling's mouth dropped open.

And just like that, the fear was gone, and Gwendolyn could move again. "Quick, through the door!" she shouted. She grabbed Sparrow by the hand, clutched the shining Figment tightly in the other, and leapt through the doorway into the unknown.

CHAPTER ELEVEN

The Mainspring Marketplace

She was surrounded by darkness. A nothingness with no up or down, no left or right. She floated. A toxic smell burned her nose. She supposed she still held the Figment aloft, but the blue light did nothing to pierce the gloom.

To her horror, she found she couldn't breathe. It was not unlike being suspended in a pitch-black pool of water, except she could feel no wetness. Only that burning in her nose, and also in her chest. There was no sign of Sparrow or Starling, though they might have been right beside her and she wouldn't have known.

Portals are supposed to go *somewhere,* she thought, fighting off panic. Then she had a burst of blue inspiration. *Perhaps I need to tell it where to go.*

It was not hard to form pictures as she floated in the nothingness. She filled the space around them with images from her book, from *Kolonius Thrash,* picturing the fantastical cities it described.

And then she felt a pulling sensation, like someone had grabbed her by the shirt and was hauling her forward. The darkness gave way to light, a shimmering whiteness full of swirling colors just beyond her vision. She could see herself again. The light seemed to be fighting back the dark, pulling Gwendolyn farther into it.

But the darkness, trying to drag her back, swirled around her hand that held the Figment. She was pulled between the two forces, light and dark, until the Figment was ripped from her grasp and she went flying forward, landing on hard stone under an orange sky.

Gwendolyn pushed her aching body up and looked around. Sparrow and Starling were with her, all three of them sprawled on hands and knees.

She was instantly assaulted by a rush of noise, clanking and clacking, voices and footsteps. She shaded her eyes from the sun, and was startled to see two of them in the sky. One sun was large and red, the other sun smaller, brighter, and yellow; their combined light turned the sky a dusty orange. Airships and zeppelins and other winged contraptions drifted lazily.

It took Gwendolyn's breath away. She got to her feet and stared up at the sky. She had never seen the sun before, not any sun, and certainly not two at once. The warmth of it on her skin. The color!

Think of all the times you have been stuck inside on a rainy day, or how nice the first bright day of March can seem after the dreary dull of February. Put them all together, and then you have some inkling of the powerful feelings that swelled inside Gwendolyn Gray as she saw the sun for the first time in her life. She sniffed and wiped her eyes, which were just watering from all that light. Probably.

Finally, she looked down. "Sparrow, Starling, are you all right?"

They climbed to their feet. "None the worse for wear," Sparrow said. "What was all that? What's going on?"

Starling looked around. "Better question: where are we?"

"Take a look," said Gwendolyn. "If I'm not mistaken, we're in the land of Tohk."

Buildings towered around them. Gwendolyn had seen tall buildings before, of course, but the kind she was used to were little more than concrete boxes. These extravagant monuments boggled her mind.

There were domes, palaces, spires, each a work of art, as if the buildings themselves were competing with each other, putting on their finery and standing especially tall. Metal lines crisscrossed over the streets and people zipped across on motorized pulley-handles.

She stood on the low balcony of some wide building, overlooking a broad avenue. Gwendolyn gaped at the bustling marketplace below, filled with shoppers and merchants of an astounding variety. Tantalizing scents wafted up to her, and she could make out a jaunty sort of music, one that made her want to tap her feet and twirl her skirt.

Gwendolyn dug the book out of her bag. She flipped to the

back, to a series of colorful maps. "Yes, see? This is Copernium, largest city in the land of Tohk." Copernium was shaped like an enormous cog, a large wheel with teeth around the edges. A meticulous pattern of streets all converged in the center at a label that read *The Mainspring Marketplace.*

She flipped to the middle of the book and found a description of the exact spot she stood now. "It worked, it really truly worked. That must be the marketplace down there."

She stepped back to soak in the splendor of it all, and Starling and Sparrow stepped up beside her.

"And you know all this . . . from that book?" Starling asked.

"Yes! It's the world of Kolonius Thrash."

"And how did we get here? Or there?" Sparrow asked, gesturing over his shoulder as if to the City. "That *was* your city I saw for a second, wasn't it?"

"Yes," Gwendolyn said. "I found a portal. What happened to you two?"

"Well, we went through that portal last night, hopped to a couple more places. We were just strolling near the aqueducts of Jonculus–"

"Strolling?" Starling shouted. "We were fleeing, because you couldn't stay out of trouble, *again*–"

"I told you, it was like that when I got there, where would I have even *found* a pair of ladies' underwear–"

"What's Jonculus?" Gwendolyn interrupted.

"Don't know, never had the chance to find out, did we? We'd just started to look around–"

"Running away–"

"—when Starling's wrist goes berserk. We turn a corner and *bam*! We're face to face with some evil tentacle monster attacking our favorite redhead. How's that for hello?"

"Well," Gwendolyn said, "I'd love to explore all this wonderfulness, but we have to go back and stop—" But when she turned to head back through the doorway, there wasn't one. Only a blank stone wall. "No! I have to get back! Those men, they're bound to erase . . . and my dress! The red one, it was in my closet . . . They knew about it, they've already been to my house, I have to help my parents, make sure they're okay—"

Starling checked her wrist. "Gwendolyn, there's no portal there. And even if there were, it wouldn't take you home, you'd end up on some random other world instead. Just be glad we got you out safe."

"But you came back for me! I can to get back the same way—"

Sparrow put a hand on her shoulder. "Gwendolyn, look, you can't—"

She shrugged him off. "No! I brought us here, I can get us back. I just need to . . ." She tried to hold the Figment to her eye, to find the doorway again, but she wasn't holding it anymore. "Oh. Oh, no. It's gone. I lost it."

"Lost what?" Sparrow asked.

"The Figment! It's some kind of magic jewel, it showed me the doorway. I lost it in the . . . what was all that we were floating in?"

Starling frowned. "The In-Between."

"And that is?"

"What it sounds like. The space between worlds. But I've

never seen that darkness before, or felt like I was the rope in a tug of war."

"So when we were stuck in that blackness, and I brought us here, that wasn't . . . normal?"

"No, it wasn't. Wait." Starling grabbed her shoulders. "Did you say you *brought* us here? Like, you chose this world, on purpose?"

"Yes, I did. Is there something wrong?"

Starling got a faraway look. "That isn't how it works. That's impossible."

"I don't care if it's impossible. I've done nothing *but* impossible things the last two days. I'll get us back!" She felt the wall for a hidden door, a secret passage, a crack, anything. But there was only smooth stone. "It can't be impossible, you came back for me!"

Starling elbowed her brother. "Tell her, you rat."

Sparrow looked exquisitely uncomfortable. "Well, we've never actually been able to go *back* to the same place before. I mean, stumbling from world to world, you can't exactly steer. We didn't expect to see you again."

Gwendolyn glared. "So you lied?" She punched his shoulder, hard, and again to hammer home each point. "You were going to leave me there? Just waiting for you? Forever? And the Mister Men! They—"

"Ow-ow-ow, I'm sorry, all right? We live rough, say what we have to." Sparrow looked like a puppy who'd been caught chewing the furniture. "But it all worked out, didn't it? We're all here, happy as can be, and everything's fine—"

"No, it's *not* Sparrow," Starling said. "Don't you get it? Gwendolyn can't get back home."

The words landed on Gwendolyn like bricks. She slumped to the ground, for once completely out of ideas. Everything had happened so fast, she just felt numb. "But . . . but what do I do? I have to *do* something."

There was a long pause. The other two shuffled nervously.

Finally, Sparrow pointed over the side. "We go down there. Down to that marketplace. It looks like a fun sort of place, we'll go explore."

"Sparrow," Starling warned.

"Come on, I'm not standing around on a rooftop all day. Plus I'm hungry. Food always helps. Rule one of interworld travel: never do it on an empty stomach."

"But my parents," Gwendolyn said, the idea still too new for her to feel it properly. "My home . . ."

Sparrow gestured to their surroundings. "Are they up here? We're going to need some help, and we'll need to get it down there. Rule two: always keep moving."

Starling shrugged. "He's not completely wrong. There's no portal up here. We'll have to look around for another. What can you tell us about this place?" Starling asked, trying to change the subject. She gestured to all the people, gadgets, and creations zooming around them. "It's, like, a whole city full of inventors." She walked over to a metal pole at the edge of the balcony and examined the zip-line that was attached to the top.

Gwendolyn sniffed. "It is, actually." She opened her book. *"Copernium was a marvelous city, renowned throughout all of*

Tohk for the skill and prowess of its inventors. Founded by the great genius Cyrio Kytain, Copernium became a home for all the greatest minds in the land," she read aloud. "They say you can find anything in the Mainspring Marketplace."

"Then let's find the way back. How do we get down there?" Sparrow asked.

Gwendolyn knew they were right. No sense sitting up here crying. If she wanted to help her parents, she'd jolly well have to do something about it.

She walked to the pole Starling was examining and pointed to a button on the side. "You're supposed to press that. They call it . . ." She stopped and flipped through her book again. "Pneumatically Enhanced High-Wire Transit Motors. The pneumo, for short."

Starling pressed the button. A metal contraption trundled up the line, a handle attached to a pair of pulley wheels. She summoned two more as well.

"Seems simple." Starling took the handle and leapt off the roof without a second thought, zipping down the line.

Sparrow grabbed hold of one and offered it to Gwendolyn. "Hurry, before she ditches us completely. A whole city of inventors? She'll be gone for days if we don't catch her."

Gwendolyn nodded and grasped the swaying metal handle. It was not any easier than her last leap from a building. Sparrow placed a not-at-all-comforting hand on her back. "Don't push me this time," she warned.

"Wouldn't dream of it." But he quickly took his hand back.

Gwendolyn took a last deep breath and jumped. She soared

down the line, picking up speed, and found herself too exhilarated to be either scared or sad. She zipped over arches and balconies and monuments, her hair flickering like fire. Soon the pneumo glided to a graceful stop against an anchor pole on the street below.

A dapper woman in a green top hat rolled up on brass wheels that were attached to her boots. "Much obliged," she said, and tipped her hat as she pressed the button on the pneumo handle. The motor whined as it carried her up another one of the wires.

Sparrow landed next to her. "Wooo! What a rush. Let's do it again!"

"Err, maybe later," Starling said. "Look."

They did. The marketplace was immense. The stalls stretched for blocks and blocks, and Gwendolyn couldn't see where it ended through the hordes of shoppers. Her eyes darted all over, never staying in one place long, trying and failing to take it all in at once. She felt pulled in a thousand directions, quite like taking your first steps into an amusement park and struggling to decide which ride to go on first.

Standing in the midst of the chaos and color, overwhelmed with sensation, she began to feel an odd sense of calm. For once, her mind had quite enough to keep it busy, and it was strangely soothing.

"It's so different! Look, they're all smiling. And there's music, and the smells!" She sniffed the delicious aromas of food and spices. "It isn't like my city at all, is it?" Gwendolyn said to Starling.

"No, it definitely isn't." Starling eyed a stall of various lenses and magnifiers. She checked her wrist. "No sign of any portals nearby." She glanced around the marketplace, struggling to keep a cool expression. "Let's explore. We might, uh, might find something useful. It's, you know, only practical." She blew her blue hair away from her eyes and retied her ponytail with a coppery band.

Sparrow gave Gwendolyn a knowing smirk.

She didn't return it. Her sense of calm was quickly replaced with guilt that she could feel anything but worry for home.

Sparrow, not entirely oblivious, noticed her expression change. "Look, it's tough, I know. But your parents are probably fine. It's you those men are after, and it sounds like your parents are model citizens. Without you there to make any spooky forbidden *chaaaanges,*" he mocked the voice of the Mister Men, "won't everything go back to normal?"

"Oh, thank you," she snapped. "Once the oddling is gone, everything will be perfect, right?"

"Hey, that's not what I—"

"Hmph," she snorted.

But secretly, she wasn't sure he was wrong. This entire mess was her fault. "I'm sorry, that wasn't kind. I know what you meant. So, where are we, really?" she asked, changing the subject as they walked through the market. "Are we in another world, or are we in my imagination now? Or are we in the writer's imagination, this Stanley Kirby fellow?" She pointed to the name on the cover.

Starling shook her head. "Not sure. All the worlds are

connected. As far as we know, this city is every bit as real as yours. Maybe there's a kid somewhere reading a book about you."

Gwendolyn hadn't thought about it that way. She wasn't sure she liked that idea.

Musicians played in the street, holding out hats for coins. Accordions and fiddles clashed with horns and drums. Barkers called out their wares, each trying to shout down the other.

"Come and see Doctor Morrillsby's Corpuscular Revitalization Tonics! One sip, and you will feel like a man of three and twenty once more. Balances the humors and restores your pep and vigor!"

"Step right up! Get your timepieces polished, get your chronometers calibrated. You can't know *where* you are without knowing *when* you are!"

"Did you hear?" said a lady in a frilly yellow dress. "Tylerium Drekk tried to raid the First Archicon Bank. But Kolonius Thrash arrived, and drove him off."

"At this rate, there won't be a single pirate left in Tohk, and good riddance. I wonder what a hero does with no one left to fight?" said her companion, dressed in elaborate violet ruffles.

"I could think of a few things to do to keep him busy. He's so dashing," said the woman in the yellow dress, cooling herself with a delicate paper fan.

"I hear the Archicon Bank lost more paying for his help than they would have lost to the pirates!"

They reached a section of the marketplace devoted to mechanical equipment, and Starling quickly dove up to her waist in a bin of spare parts, muttering to herself as she tossed bits into the air.

"Wow! Thanks for bringing us here, Gwendolyn. This place is great! Isn't it great?" Sparrow said in a clumsy and obvious attempt to cheer her up.

"Yes, it's nice, I suppose." In fact, it was utterly fantastic, a dream come true—and if she had seen it the previous morning, she would have nearly died with delight. But she couldn't bring herself to appreciate it now. Every enjoyable sight just brought another pang of guilt for forgetting to be sad for one more moment.

Sparrow took Gwendolyn by the hand. "Come on, she'll be a while." Starling had now joined a group of airship engineers and was talking much more animatedly than Gwendolyn had ever seen her do, holding her own in the circle of older sailors as they discussed the finer points of proper engine maintenance.

They found a stall where creatures barked and cawed from their cages. Gwendolyn had never seen so many animals before. There were magnificent birds and exotic-looking cats and what seemed like tiny purple lint-balls scurrying about on spindly feet. They reminded her a bit of Criminy the Falderal, and she spared a moment to wonder what had happened to him, then quickly slammed the door on such thoughts. The last thing she needed was to chase a meeping orange furball through the crowded market.

Sparrow held out his hand to one of the scampering creatures, about the size of his palm. It scurried up his arm and perched on his shoulder, chirping contentedly. Sparrow stroked it and it responded to his touch, rubbing against his hand with a soft cooing noise. "What do you call this?" he asked the shopkeeper.

"What, that? Just a little field mite. They live in the Violet Veldt, blending in with the grass, hopping across the tops of the stalks. Cheap as dirt, ten copper." The shopkeeper held out a hand.

Sparrow gently tipped the field mite into the man's outstretched palm. "That's all right. Thank you, though." He and Gwendolyn headed for the next stall, though she could hear the field mite cooing sadly after them.

"You seem to have a way with animals," Gwendolyn nodded with respect.

"I like them, they like me back. I don't know why—we never had many animals back home." His expression went fuzzy and far away. "Everywhere we've been, I've always done well with animals. They can't stand Starling, though. No warm fuzzies there; she's all gadgets and metal and *thinking*, you know?" He tapped a finger on the side of his head. "One time, we met this horse that nearly kicked her in the face . . ." But before he could tell the tale, something behind Gwendolyn caught his attention. "Ooooo, what's that over there! Come on, this will cheer you up!"

He bolted across the avenue, forcing Gwendolyn to sprint after him.

CHAPTER TWELVE

Castaway

Gwendolyn looked around at all the colors, torn between loving the marketplace, and feeling like she was betraying her parents if she let herself enjoy it. All she could picture was their faces, blank in the light of a Lambent. Maybe the Mister Men would erase everyone's memory, and no one would even miss her. Maybe they would all be better off that way, without Gwendolyn causing any trouble, and they wouldn't even have to feel sad to see her go.

Again, Sparrow must have noticed her furrowed brow and faraway look. He nudged her. "Here, see anything you like?"

They stood in front of a market stall with exotic clothing and sweet perfumes. Well-dressed ladies were *ooo*-ing and *aah*-ing over potions and dresses and accessories.

Gwendolyn made a disgusted face. "What makes you think I would be interested in any of that frilly frippery?" She sighed. "No, I'm sorry, that was rude again. You're just trying to cheer me up, and I do appreciate it."

He shrugged. "I just thought you could use a change from all the muck you were wearing yesterday. That green dress seems like it'd suit you."

Gwendolyn looked. It was an emerald sundress with a white collar, puffed sleeves, and embroidered lilies around the hem. A belt of braided golden cord cinched the waist. Contrary to her nature and her current mood, she found herself wanting the pretty thing. You have probably wanted something before, wanted it so badly you bother your parents for days on end about it. But in the City, there was usually nothing nice enough for Gwendolyn to want.

She cast a sideways glance at Sparrow. "Well it is awfully lovely, I suppose, and green *is* my favorite color—"

"Say no more! Hey, lady! Bring us that dress there, the green one!"

A woman with incredibly large hair swooped down on them in a whirl of ruffles. She snatched the dress from its hook and spread it out before them. "This one? Yes, it *is* one of my favorites. I daresay the look would be a bit bold for you, my fine boy. But it would go smashingly with your hair, dearie-girl. That red! Fantastic. If I could bottle that shade, I'd make a fortune, and every lady in Copernium would have hair like fire. And I love the wild look, very *naturale,* very *chic*. This dress would be perfect for you." She spoke with the bubbly voice of an upper-class lady but the rapid-fire patter of a salesman.

Sparrow gave her a shrewd look. "And how much do you charge for *chic*? A gifted seamstress like you would never miss a thing like that."

A huge grin spread across the pretty dressmaker's face as she spotted a kindred spirit. "Well, I've a soft spot for cheeky boys with slick tongues. So for your lovely lady, let's say, five silver and ten brass."

"What? Five silver, for that little slip?" He turned and whispered to Gwendolyn. "I have no idea how much that is." He turned back. "Outright robbery! I'll give you two silver and five brass, and not a copper more!"

Gwendolyn felt a giggle rise at his antics, but squashed it.

The dressmaker twisted her makeup-coated face into an expression of horror. "Two and five! Insulting! Clearly you haven't felt it, see how soft it is? It would be a steal at three and ten!"

"Hmmmm." Sparrow put a hand to his chin and squinted one eye, making a show of considering her offer. "I don't know, I'm not sure it's really all *that* great . . ."

Gwendolyn rolled her eyes. "He's lying, it's an absolutely wonderful dress. You're very talented. But we didn't bring any money," Gwendolyn said, looking down at her shoes. "Didn't really bring much of anything."

The shopkeeper seemed to lose interest. "Hurry back when you do, then, I—" then she looked at Gwendolyn again, scanning her up and down. "Oh, no, you're not Castaways, are you? Oh you poor dear. I'm so sorry. Lost your home?"

Gwendolyn looked up. "Yes. How did you know?"

"My dear girl, it's written all over your face! And those clothes . . . you obviously aren't from around here. What a horrid place it must be, to make you dress in *that*." She gestured to Gwendolyn's school uniform. "No, no, Iona, be nice," she muttered to herself. "I'm sorry, it's your home and I'm sure you miss it terribly. Here, sweet girl, take it, I can't bear the thought of you running around in funeral colors. I've a soft spot for the lost ones, oh, it breaks my heart. No, go on, take it," she pushed the dress toward them, "before I change my mind!"

"I really couldn't, you clearly worked very hard on it—" Gwendolyn protested.

"Here, cheeky boy, *you* take it, use that slick tongue of yours to persuade her." Iona thrust the dress at Sparrow. "Good luck, the both of you!"

Sparrow took the dress, and led Gwendolyn away from the stall. "Thank you!" Gwendolyn called.

"You are most welcome, and welcome to Copernium!" the dressmaker called after them.

They went down the street a ways, and Sparrow stuffed the dress into Gwendolyn's arms. "Here, if Starling sees me carrying that, she'll never shut up about it. Now what the heck is going on?"

Gwendolyn blinked. "What?"

"What do you mean, what? *That.* Her calling you a Castaway, and giving you free stuff? No one ever gives me free stuff."

"Well, maybe you should try being sweet for a change," Gwendolyn teased. She was feeling a bit better. "She liked my hair."

"Who wouldn't?" Sparrow grinned, and tousled it playfully.

Gwendolyn blushed. "No one's ever . . ." She choked up, surprised at the sudden swell of emotions. Her insides would have felt like they were on a roller coaster, had she known what one was. It is hard to stay sad or upset for long periods of time, especially in the face of so many wonderful things. It is exactly the reason why you never see anyone frowning while water-skiing or hot air ballooning. "Do you think . . ." Gwendolyn looked around nervously. "Could I put it on right now?"

Sparrow raised an eyebrow, but for once didn't make a joke. "There's an empty alleyway. Go down there, I'll stay here and keep watch."

"Do you promise it's the street you'll be watching?"

He rolled his eyes. "Yes, I promise. Go."

She did, darting down the deserted alleyway. The building was curved, which kept her out of sight. Quick as lightning, she changed into the green dress, tossing her school clothes into her bag.

She looked down at herself, and was stunned at how *pretty* it was. She had never felt pretty before. The dress fit perfectly. There was nothing to be done about her ugly black shoes, though.

Or was there? She stared at them and tried to picture them . . . silver. Silver shoes, soft and lovely. She held the picture in her mind, tried to summon the feeling of turning her dress red the night before . . .

But nothing happened. The shoes remained stubbornly unchanged. She frowned as she left the alley. Her imagination wasn't working.

Sparrow's face lit up when he saw her. "Wow," he said, not exaggerating this time. "I, uh, wow." Now it was his turn to blush, and he turned his face away. Which of course made Gwendolyn blush as well, and they had an extended bout of trying not to meet each other's eyes.

"Oh look, there's Starling!" Sparrow said, relieved. "Quick, before she sees another shiny invention and runs off."

They crossed the street to Starling, who had an armful of mechanical parts, and was ogling an intimidating display of swords and knives. "Hello, children. Find anything interesting?"

"Gwendolyn saw a dress she wanted, typical girl."

Gwendolyn shot him a sideways look, but let the comment slide. "I thought you didn't have any money?"

Starling grinned. "*He* doesn't have any money, as he's not allowed. I always keep a few valuables to barter with."

"Yeah, so how about something to eat? I'm famished."

"You're always famished." Starling began shoving her purchases into her many pockets.

"What can I say? I'm a growing boy. Come on, I saw a place with lots of meats on sticks." Sparrow pointed, and he and Starling started to walk, but Gwendolyn just stood there, staring.

Starling turned back. "Gwendolyn?"

"Look." She pointed to the domed building she'd changed behind. A metal sign above the double doors read *Professor Zangetsky's Imagination Engineerium and Clockwork Phantasmagoria*. "Imagination. Do you think that professor could help us?" The tiniest spark of hope flickered inside her.

Starling checked her wrist. "I *am* getting a signal from that direction."

"But I'm hungry," whined Sparrow.

Gwendolyn pulled the apple from her bag and tossed it to him. "Here."

Sparrow caught it, shrugged, and munched as they crossed the street.

The doors flew open, and a crowd of people spilled out. "That was a rip-off," groaned a boy. "Fantastic Max-o-million's Wonder Pavilion only charges a copper, and they've got a real live merman you can touch."

The children pushed through the crowd and went inside, finding themselves in a dark room with rows of benches in front of some kind of stage. Gwendolyn led them through the empty theater, thinking it a very odd sort of room indeed, for of course, the concept of "theater" was completely foreign to her. They found a door marked PRIVATE.

"Here." She led them through and down a dim corridor, then into a cluttered workshop, where they found a small man in a white coat. He was leaning over a mechanical device that resembled what you or I would know as a puppet. He was operating on it like some bizarre surgeon, muttering and tinkering. Parts were scattered across a large workbench.

"Yes, yes, yes . . . no! Darn it. Not the thermostatic relay, then. Perhaps the piston gasket? No, no, no, that isn't it a'tall!"

"Professor Zangetsky?" Gwendolyn asked.

"Who? What? Ow!" The man jerked up and banged his head on a metal pole strewn with dangling wires and tubes. He flailed about, hopelessly entangling himself. "Oh. Hello." He struggled to free himself from the wires. "If you're here for the show, I'm afraid the next one doesn't start for two hours. Maybe longer if my star here continues this mechanical temper tantrum." He aimed a kick at his workbench but missed and tangled himself further.

"Oh, no, we just wanted to meet you. I'm Gwendolyn Gray, and these are my friends, Sparrow and Starling."

"Hi," said Sparrow.

"Charmed," said Starling.

Through his goggles, the professor's eyes were magnified to a comical size, giving him a curious and deranged expression. He looked exactly as you might expect a mad scientist to look, though there were so many mad scientists in Copernium they'd had to form a union, with all sorts of rules just to keep from blowing themselves up every other Saturday. He strained against the wires and stretched to grasp Gwendolyn's hand. "Oh, well-well-well, it *is* nice to meet a fan, now isn't it? Did you enjoy my little show?"

"What show? You mean your 'Clockwork Phantasmagoria'?"

"Indeed!" he flailed toward the puppet on his workbench. "Only the finest stories, projections with my revolutionary automatons."

"Stories? How do you *show* stories?"

"Come now, surely you've been to the pictures before."

"No. Where I come from, we don't have, uh, Clockwork Phantasmagoria. We don't have stories at all." Gwendolyn helped pull his hand free of a last bit of tubing.

The professor stumbled and fell face first into an open projector. He pulled himself out and looked at her, stroking his chin thoughtfully. "No stories a'tall, you say? Hmm. Well, allow me to demonstrate. Stand back, there you go."

He slammed the projector closed and flipped a switch. White light came from the end of it, one that sent familiar shivers down Gwendolyn's spine. He pulled another mechanical puppet from where it hung on the wall, stood it up in the middle of the floor, and turned a key in a slot in its back. Then he shuffled to a horn-shaped speaker and cranked the handle on its side. His own reedy voice came out of it in a prerecorded message.

"Welcome to Professor Zangetsky's Projectraphonic Clockwork Phantasmagoria! The grandest show in all the lands of Tohk!"

The professor rolled his eyes. "Shameless self-promotion, but one must in this business."

The light from the projector grew brighter, and Gwendolyn grew even more nervous, but suddenly the light changed. Colors flickered rapidly. Red, blue, green, yellow, faster and faster. Then the rainbow of colors became images.

And the workshop disappeared.

CHAPTER THIRTEEN

Clockwork Phantasmagoria

The three of them were suddenly standing in a field of violet grass. Starling spun around, scanning for danger. Sparrow waved his hand through the grass, which flickered. Gwendolyn, who was much more used to sudden shifts in imaginary scenery, studied the puppet instead. It was a metal figure of a handsome man, wearing a cloak as purple as the grass. The three of them seemed like giants, but the scenery was the perfect size for the puppet. It began to move.

"Cyrio Kytain was the greatest inventor in all of Tohk," came the high-pitched voice of the narrator Zangetsky. The puppet gazed into a double sunset that had replaced the workshop wall, his cloak streaming in an imaginary wind. "He longed for the company of like-minded individuals. So he founded our grand city of Copernium as a haven for creators of all sorts, where none would feel ridicule or scorn for their ideas."

The domes and spires of Copernium sprang up from the grassland floor, in miniature. Gwendolyn was captivated.

"Artists, craftsmen, and inventors flocked to the city, but Kytain was hounded by admirers. Eventually he retired to a secret laboratory in the mythical Crystal Coves, safe from prying eyes."

Gwendolyn gasped as images of craggy, snow-capped mountains rushed at her, as if she were flying. They crossed a purple sea, and an island came into view, hidden in shadows.

"What spectacular inventions might he have developed in his final years? Legends speak of twelve-foot-tall mechanical men, vehicles that could traverse the inky voids above the sky, and of course, the Pistola Luminant, a weapon of purest light that could defeat even the blackest evil."

The lights faded to black. "But Cyrio Kytain was never seen again. Though it has been over five hundred years, some insist that he will find a way to return one day and dazzle us with wonders anew–"

"Wouldn't he be five hundred years old?" blurted Sparrow.

"Shhh!" Starling hissed.

"–but that, my friends, is a tale for another time. Please exit in an orderly fashion, gratuities are accepted."

The projector clicked off. They were back in the workshop again.

"That was . . . anticlimactic," said Starling.

"Yeah. And short," said Sparrow.

The professor leapt up with a *harrumph* and bustled about, putting the puppet away. "Bah. Audiences these days have no patience for documentaries."

Gwendolyn shook herself out of the trance of a good story. "Do you have more?"

"Oh yes. Everyone prefers *Horace the Bumbler,* or the *Deliveryman's Romance.* Silly tomfoolery, but who can argue with public taste with the way business is going these days."

"How does it work?"

Professor Zangetsky's eyes narrowed. "Why do you ask? Who sent you? Is it Max-o-Million again? Always trying to plunder my inventions—"

"No! It's just, your sign said you were an imagination engineer, so we thought you could help."

The professor smiled. "Ah! You're interested in my research! Finally, someone who appreciates the science."

"What *is* your research?" asked Starling.

"Imagination! Creation energy!" He rummaged through rolled parchments on his shelves. "Years ago, while traveling the Spiced Seas, I found bits of Kytain's own notes on the subject, at abandoned outposts and such. He discovered an energy field, one powered by the sentient mind. He was able to draw on it to power his inventions."

Starling checked her wrist gauntlet. "That's how you're powering your tech, isn't it? Explains my readings."

"Is that a creation energy detector?" He nearly tore Starling's arm off inspecting it. "How marvelous!" Then he cleared a space on his table. "Yes. This energy, or invention, or inspiration, or imagination. A lot of 'I' words, come to think of it, but it's all the power to change things, making something out of nothing. Of course, since everyone and their third cousin is an inventor here, there's not enough energy for a proper manifestation. But on some worlds where the energy is very strong, or very concentrated, you can create things much more literally. Physical objects from thin air! It sounds impossible, but with just the right words, you could make ideas come to life."

"Ideas to life?" Sparrow wiggled his eyebrows at Gwendolyn. "Like *magic*?"

"Exactly!" The professor cried. "Oh, it could never happen *here,* in Tohk, and most say I'm mad, but—"

"Wait," said Starling. "You're saying that telling stories is . . . magic?" She almost choked on the word.

"Magic, invention, spells, stories. It's all the same. Pulling stories out of thin air is just as much magic as pulling a rabbit from a hat! Magic equals imagination equals creation!"

Gwendolyn fidgeted. "Professor, would it be possible to drain that energy? Like your projector, only in reverse?"

He stroked his chin. "Why, yes, yes, I suppose it would be possible." He eyed her up and down. "No stories where you come from, eh? So you're from one of *those* worlds. Gwendolyn, was it? Your home, is it all awful and bleak and grey?"

Gwendolyn gaped. "Yes!"

"And everyone does everything exactly the same? Conformity, strict rules and all?"

She clapped her hands to her mouth. "Yes, yes! How did you know?"

"You'll be from the Dystopic regions, then. Similar worlds group together, and the Dystopias are a dime a dozen. Dreadful places, I hear. If I fell through the gaps, I'd hope to land somewhere in the Fantastics, much more scope for the imagination. I suppose you have some sort of sorting ceremony, yes? Some choosing ritual where you're placed into groups or jobs or houses or factions, some such nonsense?"

Gwendolyn frowned. "No. That sounds terrible. Who would let someone choose their life for them?"

Starling grunted. "Ridiculous."

Professor Zangetsky winked. "You'd be surprised."

"So you've traveled to other worlds?" Sparrow asked.

"Well, if I had, I wouldn't be able to get back *here* now, would I? It's all theoretical, pieced from Kytain's notes and my own interviews with those like you. We get our share of Castaways—"

"Castaways?" Starling arched an eyebrow.

"Yeah, what are those?" Sparrow asked.

"Why, you are, of course, I'd stake my name on it! A man of science can always tell, you know. You think you're the first to be lost through the portals? Terribly sorry, by the way, losing your world is no small thing. Ahem, as I was saying, I interview those who've fallen through the gaps accidentally, but *intentional* travel is utterly impossible. It's not like you can steer!" He chuckled. "Though they say Kytain might have managed it, and that's where he's gone off to."

But I managed to steer us here, Gwendolyn thought. She had gone exactly where she'd wanted to go. *There must be a way to do it again.*

"Speaking of, maybe it's time I wrote a Dystopian performance. Perhaps a story about a Castaway who finds herself stuck in one." He picked up a pen and began scribbling. "Have to jot that down. I always say, ideas are wild things, and if you're not careful, they take on a life of their own. Best to capture them in a cage of words, or they can quite run away from you."

"You don't have to tell me," mumbled Gwendolyn.

Starling put a hand on her shoulder. "Come on, Gwendolyn. Time to go."

"All right," she said. "Goodbye, Professor. Thank you again."

"Oh!" he said. "Leaving already? Well, you have my sympathies, dear Castaways, best of luck to you. Stop in later, so I can interview you for my research. But now, the show must go on! Spread the word!" He pushed a handful of flyers at them and shooed them out the door.

Outside, the orange sky was darkening to red.

"Yeah. Don't think we'll going back to *that* nutjob," Sparrow said, stuffing the professor's flyers into a nearby bin.

"I liked him," said Gwendolyn.

We have said how adaptable children can be when it comes to the sort of earth-shattering ideas that would leave grown-ups gibbering for their mothers, and the professor's talk was enough to boggle the minds of even seasoned adventurers like Sparrow and Starling. But not Gwendolyn; her overactive mind pieced it all together quickly, and honed in on one small detail the professor had mentioned.

Her eyes went wide. "That's it!"

"What's it?" Sparrow asked.

"He said that everyone here is an inventor, so you can't make any *proper* changes—you can't make anything come to life! That's why I couldn't change my shoes."

Sparrow frowned. "You're not making any sense."

"Imagination! It's like electricity! There's all this power, and I'm the only one in the City using it!"

Starling nodded. "Right. No one else is plugged in, so you get all the juice. Explains the readings I was getting."

"That's why I could make that leaf, and change Missy's ears, because I'm the only one not draining myself into the Lambents!"

"And that's why those faceless guys were after you," Sparrow said.

"I think so. Except here, *everyone's* imagining and creating, so I'm just . . . normal."

"Don't be gross," said Sparrow. "Normal. Yuck."

But Gwendolyn didn't hear. "That means I won't be able to use my imagination to get home." The weight of it came crashing down on her again. So she did what people usually do with difficult thoughts and emotions. She tried to ignore them.

"I'm sorry, Gwendolyn," Starling said. "We'll figure something out."

"But first, some food!" Sparrow said. "That way!"

As they walked, Gwendolyn noticed a strange tension in the crowd. Voices were hushed. People hurried furtively, heads down. An old man in a tattered cloak eyed them warily, face lost in the shadows of his broad-brimmed hat. Thunder rumbled.

"Everyone's acting strange," Gwendolyn said.

Starling nodded. "You're right. Looks like a storm. Let's find some shelter."

She steered them toward the nearest stall, which sold wind-up toys. Little clockwork soldiers paced the counter, mechanical spiders skittered this way and that, and model airships floated around the shopkeeper's head, puffing steam. He was a burly man with a ruddy face and bushy, blond muttonchops. He glanced anxiously up and down the street.

"Excuse me, sir," Gwendolyn said.

"Gah! Oh." His face softened. "Startled me. See anything you like, my dears?"

"No, we were just wondering if there was a storm coming, and if so, could you direct us to someplace to stay?"

The man didn't answer, too busy scanning the street again.

"Sir? Is something wrong? You seem quite bothered."

"Something bad is headed this way. Can't you feel it, girl? Ain't like no storm I've ever—" The shopkeeper froze.

"Um, sir?" Gwendolyn asked.

"Hello, anybody home?" said Sparrow, but the shopkeeper did not move. His mouth hung open.

Then his eyes started to glow. White light shone from empty sockets, and they heard a cold voice. It came from his throat, through his unmoving lips like he was no more than Professor Zangetsky's gramophone speaker.

"Ah. So *there* you are," the voice said. It was not the dreaded monotone of Misters Five and Six, but the childish voice of a small boy, sounding all the more odd coming from the big man's throat. It sent chills up her spine. "No more hide-and-seek, Miss Gwendolyn. Time to come home. There are other games to play."

"Uh-oh." Starling pointed.

Two men in gray suits and bowler hats were standing at the

end of the avenue. Fear shot through Gwendolyn like lightning, and thunder rumbled overhead in answer.

"What have we here, Mister Five?" said Mister Six. Just as in the Hall of Records, he was much too far away to hear properly, but each icy word found its way to Gwendolyn's ear as perfectly as though his lips were inches from it.

The Faceless Gentlemen looked around. "Color and chaos. All too much, don't you agree, Mister Five?" said Mister Six.

"Most assuredly, Mister Six," said Mister Five. "The Collector has been seeking this world for quite some time. He will want to add it back into to his collection, straighten this"—he gestured to the marketplace—"disorder. But first, there is the matter of the Gwendolyn girl. She must be erased first, to prevent any more tampering with the collection."

Gwendolyn couldn't believe what she was seeing. Slowly, ever so slowly, Mister Five and Mister Six glided down the street.

Starling whipped a hand into her pocket and brought out what looked like an umbrella handle, but at the press of a switch a sword blade sprang out of it.

"Stay back." She dashed at the men, slashed at them, but the sword passed right through, as if they were projections from Professor Zangetsky's stories.

"Do not waste our time, little construct. You have caused enough trouble. Her return is inevitable, Mister Five. She will be erased, and her power will serve the Collector."

"Most completely and assuredly, Mister Six. Though this awful place does not possess the requisite energy for a direct erasure, there are . . . other solutions."

"She's not going anywhere," growled Sparrow, stepping in front of Gwendolyn. "You'll have to go through us first."

Something twitched in Mister Five's unseeable face that might have been a smile, but the sight of it vanished like a cockroach in the sun. "As you wish."

He pushed a phantom hand straight through Sparrow's forehead, all the way up to the wrist.

Sparrow dropped like a stone.

"Our physical presence is unnecessary. The Collector has things well in hand."

"Sparrow!" Gwendolyn cried.

"Gwendolyn, look!" Starling shouted.

She whirled around. Something was moving inside the shopkeeper's open mouth. Black specks swirled behind his teeth, spilling over his lips and down his chin. The black spots swarmed together and solidified, forming writhing, black tentacles as they emerged from the man's mouth.

"Look out!" Starling said, yanking her aside. Starling collapsed her sword, and the two girls picked Sparrow up under his arms and backed down the street.

The Mister Men did not follow, but stepped toward the shopkeeper and the swarming shadows. "You will not escape, Miss Gray. Goodbye."

The oozing shadows multiplied. They now engulfed the shopkeeper's head. Liquid blackness dripped onto the street and formed a puddle. The puddle climbed up the legs and bodies of the Mister Men until they were nothing more than two pillars of shadow. There was a horrifying squeal, and the pillars exploded into black fog, leaving no trace of either the Faceless Gentlemen or the shopkeeper. The fog swirled and wafted down the street.

The people in the marketplace screamed and ran in every direction. Stalls slammed steel shutters and retracted completely into the buildings, leaving the crowds to fend for themselves in the street.

The black mist crept toward the market-goers. Behind it, the cobblestones were bleached to a dull white, crumbling as if with age.

Suddenly, the mist leapt into the air and morphed into a large fist, smashing a statue of a man on an ostrich into a pile of grey rubble. The cloud expanded again, sometimes resembling scuttling insects, sometimes swirling like mercury, sometimes grasping like claws and tentacles, but always coming closer.

Screams filled the air. People scrambled for the nearest pneumos and flying contraptions, fleeing by any means possible.

"Someone, please, help!" a woman shrieked. Gwendolyn saw Iona, the pretty dressmaker, running toward them. She tripped over her frills, stumbled, and fell. Shadows swarmed over her flailing body. She screamed and kicked. The blackness lingered, pulsing, then surged forward again. The screams stopped. Where the woman had been was now a pile of gray dust.

"Oh, no," Gwendolyn squeaked, her free hand going to her mouth. "What *is* that?"

"I-I don't know. But it can only mean one thing," said Starling.

"What?"

"More running."

CHAPTER FOURTEEN

The Shadows Fall

Gwendolyn and Starling fled down the cobblestone street as quickly as they could with an unconscious Sparrow. He was a lot heavier than his namesake.

The black cloud splashed up against the buildings like a roaring tidal wave. Wherever it touched, stone turned pale and crumbled.

"What's it doing to the city?" shouted Gwendolyn over the panicked crowds.

"No idea, but those shadows have an appetite," answered Starling. She freed a hand to root through her pockets. "Is that what we saw in the Hall of Records?"

"I think so! But how did it get here? It can't have followed us through the portal!"

"Well, clearly they found a way!" Starling called back.

The wave surged forward, tearing down a balcony. They covered their heads to avoid the falling masonry. Starling whipped around and hurled several small spheres toward the shadows.

They exploded with bright flashes of light. The shadows screeched and drew back.

The girls dragged Sparrow down a side street. The shadows had yet to touch this area. Gwendolyn's face was flushed, her heart pounding. She prayed that Sparrow would be all right. The sight of his lifeless face made her heart stutter. She checked to see that he was breathing. He was.

She had never been more terrified in her life, and she had plenty of recent comparisons to prove it. Her unhelpful curiosity wondered what would happen if she died here. What would her parents think? How long would they search before giving her up for dead?

"How many gadgets do you keep in those pockets, Starling?" asked Gwendolyn.

"Not nearly enough."

In answer, a black tentacle darted around an intersection and slammed Starling into the wall. She cried out, and Sparrow slumped to the ground. The shadowy claw lashed at her exposed back. She screamed and fell to her knees. Shadows swarmed the street, writhing, squirming, and surrounding them.

"This is bad. This is very bad," Starling mumbled from the ground, cradling her brother's head.

"Don't worry!" Gwendolyn said, trying to sound confident. "I'll think of something!"

She reached out a hand and tried to imagine blinding flashes of light like the ones Starling had used. She pictured them in her mind. But again it felt more difficult than before, like she was trying to drink through a straw that was too small.

Only a few feeble sparks leapt from her fingers, laughably tiny against the wall of shadows around them.

"It's not working! I don't have enough energy here! Starling, I'm sorry, I—" but then she noticed something in the middle of the rampaging chaos. It was a wonder she saw it at all, but of course, Gwendolyn was a clever noticer. Time slowed to a crawl again as she looked at it.

A tiny emerald leaf danced on the breeze above her head, oblivious to the tidal wave of darkness. She had no idea why, but she reached out to touch it, fingers stretching . . .

There was an explosion of light, followed by a fizzle of sparks. The shadows screamed as time sped up again. The explosion blew a hole through the cloud and someone leapt through it, carrying a long-barreled rifle.

"Get up! This is a rescue, not teatime!"

A stranger skidded to a stop in front of them, his features obscured by a tattered and floppy hat, his ratty cloak flapping as he whirled to face the monster. He fired his rifle and there was another blinding flash, followed by a sizzling fountain of sparks. The shadows screeched and reeled back again.

The cloaked figure pulled a boxy device from his belt. "Brunswick, I'm in position. Drop anchor!"

"Roger, Cap'n," came the crackly reply.

"You three! Back!" the man ordered, his talking box disappearing under his cloak. Gwendolyn pressed her back against the wall and exchanged confused looks with Starling.

Suddenly, a giant harpoon struck the ground in front of them, burying itself in the stone. Her eyes followed a thick metal cable upward to see a magnificent airship, floating effortlessly in the sky. Gwendolyn's jaw dropped.

The rifle coughed again, and another blinding flash drove the shadows farther back.

"Up the line, children!" he shouted. With a hiss of steam, pneumo handles detached from the sides of the harpoon and trundled onto the metal cable.

Starling struggled to her feet. "Go on, Gwendolyn."

"Absolutely not! Not without you and Sparrow!" she replied.

"I'll get the boy, but if you don't quit bickering and start hauling, I'll leave the lot of you behind!" the stranger growled.

"I'm not leaving my brother!" Starling tried to lift him, but she gasped, clutching the gash on her side. She gritted her teeth and roared in frustration, then glared at their rescuer. "You swear you have him?"

The stranger scooped his free arm under the unconscious boy and hauled him away from Starling and onto his shoulder. "Sweetheart, this is what I do. Now go! My crackleblast is almost spent." He braced the rifle on his side and cranked it one-handed. "What are you waiting for, an invitation?" He pulled the trigger but the rifle responded with a disappointing click. He dropped it. "Move, you ditzy brats, move!"

Gwendolyn and Starling grabbed pneumos, which each had a sort of stirrup that could be extended from the bottom. They pulled the stirrups out, slipped their feet in, and were immediately whisked into the air.

"No, wait!" Starling called down.

But the mystery man had things well in hand. He put

Sparrow's foot in a stirrup, then his own. He hugged the boy and grabbed the pneumo with one arm. With the other, he drew his longsword, and sliced the metal rope free of the harpoon. The two of them shot into the sky, away from the shapeless monster.

Gwendolyn clung tight as the pneumo climbed above even the tallest buildings in the city. The wind threatened to pull her off. Against her better instincts, she looked down.

Copernium stretched out below her. The beautiful cityscape was marred by an ugly greyish-white hole several blocks across, an unnatural clearing filled with rubble and dust. Black puddles crawled like tumors, erasing growing chunks of the city of inventors. Seeing it, she felt as though the blackness were chewing a hole in her heart as well.

The pneumo reached the hovering ship and strong arms pulled them over the side. She sprawled on the deck, trying to catch her breath.

Starling groaned and held her wound as a dark-skinned young man vaulted over the railing. He lay Sparrow gently on the deck, then whipped off the floppy hat and tattered cloak. He ran a hand over a cluster of thick, black dreadlocks with a sigh. He wore a sleeveless, white tunic that laced at the neck, black breeches with red pinstripes, and tall black boots. At his belt were several knives, a jeweled sword, and various tools. An eye patch covered his right eye, and a long scar ran under it, lending a bit of age to the young face. He leaned down to check Sparrow. "He's breathing, but unconscious. Blow to the head?"

"Something like that," Gwendolyn said, as she and Starling rushed to his side.

"Alphus!" the older boy barked. "We need a patch job over here."

"He won't wake up! What did those men do to him?" Starling asked, too worried about her brother to pay any heed to the crewman bandaging her wound.

"I don't know," Gwendolyn said. The image of Mister Five's hand buried in Sparrow's head was bright in her mind. "Probably not something any doctor could cure. Let me try something."

She brushed wavy brown hair away from his eyes and cradled his face in her hands. She tried to imagine him awake, picturing his eyes flying open, picturing him sitting up with his trademark wink and annoying grin. But she felt that same difficult sensation, like squeezing water from a dry sponge. But she couldn't give up. She remembered the Neyora, and Criminy, and she had another idea. Words came out in a rush. "Once upon a time there was a boy named Sparrow, and he was kind, and wonderful, and definitely not dead, he opened his eyes, he woke up, wake up!"

She felt a brief surge of energy, a tingle in her hands, and Sparrow's eyelids fluttered. He stirred, rolled to one side, and coughed.

Stories are magic, Gwendolyn thought, remembering the professor's words.

Starling shoved Gwendolyn aside and embraced him. "Sparrow! Are you all right?"

He moaned. "I need . . . I need . . ."

"What?" She gave him a little shake.

"Some food. I'm flipping famished." He grinned weakly.

Conflicting emotions swirled on Starling's face as she struggled to hold back both laughter and tears. "He's all right," she sniffed. She stood up and tried to look angry. "Don't ever do that again!"

The two girls helped him to his feet. "Wait, how is this my fault? Where are we?" Sparrow asked.

A burly crewman came up and patted Sparrow on the back, sending him stumbling forward. "Ah, the boy'll be fine. Welcome aboard the *Lucrative Endeavour,* finest ship in all the skies of Tohk," he said in a deep and thickly accented voice.

"The *Lucrative Endeavour*?" Gwendolyn gasped. She looked over at their rescuer, who was staring grimly down at Copernium. "Then that means . . . you're Kolonius Thrash!"

"Obviously." He crossed his arms. "Hero for hire, at your service if the price is right. Who *you* are is the question. And since I saved your sorry selves—*without* a fee, mind you, and it's a miracle we managed that much with the time we had—some explanations are in order."

"A *fee?*" Starling gaped. "You expect us to pay you for saving us? What are you, a hero or a pirate?"

He snorted. "This ship doesn't fly on dreams and happy thoughts, cupcake. I work for coin. Which will be hard to come by with that thing down there. So start talking. Who are you, and what is that thing that's attacking the city?"

Gwendolyn fidgeted. "Well, Mr. Thrash—I mean, Captain, sir—my name is Gwendolyn. These are my friends, Sparrow and Starling. We are . . . explorers." She wrestled with the decision of how much to give away, and Kolonius's stare was only making it worse. "Well, we're new to this place, you see—"

"Castaways, clearly."

"Yes, right, and we only wanted to look around Copernium, but then that monster attacked, and we tried to do our best to stop it, but it just kept coming after us, and then you showed up of course, and you're Kolonius Thrash! And I just wish that I could . . . stop . . . babbling . . ." she trailed off as Kolonius's one good eye bored into her.

"Uh-huh," he grunted. "And that monster down there wouldn't have anything to do with *you,* would it?" he said, leaning closer. He was only a head taller than she was, but he loomed much larger.

"I, um, m-maybe?" she stammered.

"Maybe. And *maybe* I saw what happened in the market, with those two men," Kolonius growled. "And *maybe* that festering abscess is bleeding Copernium dry because it's trying to get to you. *Maybe* I'm getting close?"

"Uh . . ."

"That's what I thought. Did it follow you through some portal? As if we didn't have enough trouble without Castaways bringing monsters down on our heads."

Starling stepped between the two. "Look, that abscess thingy isn't her fault, so back off," she said, planting a finger on Kolonius's chest. The taller boy swatted it away. "Just because you rescued us doesn't give you the right—"

"If you think I'm going to let you give me orders on my ship—"

"Who said we even wanted to be on your ship?"

"I didn't hear you arguing down there!" he shouted.

Both Starling and Kolonius were used to being in charge of things, so neither much liked having that attitude pointed back at them. Both were also not in the most agreeable of moods, as destruction of one's favorite city or physical harm to one's brother is likely to lead to.

"Hey!" Sparrow yelled, wincing and holding a hand to his head. "Both of you, stop shouting and do something useful, like telling me what's going on. I've got a splitting headache."

Gwendolyn grimaced. A terrible idea was gnawing at her insides. It *was* her fault. The Faceless Gentlemen were not in Copernium by coincidence. And now, an entire city was being devoured by that . . . *Abscess,* Kolonius had called it.

Kolonius straightened. "You want to be useful? Get. Off. My. Ship."

CHAPTER FIFTEEN

The Lucrative Endeavour

"W-what?" Gwendolyn said.

"You heard me, red. I should have left you to be eaten by your own monster. As it is, we'll put you down at our next landing. Which is better treatment than you deserve."

"But you can't! We just got here!" she said.

"And you'll be leaving just as quickly!"

"Erm, Cap'n, a word?" The burly first mate clunked over and stroked his fine orange mustache.

"What is it, Brunswick?" he barked.

"Well, I was just thinkin' that if'n these tykes are familiar with the beastie, they might have somethin' useful to say about stoppin' it."

Kolonius growled.

"Just give it a thought, Cap'n, that's all I ask. We don't want a repeat of what happened at Beaumont, do we now?" He gave Kolonius a significant look. As for what happened at Beaumont, that is a tale for another time.

The boy captain closed his eyes and took a breath. "Fine. New plan. You, Guinevere, you brought this Abscess here, so you'll be staying aboard until we find a way to stop it." He puffed out his chest. "After all, I can't be a dashing hero for hire if there's nothing left to save. How will I get paid?"

Starling rolled her eyes.

"And, seeing as how you owe me for bailing you out back there, you'll have to work off the debt. But for now, stay out of my way. Brunswick, are the engines prepped?"

"Aye-aye, Cap'n, primed and ready, all hands awaitin' orders."

"Take us west. Get as much distance between us and Copernium as you can. Engines full speed, open up the sails if the wind's with us."

"Already done, Cap'n." Brunswick walked away, a peg leg clunking heavily with every other step. "Sails and steam, all speed! Shift yourselves, men!"

"So, *we* don't need to do anything?" said a nearby crewwoman.

"It's a figure o' speech, Riley, give an ol' buccaneer some slack. But I don't want any slack in those bowlines."

The men and women on deck sprang to action, turning wheels and cranks, checking propellers, tying ropes, and generally doing lots of sailing-type things that Gwendolyn couldn't identify but certainly looked impressive. The children stayed by the railing, trying not to be bowled over in the frenzy of activity.

The crew were a ragtag bunch of all sizes, shapes, and shades. You might have thought it odd to see so many serious men and women taking orders from someone so young, but everyone snapped to attention when Kolonius came near, barking instructions and inspecting their work.

The *Lucrative Endeavour* was a massive vessel. Sleek wings jutted out from either side of the main deck. Each was fitted with an enormous propeller that pivoted as the ship started picking up speed. The forward prow was a long metal spike, giving the whole ship the appearance of an arrowhead of blue steel: sharp and deadly at the front, tall and wide at the back.

"Clear the mast-ways! Prepare to blow sails!" called the first mate. Three metal poles raised themselves from holes in the deck, and cables and rigging snapped into place with an audible *twang*. There was a blast of compressed air, and sails exploded from slits in the masts, instantly filling with wind.

"Pi-vot! Ten degrees starboard!" shouted Brunswick. He was the largest man on the ship, with a broad barrel chest and scruffy, orange muttonchops. He had a green bowler hat and matching vest. The goggles he wore glinted gold in the setting suns. He hobbled his way back to the bridge, where Kolonius was piloting the ship via a huge wheel behind a bank of windows. The sails angled, and the *Lucrative Endeavour* whirled like an eagle over the purple grasslands.

Starling stood with her arms folded, torn between gawking at the intricate machinery and shooting disdainful looks toward Kolonius. Gwendolyn heard her grumbling under her breath, something about "debt," "preposterous," and "windbag."

Sparrow leaned toward Gwendolyn. "So, I take it he's the reason you brought us here." He jerked a thumb toward the bridge.

"Yes! I tried to picture the portal bringing me here, into his book, but . . ."

"But what?"

"Well, he's not exactly what I was expecting," she admitted.

"Never meet your heroes, huh? What in the world happened while I was out?"

She filled him in until Kolonius burst from the bridge. "Brunswick, take the helm. Keep this course 'til we figure out where the dross we're going."

"Aye-aye, Cap'n! Steady as she goes!"

Kolonius shouted at crewmen as he passed. "Wilhelm! Wimmer! What in blazes are you doing? Quit slacking and fasten down those carrier lines! Torin! Check the rudders, I want the bearings properly greased. Carsair! We've picked up a shimmy in the port stabilizer. I want a full tear-down on the gyroscopic inverter coil by supper whistle. The last thing I need is a blown diffuser valve. This trip is already costly enough, and I'm not likely to see any pay anytime soon. And if I catch Earl, Poland, and Walker chatting in the galley again, they'll *be* our supper tonight." He stormed toward the three children. "All right, half-pints, where are we headed? How do we stop this thing?"

Starling snorted. "You're mister big hero-pants, why don't you figure it out?"

Kolonius glared at her. "Listen, missy—"

"For heaven's sake!" Gwendolyn shouted. "We'll never get anywhere if you don't stop bickering."

"So how *do* we stop it?" said Sparrow. The four of them just stared at each other. "Nothing? Come on, there must be a way!"

"The kid's right. It must have a weakness. Bullets and blades had no effect. But my crackleblast seemed to drive it back some."

"And my sparkspheres did the same," Starling said.

"Sparkspheres?" Kolonius asked with a raised eyebrow.

"Crackleblast?" Starling replied in kind.

"Well, this Abscess doesn't seem too fond of light, so that's most likely our best chance," said Kolonius.

"What, so we need some sort of light-weapons?" Sparrow asked.

Kolonius stroked his chin. "It adapted quickly when I attacked it. We'll need something much more powerful than crackleblast."

"What about Cyrio Kytain?" Gwendolyn chimed in.

Sparrow looked confused. "Who?"

"Remember? He founded Copernium. He invented 'a weapon of purest light that could defeat even the blackest evil,'" she quoted.

Kolonius rolled his eyes. "The Pistola Luminant makes for a lovely bedtime story, but we're all a little old for fairy tales. Well, *some* of us are."

"The Pistola Luminant?" asked Starling.

"Just a legend, girl. Doesn't exist."

"Ahem. Cap'n?" came a gruff voice.

"Gears and garters, what now, Brunswick?" Kolonius groaned in a very teenage manner.

"Well, there were always those stories about the Ravager."

"The Ravager?" Starling asked.

"Stonehand the Ravager, cap'n of the *Steel Dragon*, most famous pirate in history. Rumor says he found the Crystal Coves, and Kytain's hidden treasure. Course, they say he died in the findin'."

"I know what you're getting at, but it's out of the question," said Kolonius.

"What? What is he getting at?" Sparrow chirped.

"It's likely our best chance for dealin' with that beastie down there. And he owes ye a fair one."

"Who?" Gwendolyn said.

"It's too dangerous, and I'm not risking the ship and my crew to chase down a whisper of a rumor on the word of some crazy old codger."

"What are you talking about?" the three children shouted together.

Kolonius sighed. "The Dove's Nest."

"What's the Dove's—" Gwendolyn said.

"Some hero. If you're too scared, just say so, and I'll fly us there myself," Starling snorted.

"You and what pilot? The *Lucrative Endeavour* isn't a tricycle."

Starling pointed a finger at him. "I can fly circles around you any day!"

"Listen, Stripling, I've had about enough out of you—"

"My name is Starling, and if you're too thickheaded to remember, you're as stupid as you are cowardly!"

"Coward? You're calling me a coward, on my own ship?" Kolonius's face darkened. "Fine! Have it your way. Carsair!" he shouted. "Set course for the Dove's Nest. I want to see it on the horizon by breakfast tomorrow."

"Aye-aye, Captain!" yelled a large crewwoman.

Kolonius whirled back. "There. We'll indulge your little fantasy. Just pray we come out of it with our guts still on the inside." And he stormed off.

"Boys are so easy to manipulate. *You're calling me a coward on my own ship?"* Starling said, mimicking his voice perfectly. *"I'm not a coward, just a pompous, greedy windbag who's barely learned to shave."*

Brunswick chuckled. "That's him all right. Better not let the cap'n catch ye doin' that."

"What's so dangerous about the Dove's Nest?" Sparrow asked. "Doesn't sound too bad."

Brunswick tugged on his vest, trying in vain to stretch it across his barrel chest. "It's a hideout for lowlifes and pirates. Name's a bit of a joke. Also known as the Marauder's Mouth. If there's somethin' shady yer lookin' to find, t'aint no better place. Also a good place to have yer purse cut. Or yer throat."

"Oh. Lovely. They should put that on the brochure," Sparrow groaned.

"Har har har!" Brunswick bellowed, giving Sparrow another cringe-inducing slap on the back. "I like ye, lad. Ye'll fit right in."

Brunswick clunked away. Starling finally gave into the temptation to inspect some of the ship's machinery. The ship changed direction and picked up speed, slicing through the crimson clouds.

"It's so strange." Gwendolyn gazed at the colorful sky.

"What?" asked Sparrow.

"Seeing him. Here. In person. I imagined it so clearly, and

here we are. Going on an adventure with Kolonius Thrash. It's stunning."

Sparrow leaned against the railing. "You're pretty stunning yourself. You managed to bring us here, and that's supposed to be impossible."

Gwendolyn turned and caught his eyes, noticing the flecks of gold in the brown. She turned away nervously. "That's, uh, not what I meant by stunning. It's hard to believe, I mean. I'm responsible for almost destroying an entire city. It doesn't seem right that there's so much ugliness out there, when there's so many wonderful things like that."

She gestured over the railing as light from the twin sunsets painted the clouds with a rainbow of colors. The wind whipped her hair like flickering tongues of flame. Sparrow put his hands next to hers, barely brushing against each other, and her cheeks warmed.

"I know what you mean," he said. "It's hard to focus on so much awful when there's something as pretty as that in front of you. And then you feel awful for not feeling awful."

Gwendolyn was silent for a moment. "The Mister Men called that thing the Collector. It must be what is collecting all the energy from the Lambents. And now it's using that energy to attack Copernium and drain it as well."

Sparrow nodded. "The way it's attacking, like it's draining everything–it's too similar to the Lambents you talked about to be a coincidence."

"You're right. We have to help Kolonius. If we can stop this monster here, maybe we can find out how to help the City too, stop the Lambents and the Mister Men along with this Abscess-Collector thing. And then . . ."

"What?" he asked, raising an eyebrow.

"Well, if the Faceless Gentlemen were able to get through from the City, then there must be a way to get back." It seemed wrong, somehow, that something so terrible would give her a feeling of hope, but there it was. She might see her parents again after all. As long as the Mister Men hadn't already erased them. She swallowed hard. "But this is *my* mess. We can't just run away and leave it all to rot. We have to do what we can to clean it up." Gwendolyn turned to see Sparrow beaming at her, and a blush spread over her pale and freckled face. She was getting quite tired of blushing.

Kolonius came back over. They separated, embarrassed, and Starling hastily slammed shut the access panel on the machinery she'd been tinkering with.

If Kolonius noticed, he didn't say anything. "We're on our way. We should reach the Dove's Nest in a few hours. In the meantime"—he tossed each of them a mop, and indicated a nearby bucket—"you'll start paying down your debt. Happy scrubbing!" He gave them a smug smile and strode away.

Starling dropped her mop and was about to shout after him, but Sparrow threw a hand over her mouth.

"Oh, no. Unless you'd like to test one of your parabrellas from this height, keep your mouth shut and do as we're told. At least for now. He's the only chance we have of saving this world *and* Gwendolyn's."

Starling's eyes flared, but she visibly relaxed. Sparrow removed his hand.

"Fine," she said. "But if you think I'm going to put up with that arrogant, childish snot any longer than is absolutely necessary—"

"Yeah, yeah, yeah." Sparrow threw the mop at her. "Less yappin', more moppin'."

Starling growled, splashed her mop in the bucket, and went to clean a part of the deck well away from annoying captains and children.

As they mopped, Gwendolyn noticed Kolonius examining the machinery Starling had been messing with, muttering to himself. "She doubled the output . . . How did she . . ." and he trailed off as he inspected the gizmo.

"No wonder she can't stand him," Sparrow whispered to Gwendolyn. "They're exactly alike." He wet his mop and started to scrub. "Oh, uh, and by the way," Sparrow said nervously.

"What?"

He leaned in and gave her a quick peck on the cheek. "Thanks for saving me." This time it was his turn to blush, the redness spreading over his already ruddy complexion, and he hurried away to mop another part of the deck.

Gwendolyn smiled and put a hand to her cheek.

But then she remembered all the people she *didn't* save, the way the dressmaker had screamed as the Abscess killed her right before Gwendolyn's eyes, and she felt ashamed that she could ever smile again.

CHAPTER SIXTEEN

Odd Vacation Plans

Vacations are exhausting things. You spend all day seeing new sights, eating new food, and generally tiring yourself out. At the end of the day, you lie in an unfamiliar bed, in an unfamiliar room, and try to scrounge enough sleep to make it through the next day as all the memories from the last one run through your head.

Adventures work in much the same way, but with the addition of mortal peril, fearsome monsters, and even more running. Gwendolyn lay in one of the hammocks in the crew quarters belowdecks, swaying gently. Starling lay below, snoring. Gwendolyn was more tired than she could ever remember, but sleep was not her friend that evening.

She sighed. "It's overwhelming, isn't it?" she whispered to the ship. She placed a hand on the cool metal, and felt the engines hum in response. "Yes, you're right. I *did* want adventure, to go outside the City. But not like this."

Getting the things we want is no simple matter. Things seem

much less shiny and fantastic once we go from *wanting* to *having*. And now that Gwendolyn had the adventure she wanted, all she really wanted was to know her parents were safe. Maybe if the Mister Men were in Tohk, then they weren't erasing people back in the City—though it was cold comfort to know they were erasing people here. She heard the screech of the Abscess in her mind, and dark thoughts rushed to fill the stillness of the sleeping quarters.

~~~

A horn sounded from the ship's intercom. Gwendolyn fell out of the hammock and smacked onto the cold metal floor.

Wincing, she looked around. She didn't remember falling asleep, but Starling was gone and daylight streamed through the porthole, so she must have. Voices were coming through the hatchway above.

"Remind me again why we're helping this girl?" said Starling. "She dragged us into this mess. In fact, all she does is drag us into trouble."

"She's lost her home too. But she managed to bring us here on *purpose*. There's got to be a way she can get us home too. No more bouncing between worlds," Sparrow said.

"Don't get distracted by a pretty face. We aren't any closer to getting home, and now we're fighting some giant shadow monster, and I'm tempted to grab you by the shirt and find the nearest portal out of here."

"And leave Gwendolyn behind? Leave all these people to get eaten by that thing? And what if it doesn't stop at eating
~~~

one world? What if it finds our home? Besides, you didn't seem so eager to leave when you were making googly eyes at Cap'n Puberty yesterday."

"What? He's an arrogant jerk! Googly eyes? Watch your mouth, or you'll find it getting personal with my—"

But that was when Gwendolyn decided she had eavesdropped enough, and popped through the hatch onto the deck.

"Good morning, sleepyhead," Sparrow said quickly. Starling looked away, out at the sky.

"Good morning to you too," she replied, a little coldly. "Where are we now?"

"Approaching the Sundrill Mountains," said Starling, "and Brunswick says we're about to see where they get their name. Look."

Gwendolyn did, and the previous conversation was driven from her mind at the breathtaking vista. The yellow sun was coming up over a very peculiar mountain range. The craggy peaks were riddled with holes, like a worm-eaten apple. Beams of sunlight shone through the holes like hundreds of spotlights, scattering rays across the purple grasslands. It looked for all the world as though the light had drilled holes straight through the rock. They watched the spectacle until a whistle sounded over the intercom.

"Breakfast!" Sparrow said. "I'm—"

"We know," said Starling. "You're starving."

He led them to the galley where they had a quick meal of eggs, fresh bread, and a delicious but unsettlingly pink cheese. Gwendolyn marveled at the amount of food Sparrow shoveled down. She hardly touched her own. Without really thinking about it, she began drawing in her sketchbook. There was more than enough inspiration after what she'd seen in the past days.

"What's that?" Sparrow pointed with his fork.

Gwendolyn started to hide the sketchbook back in her satchel, but changed her mind, and shyly slid it over for him to see.

"Hey, these are really good!" he said.

"What? They are?"

"Yeah! I didn't know you could draw."

She took the sketchbook back and put it away. "Well, there's an awful lot of things you don't know about me, but at least now there's one less." But she was only teasing, and Sparrow grinned. In her bag, she spotted her copy of *Kolonius Thrash*. She had nearly forgotten about it, and opened it to look through its maps.

And for once she noticed something that was *not* there.

Stomachs are useful things. Sparrow's, for example, seemed capable of expanding to an almost infinite size, and communicating with a wide array of groans and rumbles. As Gwendolyn looked at the map, her stomach communicated the exact feeling of being in an elevator whose cable has snapped.

"What's wrong?" mumbled Sparrow through a mouthful of food.

She slid the book over. Copernium was gone, nothing more than a blank spot on the colorful picture. And identical white spots were growing in other places as well.

"This is all my fault. I'm the reason that monster is here, and now it's spreading!" To help emphasize this, her stomach gave her the feeling that someone had punched it. She covered her face to hide the tears that were coming. "Oh, stupid, stupid girl. All those people, all dead!"

Sparrow put his fork down, knelt next to her, and pulled her hands away from her face. "Stop it. Listen to me. You are *not* a stupid girl. I won't let anyone say it, not even you. This is not your fault. You didn't set the Abscess loose, and you didn't bring the Mister Men here. They came looking for trouble."

"Looking for me!"

"Yes, looking for you, but it's not like you invited them, is it? If you blame yourself, you're only helping them."

Gwendolyn sniffed. She supposed he was right, in a way, but it didn't lessen the guilt she felt when she pictured the dressmaker, screaming and flailing. The dark feelings returned in double size.

"Besides, this still doesn't add up," Starling said, nibbling a piece of bread.

"What do you mean?" Sparrow looked away from Gwendolyn, and she used the moment to dry her face on her green dress.

"How did they get here in the first place? Gwendolyn had to use the Figment, and we lost it in the In-Between. How did *they* get through?"

Gwendolyn perked up. "You're right! They shouldn't even have been able to see the door, much less steer their way here."

Sparrow continued to assault his food like it was an invading army. "Maybe that Abscess thing did it," he spluttered through a mouthful of egg. "This Collector person. They said he had been looking for this world for a while."

"Maybe," Gwendolyn said. "But that still doesn't explain how any of them got through. Do they have the Figment?"

Sparrow opened his mouth to reply, but Starling waved a knife at him. "If you talk with your mouth full again, I'm going to sew it up. That's your third helping! Where do you put it all?"

He grinned. "I've got a hollow leg."

"What was that?" Brunswick clunked up behind and laid a hand on the boy's shoulder.

Sparrow gulped, choked, then sputtered food all over the table. "N-nothing," he coughed.

"Too right, nothin'. Come along, sprouts, Cap'n wants you in his cabin."

"How much trouble are we in?" asked Gwendolyn.

"Yeah, is he going to throw us off the ship? Or worse, more mopping?" Sparrow said.

"Go easy on the Cap'n, lad. Seein' Copernium like that, it's enough to put anybody off. He'll be more his cheerful self today, ye'll see." He waddled away, his peg leg thumping on the deck.

Starling rolled her eyes. "Look, you two. Not a word of this book to Captain Snob. Just act natural, and don't say a thing."

Sparrow and Gwendolyn nodded, and they exited the galley. Gwendolyn's stomach delivered a dull ache that had nothing to do with food, one you may have felt if you have ever had to take the long walk to the principal's office. They reached the captain's cabin at the rear of the ship, and knocked.

"Come," he barked.

Cheerful my foot, Gwendolyn thought.

They entered. The room was as fancy as it was messy, like a

princess that has rolled in manure. An enormous unmade bed stood off to one side. A mahogany dresser hung slack-jawed with its drawers open. For every silk tapestry, there was a crumpled piece of paper, a discarded weapon, or a bit of forgotten food. A massive desk dominated the center of the room, covered in maps and charts. The expensive decor did not match the gruff boy that lived in it, but the mess seemed to suit him perfectly.

Kolonius was wearing the same clothes. An untouched breakfast cooled on the corner of the desk. He was poring over papers spread across it, and he spoke to them without looking up.

"So, what are you all hiding now?"

The children traded shocked looks.

"What? Hiding?" Sparrow blurted. "Hah! That's a laugh. Why would we be hiding–"

He looked up. "Stow it, boy. I may only have one eye, but your baby face is easier to read than this map. You, Gwennifer. Tell me."

That didn't last long, she thought. "It's *Gwendolyn.* And a please would have been nice."

"I'm not accustomed to being taught manners on my own ship," he growled, then added, sneering, "but, *if you please.*"

She looked at the other two, who shrugged. *Might as well,* she thought. He was supposed to be a hero, after all. Maybe if they started trusting him, he would trust them back. Gwendolyn removed *Kolonius Thrash and the Perilous Pirates* from her bag and dropped it on the desk with a *thump.*

Kolonius raised an eyebrow at the title and flipped it open.

Several pages of text had disappeared entirely. "Hmph. These pages are blank."

"Kolonius, let me explain, I—"

"Captain," he corrected. He gestured at the book as if disappointed. "You're all fidgety as field mites because of this?" He let out a bark of laughter and read the back cover. "'Tales of adventure from Kolonius Thrash, daring boy captain.' That's nothing new. I *am* quite daring; who wouldn't want to write about me?"

Starling gagged.

"So how does it end? Do I get the girl, slay the villain, make heaps of gold?"

"I don't know," Gwendolyn said. "I haven't exactly finished it."

Kolonius pouted. "What? Is my life too boring for you?"

"No, but I've been a bit busy, if you hadn't noticed."

"Aren't we all? You can buy books like this three for a copper in the Mainspring Marketplace. Or could, anyway. But these blank pages . . ." He flipped to the back of the book, to the map of Tohk with the growing holes. A scowl twisted the scar that ran under his eye patch. "That matches the reports coming in over the aerials. There have been more sightings of the Abscess." Kolonius pointed to blank spots on his own map. "A mysterious shadow sighted in Fultimo, in the south, as well as in the Archicon Valley to the north." He sighed and ran a hand through his dreadlocks. "Copernium has been completely destroyed. Nothing left but bleached rubble."

"No!" gasped Starling.

"That's terrible," Sparrow muttered, fists clenched.

Gwendolyn just stared at her feet. *My fault,* she thought.

Kolonius straightened and stretched. "Yes, it looks bad, but I've had my back against the wall before. We'll get out of this, if the legends of the Pistola Luminant are true. Which is still a big *if*, but seeing as I don't have any better ideas, we'll need to find it before the infection spreads any further. Destroying that thing might restore what it's taken."

Gwendolyn perked up. "Really? It could bring back Copernium?"

"There's a chance. Strange creatures play by strange rules. Right now, I have to get above deck to guide our approach to the Dove's Nest. Brunswick and I will go in and get the information. Until then, you'll all be safe here. Finish mopping the decks, then start on the galley."

The three of them all shouted at once.

"You can't just leave us here to clean your stupid ship!" Starling yelled.

"We're a part of this! We're going too!" Gwendolyn chimed in.

"I'll tell you where you can shove that mop!" Sparrow said.

Kolonius grinned and pushed past them. "Gears and garters, you're all so sensitive. You wouldn't last two minutes in the Mouth. 'Cept for you, Blue. I might need your help."

Nobody said anything.

"He means you, Starling," said Sparrow.

"Oh! Me? Why?" Starling narrowed her eyes.

"Why? I, uh . . ." For the first time, Kolonius's confidence faltered as he scrambled for an answer, the teenage boy peeking out from behind the gruff captain. "You've got a pretty head—pretty *good* head on your shoulders, and you're skilled with tech. Could come in handy. Just . . . follow orders!" And out he went.

Starling stormed after him. "I can't leave the kids behind, what if something happens to them?" But their argument faded.

Sparrow turned to Gwendolyn. "Any chance that we'll follow orders, stay put, and catch up on our deck-swabbing?"

Gwendolyn smiled a wicked smile. "Not on your life."

Sparrow grinned back. "Didn't think so."

~~~

Sometime later, Gwendolyn and Sparrow were hiding under a tarp in a longboat a hundred feet above the ground. A longboat typically takes you from ship to shore, but in the absence of any shores, or any water, four propeller struts kept the wooden craft aloft.

While Kolonius and Starling were busy arguing on deck, the two children snuck aboard, hiding under a tarp that covered the supplies at the rear. After a few more minutes of arguing, the boat was launched.

To any observer, it would seem a raggedy old man was piloting a grimy cabin boy and a very large buccaneer. In reality, it was Kolonius in his usual disguise, a floppy hat and tattered cloak. The only disguise Brunswick needed was a fake beard to cover his orange mustache, and an angry scowl to prevent unwanted questions.

Starling pulled at a hole in the rags Kolonius had forced her to wear. "I still can't believe I let you talk me into this. I don't like leaving my brother behind. And I suppose that girl
~~~

is kind of my responsibility too. You don't know them, they're going to get into some sort of trouble." Her hair was pulled up under a three-pointed hat, and she had a smattering of painted pubescent stubble.

"Come on, you could use a vacation," Kolonius said.

"Flying into a nest of pirates is your idea of a vacation?"

"It is when you're with *me*. When was the last time you got away from that brother of yours anyway, or went on a d–I mean, spent time with someone your own age? It's got to be exhausting, caring for a couple of Castaway brats."

"Hey!" Sparrow shouted.

"Wha–?" Brunswick yelped. He pulled back the tarp and picked Gwendolyn and Sparrow up by their collars. "Stowaways!" He sounded angry, but appeared to stifle a chuckle.

"You've got to be kidding me." Kolonius's face darkened. Gwendolyn expected Starling to look equally furious, but she blushed and looked away.

"What do you want to do with 'em, Cap'n?" said Brunswick. "We're on a deadline, turnin' back now'd cost us precious time."

Kolonius growled. "We leave them where we found them, and they can wait in the boat."

"What?" Sparrow said. "Look how well we hid. We can handle some mangy pirates."

"You *didn't* hide well, you got yourself caught almost immediately," Starling pointed out.

"Well, if you try to leave us here, we'll just sneak in as soon as you're gone," said Gwendolyn, "and it would be worse to have us wandering around alone, wouldn't it?"

"She's got a point, Cap'n," said Brunswick.

Kolonius glared. "I don't know how you ever made it as a pirate, Brunswick, you're nothing but a soft-hearted pushover."

Brunswick chuckled. "Lucky for you. I recall one little cabin boy who didn't mind when I took a shine to 'im."

The captain rolled his eyes with all his seventeen-year-old expertise. "*Fine.* They can come. Get them some clothes."

Brunswick did, and Gwendolyn put them on over her colorful dress. She hoped the smell wouldn't stick to it.

"If anyone speaks to you, don't answer," Kolonius said. "Keep your heads down, and try not to attract attention. Also—"

He reached into a pouch, then hurled a cloud of dirt into their faces. Gwendolyn sputtered and coughed, and Sparrow shouted something not repeatable in polite company.

"—rub that around a bit. You're much too clean." He pulled his hat low, effectively covering his face. "An' keep yer traps shut," he said with a gravelly accent. "The Marauder's Mouth ain't no place for children."

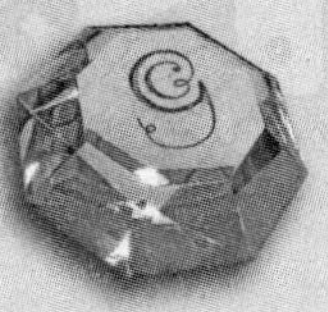

CHAPTER SEVENTEEN

Precarious Reconnaissance

As if on cue, a shadow fell across the longboat. The mountain loomed over them, and they saw a gigantic cave, one large enough to swallow a city. Which indeed it had.

Buildings ringed the top and bottom lip of the cave, looking exactly like dilapidated wooden dentures in the jaws of a stone giant. The Marauder's Mouth.

The inside of the cave looked like it had been designed by a madman with no regard for safety codes, basic good taste, or even gravity. Huts and shacks were stacked on top of each other, rickety stairs were set into the walls, entire city blocks dangled from the cave roof on wooden platforms. Ropes, pneumos, and catwalks went everywhere, and the whole chaotic mess went miles deep. The buildings resembled unruly schoolchildren, all elbowing and shoving, climbing anything in sight.

They pulled up to a metal post hammered into the rock at the entrance. Kolonius tied the ship to it, and yanked something out of the control panel.

"She won't be going anywhere without the gyroscopic inverter coil. Follow my lead. Ol' Tripp is fidgety, and I don't want you scaring him off. Brunswick, anything come in over the aerials on Drekk?"

"Nothin' since yesterday. Last we heard the *Swift Retribution* was over the Spiced Seas, raiding the harvesters." Brunswick replied, hooking pneumo handles onto lines that led into the cave.

"That's closer to us than I'd like. Let's hope he stays put. The last thing we need is Tylerium Drekk sticking his pointed nose in all this. Gather whatever intel you can, but watch our backs."

"I always do, lad." He whirred up the line and inside the cave.

"Who's this Drekk person?" whispered Sparrow.

"The most awful pirate in Tohk," Gwendolyn said, remembering what she'd read in the book. "He's Kolonius's arch-nemesis!" She looked down at the zillion-foot drop below. "Is this safe? It looks awfully . . . pointy . . . down there."

He grinned. "Safe? Gertrude, The Marauder's Mouth is about as un-safe as it gets."

"Then why are you smiling?" Starling said.

He patted his sword hilt. "Because *I'm* not safe, either." He grabbed a pneumo and whirred away.

"I think I like him," Sparrow said.

Gwendolyn grabbed a pneumo herself. "Just don't drop me, if you please and thank you very much," she said, and indeed, it deposited her safely on the platform. The other two followed, and Kolonius led them into the cave.

The Dove's Nest was a city in perpetual twilight. There were nooks, crannies, and alleyways everywhere, all in a shadowy, yellow haze from the buzzing lights hung throughout the cave. The sounds of accordion and fiddle mixed with clinking glasses, rough laughter, and the crash of some brawl.

It was crowded. Cutthroats and marauders stumbled from one tavern to the next. Some huddled in corners, whispering and watching. Nobody she saw looked particularly friendly. Or clean. Few of them had all their original body parts, instead sporting hooks, eyepatches, and peg legs.

Someone zipped overhead on a pneumo, whooping and hanging from his knees, making Gwendolyn flinch. A surly man snarled at her, revealing teeth he could have counted on his one hand.

Gwendolyn clutched Sparrow's arm.

He grinned. "That's sweet, but it might blow our cover as cabin boys."

"Oh! Right. Sorry." She straightened and tried to swagger. "So, Kolonius, who is Old Tripp? Do you really think he can help us? Why is that man lying in the middle of the street? Oh, wait, he's vomiting. That's disgusting, and this is all so dangerous, but still, that makes it a little exciting, doesn't it? Is there a word for feeling excited and terrified all at once? I've never been somewhere like this before. Of course, I've never really been *anywhere* before, and–"

Kolonius whacked the back of her head. "Quit yer jawin', Mortimer, or ye'll be cleanin' the outside of the hull *without* a harness. Got it?" His accent was fake, but Gwendolyn suspected his glare was completely sincere.

The boy captain led them to a series of stalls. He motioned

for them to stay and sauntered up to a lanky man selling questionable-looking meats. "Lookin' fer Ol' Tripp, heard tell he's been here. Seen 'im around?"

"All I see's customers. Buy somefin' or shove off."

Kolonius slapped a coin on the counter.

The lanky man spat on it.

Kolonius slapped down another. "I don't want yer stinking food, but information is always tasty."

The shopkeeper eyed the coins again. "Ask around the Slaver's Quarter." He pointed to a cluster of buildings dangling from the ceiling. "Heard tell he likes a drink at the Red-Eyed Leech now and then."

Kolonius took back one of the coins. "Thanks for little," he growled, and stomped off down the alleyway. Sparrow, Starling, and Gwendolyn hurried to keep up.

They reached a square, wooden platform. As Gwendolyn stepped on it, the whole thing lurched upward on a thick cable toward the catwalk the meat seller had pointed to. Kolonius was more grim than usual.

"What's the matter?" Starling asked.

"Hrmm. Slavers." His jaw and fists clenched.

"Slavers?" Gwendolyn asked.

"They aren't satisfied simply attacking and pillaging innocent people. They'll also take a few captive, press them into service on their ships. Force them to do all the most dangerous and disgusting jobs . . ." He trailed off, his face clouded. Kolonius had no fondness for pirates and lawbreakers generally, but he had a particular hatred for slavery. That, however, is a story for another time.

When the makeshift elevator came to a stop, Kolonius leapt out and stormed over to a tavern with a sign that read "The Red-Eyed Leech," with a childish scrawl of a mug of red ale.

Kolonius took off his sword belt. "Hold this."

Sparrow reached for it, but Kolonius tossed it to Starling. "Not you, boy, I don't trust you with sharp objects. You three wait here."

"What are you doing?" Gwendolyn asked.

He cracked his knuckles. "Wait. Here." And he vanished through the swinging doors.

They could hear men drinking and carousing. Then a crash. Then silence. Then someone shouting. Then several more someones. Then an explosion of crashing, smashing, and screaming.

Sparrow stepped forward, but his sister threw out a hand. "He might know what he's doing, but you certainly don't. Stay, like he said."

He scowled. "I can handle myself."

A man came crashing through one of the front windows and landed next to them. He sprang up and ran back inside, only to come crashing out again through the other window. He didn't move.

"Then again, here is good," Sparrow agreed.

Pirates ran out of the tavern and down the street. The crashing continued for another moment, then all was silent.

Kolonius walked out, dusted his palms, and took back his sword. "All right. Let's go."

Sparrow's jaw dropped. "Wait, d-did you find out where this Tripp guy lives? Did you take on all those guys by yourself?"

"Yes. And yes." He strapped on the belt and headed down the walkway with Sparrow at his heels like an excited puppy.

Starling looked at Gwendolyn and rolled her eyes. "Boys."

Gwendolyn laughed, and Starling smiled a little.

But then Gwendolyn noticed something in the shadows behind the tavern. Something that made her blood run cold.

It was the unmistakable shape of a bowler hat.

She looked again, but there was nothing. She quoted her mother: "Sometimes dear, your imagination gets the better of you." But this was only the sort of thing one says to make oneself feel better, and Gwendolyn walked faster than usual to catch up to the others.

"That was amazing!" Sparrow whispered to her.

"What?"

"Back there! Kolonius!" Sparrow hopped about, punching the air.

"I didn't think it was all that great." Gwendolyn had been picked on enough to develop a distaste for fighting.

"Aww, that's because you're just a gir—" He clapped a hand to his mouth in horror, but he was half a sentence too late.

Gwendolyn glared at him, crossed her arms, and looked away.

"Gwendolyn, come on, you know I didn't mean that, it just slipped out!"

"Psst . . ." came a voice.

Sparrow stopped pleading and looked around. Gwendolyn looked as well. The others didn't notice, and kept walking.

"Pssssssssst!" The whispers came from an alley on their left. Standing in the shadows was a man in a tattered cloak, a popular fashion statement in the Dove's Nest. He beckoned to them with a crooked finger.

"You children seem lost. No, not lost, not clever children like you. Looking for something, more like. Let Rog Harker here lend you a hand. Whatever you're after, I got it." He let his coat flap open to reveal dozens of gleaming trinkets and rolled parchments.

Sparrow, who lacked parents to warn him not to talk to strangers, said, "Do you have anything about Cyrio Kytain?"

"Sparrow, we need to go," Gwendolyn said.

"Kytain? Ye'd be seekin' the legendary Crystal Coves, then? I'm sure I've got somethin' here that can help. Step over here, and we'll haggle a deal."

"Sparrow, this is a bad idea." Gwendolyn pulled on his sleeve.

"He said he can get us to the Coves!" he whispered. "We could find the way before Kolonius does!"

She wrinkled her brow. She didn't think it likely that this cloaked figure had the information they needed, but even still, finding the pistol faster *could* save more lives. That was the reason they were here, after all. This might be her chance to make up for bringing the Mister Men here in the first place. If it meant saving lives, didn't she have to take every chance, no matter how small it was, no matter how shady this man seemed?

The man slunk back a little. "Look, mate, if you're not interested . . ."

"No, we're coming! Unless I was right, Gwendolyn, and you're just a girl."

"I'm not *just* anything!" She marched into the alley. "The Crystal Coves and the Pistola Luminant. What can you do for us?"

"I got somethin' that'll get you where you're going." The man reached into his cloak–

"Boys! Gears and garters, where did ye go? I've warned ye useless scum about wanderin' off!" came Kolonius's voice. He stormed around the corner. "There you are. Stay close! I swear, you're a pair of bleedin' toddlers!"

"No, Kolonius," Gwendolyn stammered, "this man might help us!"

"What man?"

They turned around. The alley was empty.

"But he was right here . . . We asked him about the Pistola Luminant, and he said he could help, and, and . . ." There is an interesting phenomenon where things that sound perfectly reasonable when you say them in your head can sound utterly stupid once you say them out loud. Gwendolyn had this feeling now.

"What?!" Kolonius grabbed Gwendolyn by the arm. "You gave away our entire mission to some alley skulker? How dim *are* you, girl? This is exactly why I wanted you rotten little monsters to stay back on the ship where you wouldn't cause any–"

"Let go, you can't talk to her like that!" Sparrow tried to get between them.

"And you! Why didn't you try to stop her?"

Sparrow shrank from his glare. "What? She just—I didn't have a chance to stop her—"

"Gah! Morons, the lot of you." Kolonius pulled out his communicator. "Torin, Brunswick. We've been had. Looks like little Red twigged us. Most likely one of Drekk's spies."

"How do you know it was Drekk's?" crackled Brunswick.

"Because it's always Drekk," said Kolonius. "Make ready for a quick getaway once I'm done here."

"Aye, Cap'n," came Torin's voice.

Kolonius stuck a shaky and enraged finger in the children's faces.

"You two. Don't. Wander. Off." And he stormed out of the alley.

Starling stood outside, shaking her head in almost parental disappointment.

CHAPTER EIGHTEEN

The Spark

They continued in tense silence as Kolonius led them through the city. The damp cave mustiness mingled with the smells of bodies, sewage, and the coppery scent of blood. Not so different from your average school locker room, in fact. The dangling street had an unnerving tendency to rock and sway.

Gwendolyn seethed. How could Sparrow have blamed her like that? All because he wanted to impress Kolonius. And that "just a girl" crack still had her steaming.

Sparrow caught her eye. He shot her an apologetic smile, but she turned her nose up at him. Sparrow hung his head.

Kolonius led them up a set of winding stairs toward the cave roof. With each step, the structure shuddered. It grew warmer too, and beads of sweat broke out on Gwendolyn's pale skin. But after several uncomfortable minutes, they reached a wooden platform anchored to the wall of the cave. The ceiling was only a dozen feet above them, but the ground was distractingly far below. A cluster of shacks and huts littered the platform. Kolonius strode to one and banged on the door.

"Open up! I know you're in there, Tripp, you ol' buzzard. Come on out with ya!" he bellowed in his disguised voice.

An answer came from within, scratchy and weak. "No need for shoutin', Thrash, ye whippersnapper. Nor for that ree-diculous accent. Nobody up here but Ol' Tripp, and me hearin' ain't gone yet."

The rickety door swung open and revealed the oldest man Gwendolyn had ever seen. His face was a sun-stained collection of lines and wrinkles, but his eyes shone bright: one green, the other a deep purple. He was bald, save for a ring of wispy white hairs that dangled to his shoulders. His clothes were as ancient and tattered as he was.

His cracked lips curled into a smile that was more gum than grin. "Weeeell, I sees ye brought me some company. And ladies too! Mighty lovely. Hello, ladies! And an itty boy near pretty enough to be a lady his own self, ain'tcha lady-boy?" He cackled and slapped his leg.

Starling grinned, Gwendolyn blushed, and Sparrow's jaw dropped as he babbled some incoherent defense.

Tripp leered at him. "Not too bright though, are they? The pretty ones so rarely are. Easier on the eyes than that oaf Brunswick, eh? Quite the upgrade. But come in, come in, get yerselves cozy." He waved them inside with a bony hand, though if anyone had ever called the shack "cozy," they were in serious need of an eye examination. And probably a flea bath.

"Whoa, there old timer," Kolonius said gently. "I'm afraid we don't have time for pleasantries."

Ol' Tripp heaved a rattling sigh. "Of course. 'Tain't nobody comes to visit, not leastaways two-and-a-half pretty ladies, not 'lessen they need somthin'. Whattdya want?"

Kolonius's tone grew serious. "We're here about this shadow monster that's destroying Tohk. We think you might hold the key to stopping it."

"Oh, *do* I now? Seems I might'a heard somethin' about that. Nasty beastie. Copernium gone, yes? Bad bit o' business. But what's it to do with me?"

Kolonius put his hands on his hips. "Don't be coy. You were on Stonehand the Ravager's crew, and rumor is he found Kytain's hideaway. We think there's something there that can stop the Abscess."

"Hmmmm, that *is* a fascinating story, ain't it? But stories are so unreliable." His tone grew cold. "And if'n I did, why would I be helpin' Kolonius Thrash? The wrench in every pirate's engine from the Spiced Seas to the Violet Veldt to the Stormlands? If word gets out that I helped Kolonius barking Thrash, well–"

"Shut up and name your price, old man."

"Fifty gold," he blurted immediately.

"Fifty? If I'd wanted to get robbed, I'd have stayed on the lower levels. I can do twenty."

"Eh, couldn't buy firewood with twenty. Forty, though, forty'd warm these old bones up right–"

Kolonius dropped a jingling pouch at the man's feet. "There's twenty-five, and ten silver. I don't have time to haggle. And you owe me." He raised the eyebrow above his eyepatch.

The story of how Ol' Tripp came to be in the boy captain's debt is a thrilling one indeed, but as we do not have the time to tell it, I shall merely say that it involved a deadly ballerina, a beautiful duchess, a runaway train, and a flock of electrified carnivorous birds.

Tripp stared him down with those mismatched eyes. Gwendolyn caught a glimpse of the pirate he must have been, the cold steel behind the liver-spotted skin, the look of a man who could kill, and had. He glanced from Kolonius to the pouch and back again. Then his face softened. "All right, young'n, no need fer all that. T'was only twerkin' yer rudder. Hold on a moment, let me find it."

He vanished inside, and they heard a clanging commotion. It was a marvel he could have enough things in that tiny shack to make such a racket. Then he reappeared with an old parchment.

"Here ye are." He unrolled it and blew off the dust.

Kolonius coughed and squinted. "An old map of Tohk? What am I looking for?"

Tripp stabbed a wrinkled finger down on an *X*. "There. That's Kytain's lair. The Crystal Coves. Ye'll want to follow this heading here–"

"I've been out that way, there's nothing there."

"Oh, thinks ye knows everything, do ye? Young'ns, always so certain. Wouldn't need Ol' Tripp if it were that easy, eh? Once yer on that headin', ye'll need to lock down yer rudders and sails. Kytain was a smart ol' bugger, and there's a sorta interference field round the island, keeps ships away. Yer instruments will lie to ye, say yer turnin' when ye ain't. Don't listen to 'em. Old Stonehand had me up in the crow's nest, guidin' him with my special talents. See?" He pointed to his mismatched eyes. "And we found it. Keep yer course manually, ye'll find it too. All that pricey tech, yers for the plunderin', hee hee!" He cackled and rubbed his hands together.

"Thank you, Tripp. But it's not plunder I'm after."

"Right, ye'd be interested in the magic pistol, wouldn't ye? Well, give that shadow beastie a jolly rogerin' from me."

"I will. And we'll be back later, just to visit, I promise. We'll sit and talk all you like. Of course, you could always come with us, join my crew."

Tripp laughed, a hoarse croak. "I'm too old and too cranky to go cavortin' about with young'ns. Don't go makin' promises ye don't intend to keep. Next I sees ye will be when ye need somethin' else. Now git!" He began to shoo them away, but stopped and grabbed Kolonius by the arm instead. "Oh, right, one last thing. That girl there."

"Starling?" Kolonius pointed. Starling looked puzzled.

"Not her, t'other one. Fiery lass. Ye know I've got the special sight. These eyes can see things, right?"

Kolonius nodded. "I've never understood it, but I know it true enough."

"Well, I'm telling ye, keep that one close. She's special, ye see? Got the *spark*. Got it strong. Dim and dusty, like a lamp covered in an old blanket. But strong enough I can see it plain, shinin' through."

The young captain wrinkled his brow. “The spark? What’s that?”

“Cripes, I can’t explain it, but it’s there, just under her skin, plain as day. Just like Kytain, if legends be true. If’n this girl dusts it off and brings it out, then you just see what she can do.”

“Maaagic,” Sparrow whispered to his sister.

“I swear to god, Sparrow, I will throw you off this ledge.”

Kolonius looked puzzled. “All right then, I’ll, um, I’ll keep an eye on that.”

“See that ye do. Now off with ye! Ye’ll ruin my reputation as an upstanding lowlife. Although you pretty ladies, you come visit any time you take a fancy. We’ll have dances and tea. You too, pretty lady-boy.” And with a cackle, he disappeared back into his shack.

The four of them clambered down the staircase. Gwendolyn’s head was spinning. The spark? Her imagination, maybe? But in a world full of inventors, storytellers, and artists, she wasn’t special, was she? She was different, sure, but there was nothing special about that. Different got you mocked and teased and pushed about. Being different just makes you lonely. She looked back up at Ol’ Tripp’s little shack. He was different, all right, and it didn’t get much lonelier than that.

They reached the bottom of the stairs and made for the elevator. Kolonius and Starling studied the map, while Sparrow leaned over to whisper to Gwendolyn.

“Listen, I’m sorry for what happened back there. You know how it is. My mouth runs away with itself, and causes all sorts of trouble.”

"I'm sure I have no idea what you mean," Gwendolyn lied.

"Look, I'm trying to apologize here."

Gwendolyn folded her arms. "You wouldn't have to do so much apologizing if you'd do more thinking first. Go apologize to Kolonius, he's the one you want to impress."

Sparrow sagged.

Bull's-eye, Gwendolyn thought with a bitter taste in her mouth. She'd been too hard on him, and she knew it. After all, who was *she* to criticize anyone for acting impulsively? "Sparrow, I'm sorry. It's just, I thought that you and I . . ."

She stopped, suddenly quite unsure how she wanted to finish that sentence.

He raised his head, and an eyebrow. "What? Go on. What were you thinking about me? And you? Us?"

She waved him off. "Nothing. Never you mind what I was thinking."

"Come on, you can tell me!" But Sparrow was so intent on Gwendolyn, he did not notice the pirate that stumbled into his path, and they slammed into each other.

The grizzled man was twice Sparrow's size, with a battered trench coat, a sword at his waist, and a drink in his hand. A drink which was now splattered all over him. The pirate glared down at Sparrow through a face full of foamy suds. The smell of sour ale washed over them.

"Wot do you think yor doin'? Watch where you're goin', you brat!" He pulled Sparrow's face close to his unshaven one, spitting with every word.

"I'm sorry, sir, it was an accident."

“Don’t *sir* me, you snot-nosed puke! I’ve got boogers bigger than you in my ’ankerchief. Who’s gonna buy me a new tunic, and a new drink?”

By now, several other men had gathered behind the first, none of them looking particularly friendly. Kolonius pushed his way between them. “Wha’ssa fuss?” he grumbled in his disguised voice, keeping his hat low. “What ye botherin’ me cabin boy fer? Ye’ve a problem, ye can jolly well dross off. Come, boy.” Kolonius tried to pull Sparrow away, but the man yanked on Sparrow’s collar.

“You ain’t goin’ nowhere. You gonna pay for yor little runt? And I think me boys’ll be wanting a round a drinks too, seein’ as how they’ve been traumatized with this whole ordeal.”

The men gave scattered laughs of approval.

Kolonius dropped some coins in the street. “Ye’ve had enough, ye ask me, but that’ll cover your drink and your tunic. ’Fraid your crew will be buyin’ their own tonight.” He tried to go, but again, the man hauled Sparrow back.

“Oh, don’t think yor goin’ just yet,” the pirate slurred. He twisted an arm around Sparrow’s neck and put a dirty knife to his throat. “We’re owed a little fun, ain’t we?”

There was a roar of agreement as more pirates gathered, like sharks scenting blood. Two of them grabbed Sparrow and flipped him upside down by his ankles.

Sparrow’s cloak flapped into his face. “Hey! Let me go, you stinking cave rats!”

The leader twirled a finger in the air. “Send ’im for a ride, buckos!”

The men hauled him to the pneumo at the edge of the catwalk and dangled him over the drop. Sparrow screamed and squirmed, then looked down, and grew remarkably still. "Guys! Hello! Little help?"

Starling's hand went to her pocket, and Kolonius's hand crept toward his sword, and Gwendolyn's hands started to sweat. Three pirates squared off in front of them.

"They won't be helpin' you none," the leader jeered. "Make sure to pull the safety. He looks like he likes a bit o' speed."

The pirates tied Sparrow's ankles together, and hung him on a pneumo handle.

"You'll be lettin' my boy go now," Kolonius growled.

The leader shrugged. "If you say so!"

He kicked Sparrow in the back, and the boy went zipping down the line. "Gwendolyn, heeeelp!"

Kolonius burst into action. In one smooth motion he flung off his cloak and drew his sword, a long, jeweled affair with a corkscrew blade. He pressed a button on the hilt, and the sword's spiral blade began spinning like a drill. He slashed at the pirate on the right and kicked the middle one into his companion on the left. "Girls! Get Sparrow!"

"Cripes! Tha's Kolonius Thrash!"

"Get 'im!" the pirates roared.

Kolonius cut a path through the mob, and Starling and Gwendolyn ran for the pneumo. They grabbed handles and jumped.

Farther down the line, Sparrow was sliding much faster than was safe, heading for the cave mouth.

Gwendolyn looked back. Kolonius was holding off five pirates at once, his spinning spiral blade whirling and cutting and deflecting every blow. He threw something to the ground, and there was an explosion of orange smoke. A moment later, Kolonius zipped out of the cloud on a pneumo.

"I gave him that," Starling shouted with pride.

"We'll never catch Sparrow!" Gwendolyn shouted back. "He's going right out of the cave!"

"That's not our only problem! Look behind us!"

Pirates were zipping down behind Kolonius, and they did not look pleased. There was a large gap between them, but on the ground they'd catch up quick.

Gwendolyn swung her feet, urging the device to go faster, faster. Sparrow was almost out of cable, and out of cave. He was swinging his body up to try and reach his feet.

She tried to imagine Sparrow stopping safely, tried to picture it happening. "Once upon a time, there was a boy named Sparrow, who definitely did *not* fly out of the cave and fall to his death on the rocks bel–"

Suddenly, the cable went slack. Gwendolyn shouted in surprise, and she and Starling fell the last ten feet to the ground, landing in a heap. Farther back, Kolonius dropped, rolled, and came up running, heading for the entrance. "Nap time's over, girls. Go!" he roared.

Gwendolyn looked back. The pirates had only been halfway down the line, and had a much farther fall. There was no sign of them. She got up and ran after Kolonius.

Burly Brunswick was standing at the lip of the cave holding

Sparrow by the feet in one hand, a sword in the other. On the ground lay the pneumo cable, cut from its anchor.

"I think you ladies might 'ave lost sumthin'," he said, a toothy grin sprouting under his orange mustache. He cut the ropes on Sparrow's ankles, and the boy dropped.

Sparrow got up and flung his arms around Brunswick. "Thank you thank you thank you!"

Brunswick tipped his hat awkwardly. "All right, 'nuff o' that. Back to the longboat, hurry!"

Dozens of pirates were racing toward them. Gwendolyn and Sparrow ran down the ramp and out of the cave. Kolonius and Starling were already reinstalling the gizmo Kolonius had pulled out.

He slammed the engine cover shut. "All aboard!"

"Did we get what we came for?" Brunswick asked.

"We did. Take us out. I'll raise the *Endeavour* on the wireless and let them know we're coming."

Brunswick took the controls, and the longboat puttered into the orange sky. Starling grabbed Sparrow by the shoulders. "Are you all right?" she said, checking him for injuries.

"Ugh, I'm okay, quit it," Sparrow said. "It's not the first time I've gotten in a scrape."

"It better be the last time, or you'll see how bad *I* can hurt you."

"Lay off, I'm fine."

"You won't be for long," said Kolonius. He brushed Starling aside and grabbed Sparrow by the shirt. "Next time, when I say stay on the ship, I mean Stay. On. The. Ship. Or you'll be leaving it faster than you'd like. Got it?"

Sparrow gulped. "Got it."

"Now let go of him," Starling said, slapping Kolonius's hands away.

We did it, Gwendolyn thought, though she still didn't know if it was Brunswick or her story that had saved Sparrow. Either way, they had the map, and they might actually pull this off.

But then she looked back at the Dove's Nest, and her breath caught in her throat. "Look!"

Creeping from the dozens of caves that dotted the mountainside, particles of liquid shadow swarmed toward the pirate stronghold.

"No, the Abscess!" Starling said.

"What about Tripp?" Gwendolyn asked. "We have to go back for him! Kolonius!"

But the boy captain said nothing. His face was as cold and hard as the mountain itself. He just stared straight ahead as the Abscess poured into the Marauder's Mouth.

CHAPTER NINETEEN

Sunset on the Spiced Seas

There is a vast difference between knowing a thing and seeing a thing. You may *know* that a friend has moved away, for example, but actually *seeing* their empty house sends you into tears. Gwendolyn knew that the Dove's Nest was being destroyed, but this was much different than seeing it for herself. It can be hard to fit something so big into your head, or your heart.

And so the five of them arrived back at the *Lucrative Endeavour* in a tangle of emotions as they all struggled to—as grown-ups say—process the situation.

"Kolonius!" Gwendolyn shouted as they landed in the *Endeavour's* hangar bay. "We have to go back! We have to rescue Tripp!"

Kolonius whirled on her. "Look, little girl, I will not risk the lives of me and mine on a suicide mission! Tripp made his choice. He could have come with us. You think I like it? After you gave us away back there, we had to get out of there. Now." He stormed off, barking orders, smothering his conflicting emotions with a blanket of anger, the standby of teenage boys everywhere.

Gwendolyn clenched her shaking fists. She pictured the dressmaker from the Mainspring Marketplace screaming, turned to ash. The toymaker, eyes glowing and black spots pouring from his mouth. And now it was happening again. *My fault. It's always my fault.* It was seeing those things, even in her memory, that made hot tears appear at the corners of her eyes.

Sparrow put a hand on her shoulder. "He's not wrong, Gwendolyn. It's harsh, but we need to move on."

"Shut up, Sparrow." She shrugged him off and walked away.

Sparrow started to follow, but Brunswick stuck out a beefy arm. "Leave her be a minute, lad. We could all use some time to cool off. Get those rags off, scrub yerselves, grab some grub, then come up to the bridge. According to the map, we'll be at the Coves come nightfall."

~~~

Kolonius pored over maps and charts. Brunswick was at the helm, manning the large wheel. The ship was passing the grasslands and heading out over an ocean of sapphire waves. Starling gaped at the control consoles filled with switches, dials, and more gadgetry than she could wave her wrist at.

"Where are we?" Gwendolyn said.

"Just enterin' the Spiced Seas," Brunswick answered.

"Look. This came in over the wireless from some contacts at the Archicon Archives." Kolonius pointed to a map of empty ocean, marked by dozens of red Xs. "These are all the ships
~~~

that have gone down in the area." He drew a circle around the Xs. "The Crystal Coves are somewhere in there. Some trap of Kytain's has likely been bringing down ships for years."

He rustled through some other parchments. "Tripp said there's an interference field, which explains all these downed ships, so I'm putting the *Endeavour* at minimal risk, flying in low for a visual before we take the longboats in. I'm not sure what we'll find, so we'll be wary, well-armed, and this time you'll follow instructions to the letter."

"And what if we run into whatever destroyed all these ships? Giant monsters, booby-traps?" Starling asked.

"You mean what if it all falls apart and we're forced to improvise and fight to get out alive?" He grinned wickedly. "Well, we call that Tuesday. Now go get some rest, we should reach the Coves just before first dawn."

Starling was examining the big wheel that steered the massive vessel. "If it's all that dangerous, maybe I should pilot us into the Coves. I could probably fly this thing better than you," she teased.

Kolonius scoffed and stepped behind her. "I'd like to see you try."

Starling raised an eyebrow at him.

"Fine," Kolonius said. "Brunswick, move over. There you go. Put your hands right here, like this."

Sparrow leaned against a console at the rear of the bridge, well away from where his sister was getting her flying lesson. "Ugh. I can't even tell if they're fighting or flirting anymore."

Brunswick joined Sparrow and Gwendolyn. "Oh, the Cap'n's

sweet on her, all right. But he's got no experience with lasses his own age. No idea how to handle 'em." He chuckled knowingly.

"And you're a romance expert?" Sparrow quipped.

Brunswick reddened a bit. "Uh, right. Work to be done." And he clunked off.

Sparrow scoffed.

Gwendolyn leaned up next to him. "Why so bothered? Not jealous, surely? Someone else getting your precious sister's attention?"

"No, it's not that, it's . . . I don't know. I guess it's sweet, in a weird and completely gross kind of way. Look, I, um," Sparrow stammered. "I'm sorry. Really. For back at the Nest. You're not just some girl. You're pretty, um, pretty—"

"Pretty what?" Gwendolyn asked, hoping that might have been the end of his sentence.

A speaker on the console next to them crackled to life. "Captain, we've got the course plotted. Instruments already acting strange. They say we're turning, but the rudders and sails are locked."

"Ah, what's this?" Sparrow winked at Gwendolyn and snatched up the microphone, grinning his wolfish grin. He slapped a large red button on the console. "Ahoy-hoy, this is Sailin' Sparrow. Listen up, *Lucrative Endeavour*, we're headed for certain death in the Crystal Coves, but don't worry, because Captain Dreadlocks has a plan, so get your checkbooks ready, because he doesn't come cheap, if you get my drift—"

Kolonius slapped the microphone out of his hand and slammed Sparrow against the console. "What. Are. You. Doing."

Sparrow's wolfish grin turned sheepish. "Starting a lucrative career in airship radio?"

"That's not an intercom, that's a wide-band broadcast!"

"And that's bad because?"

"Because Tylerium Drekk would cut off his left hand if he could get his right one on Kytain's plunder, and you just broadcast our position to half the continent. You better pray he wasn't in range or the only thing he'll be cutting is our throats. If you were one of my crew, I'd be giving you lashes for everything you've pulled today!"

The color drained from Sparrow's face.

"You're not whipping my brother," Starling said casually.

Kolonius groaned and let him go. "But you're *not* one of my crew, unfortunately. So you know what that means?"

"More mopping?" Sparrow asked hopefully.

"You wish. You'll be cleaning the head."

"Aaaaand what's that?"

Kolonius smiled a wicked smile.

"It's boat-talk for toilet," Starling called over her shoulder, still steering the ship.

"All of them," Kolonius added. "With a toothbrush. Now get out of here."

Sparrow nodded and scampered out, dodging a kick from Kolonius, who went back to showing Starling how to steer.

Gwendolyn rolled her eyes and headed out on deck. Sparrow was staring out at the waves. It's hard to stay mad at something that looks so utterly miserable, like a puppy that's been kicked. She walked over and punched him in the arm. "You are an idiot."

He sighed. "You were right. I wouldn't screw up so much if I'd actually think first. I was just trying to be funny."

"Just trying to show off." *For me,* she added silently.

He blushed. "Maybe. You ever feel like no matter what you do, you just make things worse?"

Gwendolyn nodded. "Absolutely."

"Friggin' toilet duty," Sparrow said. "You gotta be kidding me."

The yellow sun was going down, its larger, red companion not far behind. You have likely never seen a binary sunset, but they are breathtakingly beautiful. The sky darkened from orange to red. The Spiced Sea looked like it was made of rainbow fire. The waves were covered in floating patches of something like yellow grass, and men skimmed over the patches on harvester machines with long pontoons, gathering the spices for which the sea was named. The two of them watched together.

"Sparrow?" Gwendolyn asked.

"Yeah?" he murmured.

"I've been wondering . . ."

"Pfff. Aren't you always?"

"True. Where do you really come from? You and Starling?"

Sparrow didn't answer. He stared over the side for a minute, then glanced across the deck to where Starling was helping Kolonius fiddle with one of the masts. He smiled, not his usual cocky grin, but one with more sadness than was fair for a boy so young to carry.

"Another world, like we said."

"What was it like?" she pressed.

“I don’t remember a lot. Kind of like Tohk, but less clockwork and steam and more wires and electricity. I remember a big city, like yours. Dark skies. Streets, all shiny and wet, streetlamps creating little halos in the rain. Lots of lights. Thousands of them, all over the skyscrapers, in all different colors. Big glowing neon signs. My parents were engineers. They worked on airships.”

“Like this one?” Gwendolyn asked.

Sparrow squinted. “Kind of. I remember they all had these big balloon things holding them up. People would dock them at the top of the skyscrapers. You could see everything from up there.”

“How long has it been?”

“Well, Starling’s sixteen, I’m thirteen now, and I was six then, so . . .”

“You’ve been looking for your home for *seven years*?” Gwendolyn gaped. “Why did you leave?”

“Look who’s full of questions all of a sudden.”

“No, I’m full of questions always, and you didn’t answer that one.”

Sparrow heaved another sigh. “Because I was stupid.”

“I believe you,” Gwendolyn joked. “But can you be more specific?”

“Our parents had taken us up on one of the tallest buildings, to a fancy new zeppelin that was docked at the spire. They took us around, showed us how all the engines worked. Starling was fascinated, but I got bored and wandered off. And on the other side of the ship was one of those portals, all glowy and shimmery, like a hole in the air. Starling was sent to find me, and she did, but I went through anyway, too stupid to listen to her. She followed me, the portal closed, and we were stuck. Orphaned and homeless. Not to mention in a world we'd never seen before."

His eyes grew wet as he stared at the ocean.

Gwendolyn was reminded of the time Father showed her his office when she was younger. The big room with all the grey cubicles, hundreds of people in little boxes chattering away on typewriters. And now she didn't know if she would ever see him again.

"We were lost and alone," Sparrow said. "But Starling made us carry on. She took care of us as best she could. She's always great at figuring things out and inventing stuff, always scrapes enough to get by. And we found more doors, more worlds. We've been stumbling from place to place ever since, trying to get back home."

Gwendolyn took a moment to swallow that. Strangely, it felt as though she'd known it all along. She put her hand on the rail and covered his. "Your parents must be worried sick." She hoped her own were all right, and still remembered they had a daughter to worry about.

"I can barely even remember what they look like. When I think about it—well, I try not to. But Starling does. Sometimes I catch her staring off at nothing, and I know she's thinking and remembering and missing. But you know what? No matter how bad things got, no matter how mad she was, or how much she might yell at me for being stupid, Starling has never blamed me for getting us stranded. Not one time."

After a few moments of silence, Gwendolyn spoke up. "Sparrow? I think you should stop blaming yourself, too."

He sniffed, and his words came out in a choked whisper. "It's not that easy. I mean, you saw what happened back there, I might have ruined this whole thing, just because I wasn't thinking."

"Then I guess you'll have to start thinking, stupid boy," Gwendolyn teased.

Sparrow barked a soft, wet laugh. "Yeah. I guess I will."

"Besides, now you've got me to help! Between the three of us, we're bound to get you home. We'll need something to do once we've saved Tohk, after all. One must keep busy."

"That sounds brilliant. I can't wait." But his tone lacked enthusiasm.

"And Sparrow?" she asked.

"Yes?"

"Once we find our ways home, will you come back for me?"

He gave her a sideways look. "Running away? What about your parents and everything?"

"No. I'm done running away. We'll stop the Mister Men, both here and in the City. But . . . when we're all done, and I go back, promise you won't leave me there forever. I'm not sure I could stand it alone. Just promise me, no matter where you go, you'll always come back."

Sparrow looked at her, his brown eyes warm as a summer afternoon, meeting Gwendolyn's sparkling green ones. Sadness flickered across his face, just for a moment, and then his cocky grin wiped it away. "I'm with you 'til the end, Miss Gwendolyn

Gray. Come on, let's get some rest before we reach the Coves. It's going to be a long night."

They walked toward the hatch, but Gwendolyn spotted Starling by one of the sail mechanisms with Kolonius, the two of them acting remarkably friendly. She ran over and gave her a fierce hug.

Starling looked bewildered, but didn't struggle. "What's this for?"

Gwendolyn looked up at her. "From your brother. He's too much of a boy to do it himself." And with that, she disappeared belowdecks.

Starling looked at Kolonius, and they both shrugged.

~~~

Lying once more in her cozy hammock in the crew quarters, the ship feeling ever more like a home, Gwendolyn's thoughts melted into dreams of the past days. The marketplace. The bathysphere. The Edge. A flash of scissors, a lock of hair.

And then darkness, the kind that makes you afraid to peek under your bed. Gwendolyn stood in the middle of a vast desert. Thunderclouds fought overhead. The ground was blackened and cratered. A bitter wind cut through her dress. The same nightmare again. And she realized that she'd seen the Abscess once before it attacked the Mainspring Marketplace—she'd seen it here.

Again, slithering tentacles emerged from the clouds, engulfing her, smothering her. A voice whispered in her ear, a voice she recognized from the marketplace. It was a child's voice, but
~~~

old, so very old. "Come and see me soon. We have so much to do, we do, we do. Much to say, and much to play, Gwendolyn Gray. Gwendolyn."

"Gwendolyn!"

She woke. Starling was shaking her. "Gwendolyn, are you all right?"

"Wha?" she muttered. "I-I think so."

"You were screaming."

"Was I?" Gwendolyn said, embarrassed. "I-I'm sorry." She rubbed her eyes. "Just a bad dream, that's all. Where are we?"

"Approaching the Crystal Coves."

"Is it morning already?"

Starling snorted. "Nope. Adventures don't keep regular business hours. Come on."

Above deck, the night air was warm and sweet, wicking away the last of the nightmare sweat. The ship flew over an endless sea of inky blackness. In the dark it was quite impossible to tell how fast they were going, and if it weren't for the wind, she'd have sworn they weren't moving at all. Strange new stars twinkled in the sky above Gwendolyn's head, and a pale moon with thin, glittering rings seemed to have put on its finest jewelry just for her.

She took a moment to soak it all in; she still wasn't used to seeing anything but clouds overhead. For the first time, she felt the sense of infinite smallness that we have all felt when staring at the stars. Then she imagined a cloud of black smoke blocking them out, one by one, and gritted her teeth. She would not let that happen.

On the horizon, they could see an island, a single great mountain jutting from the sea. The entire island glowed with an unnatural violet light.

They found Kolonius on the bridge. He pointed. "The Crystal Coves of Kytain. The lost laboratory of the most famous man in the history of Tohk."

"He invented 'a weapon of purest light that could defeat even the blackest evil,'" Gwendolyn quoted from memory.

"Let's hope you're right, Gretchen. We've been holding steady, ignoring our instruments, just like Tripp said." He gestured to the control panels. Gwendolyn saw needles and compasses dancing and jumping as if to some hidden music.

"If it weren't for him, we'd have circled around this place and never noticed. Clever. We might actually pull this off."

"I don't see anything dangerous. What's so bad about this place?" Sparrow said.

As if offended by the boy's doubts, the glow at the tip of the mountain went from a dull purple to a shocking pink.

"Uh, what's that?" said Starling.

"Hold on!" shouted Kolonius.

A bolt of violet lightning erupted from the mountain top and struck the *Lucrative Endeavour.*

Electricity rippled over the ship. The lights went out. The engines squealed once, and all was silent, save for the rushing of the wind as they fell.

PART THREE: RED

CHAPTER TWENTY

The Crystal Coves of Kytain

It might have been oddly peaceful, bobbing on the waves without even the sounds of the engines, except for the adrenaline pumping through them all as they lay sprawled on the floor of the bridge.

"Must every adventure involve either running or falling?" Gwendolyn murmured.

"In my experience? Yes," said Sparrow.

"Status report," groaned Kolonius.

"Instruments are shot," croaked a crewman. "I'll check the rest of the ship. Good thing we came in low."

"Blast it, Tripp, you could have mentioned the mountain-sized lightning gun. All right, see if there's any injured, report back. The rest of you, drop anchor! Oars to the longboats! We'll have to row in. Brunswick, Torin, Wilhelm, Carsair, you're with me. The rest of you, get the systems back online. I want my ship ready within the hour."

"Will do, Cap'n!" shouted a woman who rushed to take the helm. "But won't that mountain just shoot us down again?"

"Let me worry about that, Ching. You have your orders. Move out!"

They prepared to go ashore. Gadgets were checked and re-checked. Starling's pockets bulged even larger than usual.

"All right," she said to Gwendolyn and Sparrow. "We'll find the pistol, and be right back. Don't get into any trouble while we're–"

"Oh no," Sparrow said. "You're not leaving us behind again. It didn't work last time, and it's not going to work now."

"You need me!" Gwendolyn said. "Tripp said I had the spark! I don't know what it is, but he said Kytain had it too. It could be important!"

Starling's jaw tightened. "Fine. *You* can come. You'll need this," and she tossed Gwendolyn a small dagger, which she tucked into her belt. "But after your mishaps, Sparrow, you're staying put."

Sparrow said some words that I will spare you from. "You're not Mom, so stop trying to act like it. I'm going. And if you don't take me, I swear to cause as much trouble here as I can. And you know I can cause a *lot* of trouble."

Starling seemed torn, but eventually threw up her hands. "Fine. Do whatever you want, see if I care." She walked away muttering, "I don't know why I bother, I really don't, it's not like

I ever get a *Thank you for taking such good care of me, Starling,"* she said in her brother's voice.

When preparations were finished, two longboats were laid into the water. On one rode the three children and Kolonius, and on the other were Brunswick and the crewmen Wilhelm, Carsair, and Torin.

Torin seemed like a capable crewman, his face set and serious. Wilhelm was scrawny and practically trembling. Carsair was an intimidating woman who towered over the rest of them, with tattooed arms, close-cropped pink hair, and the kind of build that steamrollers dreamed of. Starling and Kolonius took turns rowing toward the glowing island, while Carsair propelled the other boat by herself.

Dozens of rotting old ships bobbed around them. "That mountain blaster must be the cause of all the disappearances in this area," Kolonius said, gesturing to the shipwreck graveyard.

"Were they all looking for Kytain's lab?" Gwendolyn asked.

"Might be. The legend always proved a particular fascination for treasure hunters."

"But surely this means the legends are real?"

Kolonius rubbed his pubescent stubble and nodded. "This plan just got a lot less stupid. Hopefully the Pistola Luminant is real as well. We'll grab it, then find a way to shut down whatever that was that shot us down."

They reached the shore and pulled the boats onto dry land. They found themselves surrounded by giant crystal spires. It was these crystals that cast the eerily beautiful violet light. They grew everywhere, sprouting in clusters from the rocky ground, stretching even taller than Brunswick.

Gwendolyn dashed ahead to get a look at one. She could hear a high-pitched whine that sounded almost like chimes. She was mesmerized by its neon purple glow, and she reached out to touch it.

"Ow!" she cried. "It zapped me!"

"Watch it, Grundolyn," Kolonius said. "This place is dangerous. No running off on your own. The two of you are only here because Starling swore you'd behave and be useful."

Gwendolyn nodded and cradled her hand. Two of the fingers were numb and tingling. She hoped it wasn't permanent.

Starling, of course, was inspecting the crystals anyway. She pulled on a pair of thick rubber gloves and produced a hammer and chisel from somewhere. She lowered her goggles and broke off a sliver of crystal, which continued to glow as she slipped it into a pouch.

Kolonius grunted. "You're setting a bad example for the munchkins. Come on, help me take the lead. Brunswick, you bring up the rear. Stay alert."

The ground was covered in sharp and shiny black stones, which shifted treacherously as they walked. Suddenly, a crystal spike on their left began to glow more brightly, humming louder and louder. A bolt of purple lightning lashed out, a miniature version of the one that had struck the ship. Kolonius threw out his arm to protect Starling, and the lightning hit the ground in front of them, leaving a crater of black and purple glass.

Kolonius sighed. "Watch out for . . . that."

"It's got a real 'keep out' sort of vibe, doesn't it?" Sparrow whispered.

"Not a terribly friendly place," Gwendolyn replied. "Which I suppose is what you want in a secret island hideaway." She shivered, and not just from the cold sea air.

A few minutes passed in tense silence as they picked their way along the uncertain ground. A crystal started to glow, and from their left came another bolt. Sparrow dove out of the way. It hit another crystal, forming a crackling energy strand between the two. The bolt shot out of the second crystal and passed through a third as well, then shot out again and hit Torin squarely in the back.

His mouth opened in a silent cry, and he fell forward. He didn't move.

"Torin!" Kolonius yelled. "Carsair, get him up." She nodded, and effortlessly lifted his limp body.

Allow me to assure you that Torin will be quite all right, and that no one will be seriously injured for at least ten more minutes. All of them will die, of course, but some of them might be very old and safe in their beds when that happens. In fact, Torin was already blinking and coughing. "M'okay, Captain. All numb. Can't feel a thing."

"Carsair, get him back to the longboat, patch him up, and catch up."

She nodded silently and headed back toward the shore. Kolonius tried to radio the *Endeavour,* but all he got was the crystalline whine coming through the earpiece.

"We move on," Kolonius ordered.

Eventually, the party arrived at the base of the mountain, facing an imposing wall of rock. Carsair rejoined them there. An opening was barely visible high up in the craggy cliff.

"If I were a mad scientist, that cave up there would be ideal secret laboratory real estate," Sparrow said.

"I agree," Kolonius nodded. "The opening's too perfectly round to be natural. Time to climb."

"That's my cue," said Starling. She reached into several pockets, and brought out all sorts of metal components, unfolding and connecting them. Soon she held a launching device with a cable and spike. She squinted, pulled the trigger, and the spike shot up. It stuck in the rock above the cave entrance, and several smaller spikes sprang out from the sides and dug into the wall.

"A fine shot," said Kolonius.

"Jealous?" teased Starling.

"Not hardly. Hand out the graspers." Those turned out to be small metal clasps that attached to the climbing belts Brunswick had carried.

Starling helped Gwendolyn put hers on over her dress, tightening straps and attaching the grasper. "We'd use pneumos, but the blast that hit the ship scrambled the climbing mechanisms," Starling explained. "So I whipped up these non-electronic nifties."

Kolonius was already several feet up the wall. Starling and Sparrow followed, and then it was Gwendolyn's turn. Brunswick gave her a lift up.

She found the climbing difficult, but not impossible. Her dress was certainly not the right attire for this sort of thing, and her school shoes slipped on the rock. The grasper kept her from sliding back down every time she pulled herself up. The higher they went, the more the line began to sway.

She looked down and saw Brunswick, climbing with the strength of his arms alone, his peg leg detached and slung across his back. Then she saw how far down the ground was, and regretted the look.

Sparrow fidgeted with his belt. "Ow. Stupid thing. These straps are too tight."

"Don't mess with those, I made them as tight as they should be," Starling called down.

"Just give me a moment, I need to—Yaah!" he cried out as his grasper broke free of the line. Sparrow dropped.

Fear shot through Gwendolyn like a bolt of purple lightning. "Sparrow!" she yelled. She pushed off the wall and managed to grab him around the waist as he fell toward her. Her arms felt like they would be yanked from their sockets. The line swung back and the two were smashed against the wall, hard enough to rattle their teeth. Despite the pain, Gwendolyn held on.

After some fumbling, Sparrow managed to grab the rope and reattach his own grasper. He breathed a sigh of relief and they swung together, their faces inches apart.

"Thanks, Gwendolyn. I thought—"

"Just climb, and listen to your sister," she said, trembling. "Maybe we *ought* to have left you on the ship."

Sparrow clamped his mouth shut, nodded, and climbed back up.

Soon, though not soon enough for Gwendolyn's tastes, they

reached the mouth of the cave. Kolonius was first over the lip, and he helped Starling in. Together they pulled in the rest of the crew, though there was a tense moment when one-legged Brunswick nearly toppled backward out of the cave. He windmilled his arms, trying to balance, before Carsair pushed him in from behind. He nodded gratefully, too breathless for words, then sat and began reattaching his leg. Kolonius called a brief rest.

Gwendolyn brushed herself off and looked around, glad to be rid of the climbing belt. The cave was a cramped stone tunnel, all smooth walls, which were slightly slimy to the touch. Smaller crystal clusters jutted out here and there. The light was bluer here, and cast strange shadows on all their faces.

Her mind as restless as always, Gwendolyn thought about Sparrow. So kind and sweet, but also thoughtless and impulsive. She remembered the way his hand crept next to hers as they watched the suns set, and how he had yelled at her for calling herself stupid. She supposed she was pretty thoughtless and impulsive herself, at times.

She noticed Starling leaning against the rock, tapping her foot impatiently. She acted so tough, but Gwendolyn knew she cared for her brother. She wondered if the older girl even liked her at all. Did she see Gwendolyn as just another burden? Or a distraction, keeping them from finding their way home? She was always so gruff, it was hard to tell what was going on under that blue-streaked hair.

After a moment, Kolonius led them onward. There was a pungent smell to the cave, sharp and unpleasant. Starling turned on her goggle-lamps as they came to a fork in the path.

“Which way do we go?” asked Wilhelm timidly.

“Georgette, which way do we go?” Kolonius barked.

“It’s Gwendol–oh never mind. How should I know?”

“You’ve got the spark, or something, and so did Kytain. Isn’t that why you convinced me to bring you along in the first place? Make yourself useful.”

“Wouldn’t be the first tunnels you’ve gotten us out of.” Starling tapped her wrist gadget.

“What’s that?” Kolonius asked, getting close to Starling to take a look.

“Oh, just a little something I threw together.”

“You’ll, uh, you’ll have to show it to me sometime.”

Sparrow rolled his eyes.

“Right. Wonderful. All up to me,” Gwendolyn muttered. She looked at the two tunnels, but hadn’t the slightest idea which one to take. She closed her eyes, and tried to imagine going down each one in turn. *What if* . . . she thought.

Now, *what if* is a particularly powerful set of magic words. It is responsible for all the best stories and inventions. Before there can be a *once upon a time,* there must always be a *what if.* It is a magic spell that children are especially good at, but only the best adults are capable of.

As it so happens, Kytain had been a master of the *what if,* and the tunnels responded to Gwendolyn’s imagination. A flash of blue seemed to flicker down the left-hand side. It somehow felt like the better idea.

“We should go that way.”

"Hope you're right, or we might be here a long time," Kolonius grunted, marching ahead.

Sparrow rolled his eyes again. "He's a real ray of sunshine."

"Stop, children, what's that sound?" Kolonius hissed.

Starling groaned. "Again, you're only like a year older than–"

"Shh!"

"I can't hear anything but these crystals. That buzzing's giving me a headache," whispered Wilhelm to Carsair.

"Silence. No whining," she rumbled.

Suddenly, a huge section of wall exploded outward, showering them with stone and crystal. Something monstrous appeared in front of them. It was huge, twice the size of a rhinoceros, nearly filling the tunnel. It gnashed flat teeth in a long snout. Too many milk-white eyes dotted its wide head. A long, spiral horn jutted from its snout, two more from the sides of its jaw. Its skin was white and clammy, shot through with mottled blue and violet, and it dripped some sort of slime onto the floor of the cave. Each of its six legs had long, sharp claws. It pawed the back two, preparing to charge, and bellowed.

"What is that?" shouted Carsair. She unstrapped the weapon on her back, an enormous long-shafted thing halfway between war hammer and sledgehammer.

"Whate'er it is, it's in our way. To battle!" shouted Brunswick. He barreled in and slashed at the beast with a great two-handed blade. The beast smacked him away with one of its six legs, and he went flying back down the tunnel and landed with a wet thud. "Is that all ye got, ye great beastie?" Brunswick roared, a bit more feebly.

Kolonius drew his spinning longsword. He sprinted down the tunnel, ran three full steps up the wall, then vaulted off and lunged at the beast, but was knocked aside. He recovered, and sprang to his feet. "Don't just stand there! Fight!"

Wilhelm drew a dagger with a shaking hand, but didn't exactly leap into action. Carsair didn't hesitate, though, and swung her hammer at the beast's head. Blind as it was, it must have sensed the blow, and it jerked backward just in time. The hammer blasted an impressive crater in the tunnel wall instead.

"You two! Stay back!" Starling called to Gwendolyn and Sparrow.

Gwendolyn drew the dagger Starling had given her but couldn't bring herself to use it. *He might look fearsome, but we* are *in its home,* she thought. *I might look fearsome too if someone stormed into my bedroom and began slashing at me.* She looked at its milky eyes.

"I think it's blind! It must be, living in these dark caves," she said to Sparrow.

"And I'd bet those claws are more for digging than fighting. Not that it seems to mind some of both," he said.

The beast lunged at Starling. She dove over one of the beast's legs and slid feet first under another, but slipped on the slime that dripped from its skin. Her momentum carried her under its belly, and she slid out the other side, catching a nasty gash on her shoulder from its spiked tail. She rolled away and clutched at the wound, wincing.

A sudden brightness filled the tunnel. "Down!" shouted Gwendolyn. They ducked, and a bolt of blue burst from a patch of crystal and zapped over their heads. The beast's milk-white eyes glowed blue. It grabbed the crystal in its massive jaws, tore it from the wall, and crushed the glassy spike in its large flat teeth, devouring the jagged fragments.

"It eats the crystals," Gwendolyn called. "Starling! It eats the crystals!"

"I hear you!" she said. "I don't see how that's helpful at the moment!"

"Just stop fighting!" Sparrow shouted. He rushed forward and stood directly in front of the creature.

"Sparrow, don't!" Starling warned.

But as usual, he didn't listen. He put a hand on either side of the creature's wide head. He looked deep into its milky eyes and whispered softly as it pulverized the crystal shards into blue powder. He stroked its horn gently.

Gwendolyn tensed, thinking how easily that same horn could impale him if it wanted to. The rest of the crew seemed equally tense, but none of them moved to interfere.

"There, now," Sparrow said. "Calm down. You're all right. Starling, give me that shard you took."

Starling opened her mouth to protest, but was too stunned to say anything. She pulled out the pouch and tossed it. Sparrow caught it and dangled it in front of the beast. Its milky eyes began to glow again, violet this time, like the crystal in the pouch. "That's what you want," he said. "Here you go! Go on now!"

He threw the pouch as hard as he could, back the way they had come. The beast barreled down the tunnel, picked up the pouch in its jaws, then lumbered into the wall with a tremendous crash, digging a new tunnel.

"Starling, you're hurt," said Kolonius. He fetched bandages from Wilhelm's pack and inspected the damage.

"It's nothing, really," she said as Kolonius dressed the wound. She winced. "Ouch, okay, it's not nothing. Thanks. It's almost like you care, or something."

Kolonius grunted, but Gwendolyn saw a flicker of a smile. "This is the second time we've had to patch you up."

"Yeah, well, keeping my brother safe is usually a hazardous job, so it probably won't be the last."

"Right good thinking, lad," Brunswick said to Sparrow. "Ye got a way with beasties, eh? Reckon ye've made a new friend!" He laughed and slapped Sparrow on the back.

"Yes, the boy's not completely useless," Kolonius admitted. "Let's move out."

"Can we have a moment to catch our breath?" said Wilhelm.

"No. Which way, Gabriella?"

"Oh come on, that one's not even close." Gwendolyn sighed, then looked at the tunnels, asking again, *What if . . . ?* "Straight ahead," she said. She could feel it. "Are you all right, Starling?"

She cracked her neck. "I'm fine. Let's go."

Kolonius's eyes narrowed. "This is getting dangerous. Be careful. I don't want you—I don't want anyone getting hurt," he said.

Starling raised an eyebrow. "Careful? Now, Kolonius Thrash. Where would be the fun in that?" She planted a quick kiss on his cheek, turned away with a playful toss of her hair, and strode casually down the tunnel. Kolonius stared after her, his mouth hanging open.

"Seriously?" Sparrow groaned, catching up to her. "You're supposed to be looking after *us,* not him."

"Shut up," Starling hissed. "I don't tease you about the redhead. Let me enjoy the moment. Is he still looking?"

Sparrow checked. "Yeah."

"Good." She strutted, head high, eyes forward. Her foot snagged a rock and she stumbled a little, but she recovered.

Sparrow and Gwendolyn exchanged looks. He rolled his eyes. "'Don't get attached, Sparrow,'" he mocked. "'We won't be here long, Sparrow. We'll never get home if you keep picking up strays, Sparrow.' Hypocrite."

Gwendolyn struggled not to laugh.

They walked, occasionally passing a cluster of glowing blue shards, but had no more random encounters with crystal-eaters. Soon they reached a dead end with an iron door set into the rock. Slumped next to the door was a skeleton.

"Aaah!" Wilhelm screamed. Everyone shushed him, and he blushed.

Gwendolyn and Kolonius knelt down for a closer look. The skeleton's clothes must have been elegant once. Now they were decayed and tattered scraps. Kolonius pointed to its hands. The left was as bony as the rest of him, but the right was a solidly carved piece of marble, sculpted into a closed fist.

"See that? This is Stonehand the Ravager. Or was. The most feared pirate in history," Kolonius said.

"What about Tylerium Drekk?" Gwendolyn asked.

Kolonius snorted. "He wishes."

"Is there any sign of . . . whatever it was that killed him?" She glanced around the tunnel, wondering what else the ancient Kytain could throw at them.

Kolonius scowled. "None. All the more reason to be ready." He drew a pistol from his belt, then tried the door handle. "Locked."

"Starling? Think you can open it?" Sparrow asked.

Starling mimicked the eerie monotone of the Faceless Gentlemen. "*It is most unwise to doubt my abilities, little boy.*"

Sparrow shuddered. "Don't ever do that again."

Gwendolyn giggled nervously.

Starling reached into a pocket and produced a complicated-looking set of hooks and rods. Quick as a flash, Starling had her hooks into the door, picking the lock. She stepped back and bowed to Kolonius.

He raised his pistol and reached for the handle again when Gwendolyn shouted, "Wait!"

He paused. "What?"

"Something doesn't feel right." She stepped forward and put a palm against the metal, probing that feeling, wondering what they might find on the other side. There could be any number of inventions, traps, and weapons. She tried to picture the door opening, just like back on the train, imagining it swinging open with a metallic squeal, light from inside bathing the tunnel—

And the door opened, revealing an enormous cavern of glittering technological treasure.

Kolonius burst through the doorway, leveling his gun at

anything inside. Most of the mountain appeared to have been converted into a laboratory, filled with a spectacular array of machines and equipment that would have made Professor Zangetsky drool. The walls were covered in instrument consoles and the rocky ceiling looked like a snake's nest of pipes and tubes. A thick layer of dust had settled on everything, and some sections had caved in.

"Kytain's secret lab," Kolonius whispered in amazement. "You were right, Red. Just look at all this stuff. It would bring a fortune on the open market."

"Which is *not* what we're here for, right Cap'n?" growled Brunswick.

"Right," Kolonius said reluctantly. "Another time."

Gwendolyn looked back at the door. The inner frame was covered with an intricate mechanism of wires, leading to a tank of green liquid above the door.

"Acid," Kolonius said quietly. "If I'd turned that latch, it would have sprayed all over the tunnel. That explains old Stonehand out there. Nice work. Way to earn your keep, girlie."

Gwendolyn scowled.

Starling inspected it. "Hmm. An imagination lock. Clever. Sort of an 'inventors only' precaution."

All around there were work benches littered with equipment, gadgets, and inventions. A mechanical man stood motionless in the corner. Three half-finished airships hung from the cavernous ceiling.

"Gears and garters, I can't believe we're standing inside a friggin' fairy tale," Kolonius whispered.

They stepped over fantastic inventions that were little more than dusty junk after centuries of neglect. Sparrow skirted an old steam engine, and Gwendolyn eyed a spindly model of planets and moons that was still revolving quietly to itself.

Step by careful step, they moved into the center of the cavern, which held an enormous glass bulb, thirty feet high, all dusty and dull. Cables as thick as Gwendolyn's waist were connected to the bottom of it. A long crack ran down its side.

Inside, protected from the ravages of time, was a gleaming, golden pistol.

The pistol was covered in hoses and dials, with three tube-shaped bulbs on top. It was beautifully made, with gold plating and a pearl handle. Flowered stenciling ran from the stock to the ringed barrel and pointed tip, which looked more like an electrical conductor than the business end of a weapon. Gwendolyn brushed dust from a plaque on the base of the bulb. "The Pistola Luminant," she read.

"Gears and garters," Kolonius said again, breathless with wonder. "It's real. We found it."

"And not a moment too soon," added Starling.

"I couldn't possibly agree more!" came a voice from behind them.

CHAPTER TWENTY-ONE

Tylerium Drekk and the Pistola Luminant

They spun around. Twenty bandits surrounded them, with weapons that gleamed with the kind of careful cleaning the men themselves were clearly unaccustomed to. They sneered, and Gwendolyn quickly gave up trying to count the missing teeth.

Standing in the center was their obvious leader, since he was taller, better dressed, and not covered in filth. He wore a blood-red longcoat with gold trimmings. His boots glistened, and his periwinkle tunic had so many ruffles that it resembled a bird puffing itself up for a mate. His lip curled and his perfect smile flashed nastily at them.

"Well, well. Kolonius Thrash. I daresay, you have once again proven to be a most *lucrative* asset." His voice dripped like honey from a nest of angry bees. "I really should start paying you. Of course, if you so much as flinch, you'll be paid in full immediately, but I fear you'll find the currency more leaden than you prefer."

The pirates beside him exchanged confused looks and mutters.

He rolled his eyes. "Bullets, you idiots," he sneered.

Kolonius scowled. "Drekk, you windbag, you–"

"Tut-tut, surely we're on first name terms by now?" He pointed to himself. "Tylerium." He pointed at them, but with his pistol. "Kolonius. Now that the formalities have been disposed of, step aside, or you will find yourselves likewise disposed of."

"Do what he says," Kolonius growled.

"Why the–" Starling said.

"Just do it!" he snapped.

Slowly, Gwendolyn and the others moved away from the glass bulb. Brunswick grumbled darkly. Carsair's muscles rippled as her hands tightened around her hammer, longing for smashing.

Three pirates herded them into a corner, while the rest of the men surrounded the bulb.

"Don't! That's the only way to stop the Abscess!" Gwendolyn shouted.

Drekk motioned his men to stop. "Oh, is it now? I presume you're referring to the monster that destroyed my dear Dove's Nest?"

"Yes! And the Pistola Luminant can stop it."

"Interesting. This trinket? The key to Tohk's salvation? Well." He looked at his men, who chuckled and jeered. "After Copernium, I'm sure Archicon would pay handsomely for such protection, or perhaps Vernius. Not everyone could afford it, of course, but overpopulation is a *serious* problem these days."

"You can't!" Gwendolyn shouted. "The whole world could be destroyed."

"Utter nonsense. It's always 'saving the world' with you heroes, isn't it? If the world needs as much saving as you claim, it will take more than a few prepubescent snot rags to do it. Whatever this monster is should be easily dealt with by someone with my ingenuity."

"You don't understand–"

"Silence. So, Thrash is recruiting little girls to join his crew. That *is* fitting, isn't it? You simply must be more careful about what you say to strange men in alleys, or on the wireless. By the way, which of you is Sailing Sparrow?"

His crew roared with laughter again. Sparrow blushed. With another gesture from Drekk, two men stepped forward.

"Thank you again, Kolonius. Watching the *Endeavour* get shot down was quite instructive, allowing us to land out of range of that lightning trap. You're much more useful now than you ever were as my mewling cabin boy. Smash away, men," he waved.

The pirates slammed their sword hilts against the crack in the bulb. A spiderweb of fractures appeared. They struck again, and the bulb exploded, the glass shattering into a thousand flying shards. The pirates dove to the ground, shouting in surprise, covering their faces to avoid the spray.

With that sudden distraction, while everyone else was preoccupied with the threat of flying glass, Gwendolyn's hyperactive mind saw an opening. Thinking as fast as only she could, Gwendolyn dashed forward and snatched up the golden weapon before anyone could react. She waved it around. "Don't move or I'll shoot!"

Drekk pointed his own pistol at Gwendolyn as his men encircled her. "Come now, dolly," he sneered. "You give that lovely shiny to your Uncle Tylerium. Little girls shouldn't play with guns. It's dangerous."

"Don't give it to him, Red! Blast him!" Kolonius roared.

"Keevers, if he speaks again, cut out his other eye, then slit the girl's throat."

"But she's got that Pistola thingy, she'll shoot me," said a mangy-looking pirate.

"Not *that* girl, the one with the blue hair—oh, never mind." He massaged the bridge of his nose. "Look, girl, just give it to me, or somebody's getting shot. They may be morons, but at least they can aim." He stepped closer. "You, on the other hand, won't be shooting anyone. Murder's not as easy as everyone thinks. I'm sure a precious little thing like you hasn't had much practice, whereas I could teach advanced courses on the subject of killing. So hand it over before I flunk you."

He fired a shot at her feet. Gwendolyn flinched and nearly dropped the pistol. The shot echoed in the open space.

She didn't see any choice. She didn't even know how the pistol worked, and the pirates outnumbered them five-to-one. "Promise you'll let us go!"

"Don't! He'll kill us anyway!" shouted Kolonius.

Drekk snorted. "I don't make promises." His next shot

whizzed past her ear, and she flinched again. "But you'll certainly die if you don't."

She looked at Sparrow, then at Starling, avoiding eye contact with Kolonius. She put the pistol on the floor.

"Good girl. Now slide it over."

She did.

"No!" Kolonius roared.

A clanking and shuffling noise came from somewhere in the lab.

Drekk delicately picked up the Pistola Luminant. "Thank you. He was right, you know. I'm still going to kill you all." He cocked his weapon and aimed it at her chest.

"Weapons-fire-detected. Initiate-*click-whirr*-defensive-protocols," said a mechanical voice. Drekk turned as a twelve-foot metal man charged into him, knocking his gun away. Three more clockwork giants, all in various unfinished states, clanked up behind the pirates. Through gaps in their brass plating, Gwendolyn could see gears and pistons whirring. They looked a bit like giant versions of Professor Zangetsky's puppets. "Intruders-must-be-*click*-neutralized."

The pirates opened fire, but their bullets pinged harmlessly off metal skin. The automatons plucked their weapons away as easily as picking flowers, and crushed them just as easily. The three pirates guarding the crew watched the battle, unsure what to do.

"Drop your weapons, you fools!" Starling yelled, expertly mimicking Tylerium Drekk's voice.

Two of them did immediately, but the third spun around. "Who said that?"

Brunswick hit him across the jaw and the pirate fell. Carsair swung her hammer and dropped the other two in a single swipe.

"Nobody move," Kolonius warned. "Don't do anything to make yourselves a threat—wait!"

But Starling leapt into the fray, fighting her way to Gwendolyn's side. "Hang tight," she said. "It'll be over in a second."

Drekk picked up his fallen pistol. He shot one of the mechanical men in its faceplate, putting out an illuminated eye. "You know? I think blue-hair might be right." He dashed over to them. Starling slashed at him, but he ducked under her sword, twirled behind her, and hit her with the butt of his pistol. Her head jerked forward so hard her goggles fell off. Starling slumped unconscious into the waiting arms of the pirate captain.

"Starling!" Sparrow cried, but his path was blocked by two pirates dueling a flailing automaton.

"No you don't!" Gwendolyn shouted, hitting Drekk, yanking at Starling, but he flung her easily away. She went reeling into a mechanical man. The force of the impact knocked them both over, sprawling at the feet of Kolonius and the rest.

Drekk fired at them, but the automaton lurched up into the bullet's path. The pirate tossed the unconscious girl over his shoulder. "Thank you, cabin boy! I'll be taking this one for insurance. Pretty thing, about your age? You must have feelings for her. If I catch a glimpse of sail on the horizon, I'll cut out her clever tongue. Then throw her overboard, or something. To the ship!" He ran for the door, firing blindly behind him as he went.

"Run! Deeper into the lab!" Kolonius yelled.

"Deeper? Why deeper? We have to save my sister!"

"Are ye' lookin' to be shot, boy?" Brunswick said. "We can't leave 'til we shut down the island's defenses. We'll be zapped out'a the sky!"

They scampered between worktables, vaulted over half-finished equipment, and passed a strange door wired up to an even stranger-looking control panel. They could hear the automatons clanking behind them.

"We'll get her back," said Kolonius, "but we'll need our ship to do it. There's got to be a control system somewhere! Look around!"

Behind them, two metal men were overturning tables in their way, sending potentially world-changing inventions clattering to the floor. "Apprehend-*click-whirr*-intruders. Maintain-laboratory-integrity. Protect-*tick-tick-tick*-doorway."

Fortunately, half-finished clockwork automatons are not particularly quick. The first had only one arm attached, and the second was missing a foot. *But with nowhere to go, that won't matter much,* Gwendolyn thought.

"There!" Sparrow pointed to a large console covered in screens and dials, obviously some kind of central control. There were two glass plates on either side of a golden keyboard with pearl buttons. He raced over to it.

"Shut down those metal men!" Kolonius said.

"I don't know how this blasted thing works!" Sparrow

pounded the console. "This is exactly the sort of thing we need Starling for!"

Kolonius shoved him aside and fiddled with the controls. The mechanical men were getting closer again. "*Click-whirr*-intruders-must-be-neutralized."

"Let Gwendolyn try!" Sparrow said.

"What?" Gwendolyn said.

"You found our way in the tunnels, you deactivated that trap on the door."

"He's got a point, Sparky. Hurry!" Kolonius stepped aside.

"O-okay." She stepped up to the console. She didn't know what to do, so she placed her hands on the two glass plates. "Hello?" she asked. She had talked to plenty of objects before, but never anything like this. Mother always said politeness was the best way to handle strangers, so she hoped that applied to strange devices as well. "Excuse me? Mister Control?"

Nothing happened. The metal men were only twenty feet away.

"Come on, girl, you can do better than that," Kolonius urged.

"Right. It would be very nice if you would stop those mechanical men from chasing us. Please?" She tried to imagine the automatons freezing in place.

"*Click*-spark-detected-*whirr*-command-accepted." The metal men stopped and stood at attention.

"O-okay then. Thank you very much," Gwendolyn said.

"Shut down the defense systems!" Kolonius said.

"Oh, yes!" She tried to imagine what she wanted, but it is very difficult to picture something *not* happening. Gwendolyn did her best to imagine the island staying very calm indeed while they left, and definitely *not* blasting the *Endeavour*. "I would very much appreciate it, Mister Control, if you would please let us leave?"

The metal men spoke again. "*Click*-spark-detected-*click-whirr*-command-accepted-*click*-defenses-deactivated. The-spark-must-be-served."

"Back to the ship!" Kolonius said.

"Who would have thought that talking to objects would actually get me *out* of trouble for once," she muttered.

They bolted back through the laboratory, and Gwendolyn noticed Starling's goggles, lying forgotten on the ground. She scooped them up and ran to catch Kolonius as they reached the stone tunnels again. "So how are we going to save Starling?"

He growled as he ran. "She wouldn't need rescuing if it weren't for you and your boyfriend."

"He's not my boyfriend," Gwendolyn mumbled. "But you have a plan to rescue her, right?"

"I'll figure it out when I'm through rescuing *us*. Move!"

They reached the mouth of the tunnel, the crystal light shifting again from blue back to violet, and slid down the ropes faster than was strictly safe. On the ground, the loose stones slowed their progress. They moved carefully while lightning bursts struck the ground around them.

"I thought we deactivated all the defenses!" Wilhelm said.

"These things grow here, they're not inventions, so I don't think the laboratory controls them. Maybe it draws power from them," Gwendolyn said.

"We're going too slow, he's getting away!" growled Kolonius.

"We can't help her if we're roasted alive," said Brunswick.

"Um, Cap'n," muttered Wilhelm.

"Not now!"

"But Cap'n, I think–"

"Don't think, just run!" Kolonius barked.

Wilhelm tugged the back of his shirt. "But Cap'n, you need to look–"

A deafening roar shook the ground. They looked back. An enormous crystal-eater was charging toward them.

"Never mind," said Wilhelm.

CHAPTER TWENTY-TWO

No Room to Run

"Run!" bellowed Brunswick.

Caution forgotten, they sprinted toward the shore. The creature's six legs were a blur, kicking up bits of stone. This one was several times larger than the one in the caves, and the eyes dotting its head were glossy black. It roared again, lowered its massive spiral horn, and shattered a cluster of crystals.

"That's . . . a big one . . ." Sparrow gasped between breaths, covering his head against flying purple shards.

"And I'd say its eyesight is just fine," Gwendolyn panted. Her lungs and legs were burning. "Maybe the first one . . . was just a young one . . . and I fear we've rather upset the mother."

In answer, the creature roared and charged, closing the gap.

"Ahh!" Wilhelm screamed in fright. He was not as quick as the rest of them, and the creature was close on his heels.

Carsair turned and allowed the others to run past her. The creature charged straight at her but she just planted her feet and rolled her massive shoulders. Then she punched the crystal-eater right in the side of the head.

It didn't stop the creature's charge, but the blow lifted its front paws off the ground. It veered off course and charged into a large crystal growth, scattering purple lightning. It scrabbled on the loose shards, trying to turn around.

"She didn't even use the hammer," Sparrow panted in awe.

They were almost to the shore now. Gwendolyn could see the longboats bobbing lazily. Torin was waiting for them, apparently recovered. His eyes went wide, and he scrambled to ready the boats.

There was a stinging pain in Gwendolyn's side, and her hair whipped her face, but she gritted her teeth and pushed on. "We're going to make it!" she said, unaware that this is the absolute worst thing one can say in these situations. As if to punish her insolence, a lightning bolt shot from a crystal and struck her in the knee.

She fell and slid, scraping herself raw on the sharp stones.

"Gwendolyn!" Sparrow whirled and ran back to her side. The beast was gaining again.

Sparrow stood over her. He took off his yellow scarf and waved it like a matador to distract the creature.

"Get up! Go!" he said.

She tried, but her numb leg refused to hold her weight. "I can't!"

The beast charged, but Sparrow yelled and waved, drawing the monster's attention. As it passed, he twirled his scarf to the side, and the beast sped past, clawed feet just inches from Gwendolyn's head.

It skidded to a stop, and came around again. Sparrow had its full attention now.

Gwendolyn crawled under an outcropping of rock while Sparrow lured the beast away. It charged him again, but he leapt straight at it and grabbed the tree-trunk-sized horn. It stomped around in a blind rage, flinging its head from side to side to dislodge the pesky insect on its nose.

Gwendolyn tried to stand again, but her leg collapsed with a vicious twist of her ankle. Suddenly, Carsair was there, enormous hammer in one hand, plucking her up by the back of the dress with the other. She slung Gwendolyn over her shoulder and onto her back as easily as an empty knapsack. Then she ran toward the boats.

"No, wait! We've got to help Sparrow!" Gwendolyn said.

"Boy is doing fine," Carsair rumbled. "Get you safe first."

They reached the boats, and Carsair set her inside with surprising gentleness. She turned back, but the beast was charging the shore.

Sparrow had his legs wrapped around the horn, clinging for dear life. "Go!" he yelled. "Push off!"

"No! We can't leave him!" Gwendolyn screamed.

"Do as he says!" ordered Kolonius. Brunswick and Carsair helped him push the boats into the water. Gwendolyn watched in horror as the monster barreled toward the water's edge.

It reached the shoreline, and the crystal-eater slammed all six legs into the ground, digging its claws into the rock with a bone-jarring halt. Sparrow flew off the horn, sailed over the boats, and splashed into the inky water.

The creature roared and touched a claw into the water. It shuddered, roared again, then lumbered back up the slope. It bit off a crystal spike and ground it to pieces in its brick-like teeth. The shards that fell to the ground faded from purple to black, adding to the sharp, glossy stones that littered the island.

"Go!" shouted Kolonius. They rowed to where Sparrow bobbed on the surface. Brunswick picked him up by his collar and dropped him into the boat.

He coughed and sputtered. "Like Kolonius said, I'm not *completely* useless." He tried to force a grin, but he was nearly knocked overboard as Gwendolyn flung herself around his neck in a crushing embrace.

"Of all your stupid stunts, that was by far the stupidest," she whispered. "Thank you."

He hugged her back. "I lost Starling. I'm not losing you too."

"You're all wet," she said, feeling icy water soak into her dress.

"Does it matter?" he said.

"Not a bit." She squeezed him tighter, then noticed that everyone was staring at them.

Her cheeks turned color to match her hair.

Brunswick barked a laugh and slapped the two of them on the back. "Ha! Young pups. All right, you lot, mind yer business and yer oars. Pull for yer lives!"

When they had distanced themselves from the crystals, Kolonius radioed the ship to make ready for high-speed pursuit.

The propellers were spinning and sails unfurled when they arrived.

"Drekk's ship stayed out of range of that weapon," reported Ching, "and being dead in the water, there wasn't much we could do to fight them off. But repairs are complete, and all our systems came back online a few minutes ago."

"They must have come on when we shut down the interference field. Drekk clearly knew we were here," Kolonius shot a withering glance at Gwendolyn and Sparrow, "and they've got a head start, so get us in the air *now*. Follow their last heading."

"Aye-aye, sir!" she saluted. Brunswick adjusted his green bowler hat, then clunked about the deck barking orders.

"You two." Kolonius pointed to Gwendolyn and Sparrow. "My cabin. Now." He stormed off, not bothering to see if they were following. They looked at each other nervously, then trotted after him.

He entered the cabin and pounded his hand on the desk. "Boy! Girl! You completely sabotaged this mission every step of the way! It's your fault Starling's in the hands of that, that monster." Teenage boys are not known for acting rationally under pressure, but he sounded less like the boy he was and more like Father when he was angry.

Sparrow fidgeted, dripping on the floor. "Kolonius, we didn't mean–"

"No excuses!" He picked up Gwendolyn's book from his desk and flipped through it; larger sections were now blank. "Look. At this rate, the Abscess will devour the entire world." He flung the book at them in disgust. It hit the floor and skidded to a thump against Gwendolyn's shoe. She picked it up.

"I know you're just Castaways here, but this is my home. You brought this monster, you gave away our position, you just *handed* Drekk the pistol, even though I told you he would kill us anyway, and now he has Starling and I'm honestly beginning to wonder whose side you're on!" he roared.

Sparrow went red in the face. "How dare you! She's my sister, I ought to–"

"Ought to what? I'm not the one who got her captured. If little Red there had listened and waited another second, those automatons would have finished him for us, and we'd still have your sister *and* the pistol!"

"And how the heck could we have known that a bunch of metal men were going to jump in?" Sparrow shouted back.

"I don't care! I'm tired of Tylerium-blasted-Drekk taking everything that I care about!"

"Both of you, stop it!" Gwendolyn shouted.

They turned to look at her.

"He's right," she mumbled. Tears rolled down her cheeks to splash on the open book. She wasn't even listening anymore, but was looking at the map of Tohk. The white spots were visibly growing, and more than half the page was blank. "W-what if we can't stop it?" Gwendolyn sobbed. "What if it's too late to save Starling, because it's too late to save Tohk at all?"

The boys stood in tense silence.

Gwendolyn sniffed and rubbed her eyes. She looked around the cabin, at all the little details of Kolonius's life, his clothes, his bed, the uneaten food, and realized how much *more* he was. How much of him was not in her book, could not be contained by any book. He was a real person, not just some character. She looked back at the book in her hand. In the other, she still held Starling's goggles.

And at that moment, it fully struck her just how much had truly been lost, and how much more was in danger. A danger she had caused. She had understood it in her head, but had kept the emotional weight at bay by acting. Now, somewhere inside her, a dam burst, and the awful feelings washed over her in a tidal wave. A small, dark voice whispered in her ear, a voice that was entirely her own.

All your fault.

She turned and ran out of the cabin.

"Gwendolyn, wait! Stop!" Sparrow yelled, but as usual, she didn't listen. She ran like she always did. She would have kept running too, until she escaped from the feelings that threatened to drown her.

But there's only so much space to run on a ship. She reached the prow, collapsed against the railing, and sobbed helplessly into the night.

Eventually, she heard footsteps. Sparrow appeared, sat down, and leaned against the railing next to her. He tried to slip his hand into hers, but she pulled back and turned her face away. "I can't do it, Sparrow."

"What do you mean?"

"This. Any of it. Fighting pirates, saving people. It's all so . . . real. People are really dying, and it's all my fault." Her throat closed in a choked sob.

"You *can* do this. You're strong and brave. You're the champion of the City, the best they have to offer."

"Stop it, this isn't some story. I thought adventures would be fun, but it's all just danger and running, and . . ." She turned back. "What if I just found another portal? Went back to the City, or anywhere else?"

He frowned at her. "I thought you were over this running away stuff. You'd just leave Starling to . . . to . . ."

"Not running away, just getting *out* of the way. Every time I try to help, I make things worse. What if it's my help that gets Starling killed? Or you? Or everyone in Tohk? I'll leave, and let you and Kolonius save your sister without me messing everything up."

"And what about Tohk? You wouldn't let all these people be eaten by the Abscess."

"But I'm the reason the Abscess is here! If I leave, maybe it will follow me back and leave everyone alone. Anyway, Kolonius is the hero, he'd do better without me."

"What if Kolonius can't use the Pistola Luminant? You're the one with the spark."

"But we don't *have* the pistol, do we, and whose fault is that again? Oh yes, it's mine."

She looked out at the dark ocean below them, waves glistening in the light of the ringed moon.

It was silent for a while.

"You're not really going to leave, and we both know it."

Gwendolyn sniffed. "No, I'm not. So just shut up and hold me."

He put his arm around her and pulled her in close. She snuggled against him, warm in the chill night air.

"It's not true, anyway," he said.

"What?" she asked.

"You making everything worse. It's not like you meant for all this to happen. Look at the Coves: you figured out that stuff about the crystal eaters, you opened the door to the lab, you shut down the defense systems, and you grabbed the pistol when everyone was distracted. I didn't see Mr. Thrash do much besides bossing everyone around."

"But I gave Drekk the pistol. I got Starling captured."

"Sometimes there are no good choices, and doing your best means doing what's right, and not giving up when things don't go your way."

She thought about that for a long moment. "I'm sorry about Starling," she said.

Sparrow gave her a reassuring squeeze. "We'll get her back. Besides, it's my turn to save her for a change." But his tone was not as confident as his words.

After a while, she noticed Kolonius standing awkwardly off to one side. Gwendolyn ignored him and buried her face into Sparrow's jacket, breathing in the smell of the leather, wanting to freeze time as long as she could. But she knew she would have to face Kolonius eventually. She would have to face everything. Running away had never solved her problems, and it never would. And no matter how bad it felt, there wasn't a single part of her that could leave all these people to die. This was all so much more important than her feelings.

Kolonius coughed and took a step toward them. "Ahem. Look, scraps, I guess I was a little hard on you. I know it seems bad. But as long as we've got some fight in us, we're not giving up." He pointed a finger at Gwendolyn. "You still want to help? Want to fix this mess?"

For once in her life, she hesitated and thought very carefully before answering. She looked deep inside and found the part of her that would always keep going, keep trying to save the mice and the Missys of the world, no matter what the outcome. "Yes. I'll help."

"Then listen up, cause here's how we're going to make that thing pay. And if we're lucky, we'll take Tylerium Drekk along with it."

One of the crew came up behind them. "Captain, we've picked up Drekk's ship on the sensors," she said. "We're holding course. He won't be able to shake us, but we won't overtake him until morning."

"Thank you, Riley. I'll be there in a minute." Kolonius rubbed his temples. "Look, I've got a plan, but I'm going to need . . . " He looked up to the stars, as if praying for strength, and spoke through gritted teeth. "I'll need your help. Both of you. But it won't be easy, and it won't be safe. Are you up for it?"

Gwendolyn took a deep breath, and let it out slow. Then she straightened. "I can do it. I won't let you down, Captain." She threw in a salute for good measure.

Kolonius actually smiled at that. He returned her salute. "Good. Let's get to work."

CHAPTER TWENTY-THREE

Rising Tides

I will not bore you with the details of the preparations that followed, as I am sure you would much rather see pirates fought, battles won, and villains vanquished. So we shall skip over that night's tedious conversations in Kolonius's cabin, and we will skip ahead to, as you might say, the good part.

As the long night came to an end, Kolonius led them onto the bridge. The three of them looked out the forward windows and watched the red sun tint the eastern horizon.

"Hrm. A red dawn," Brunswick said from the helm. "Normally the yellow one rises first," he explained to the children. "This be a bad omen."

"Let's hope it's bad for Drekk. Look." Kolonius pointed. "The *Swift Retribution*."

If the *Lucrative Endeavour* resembled an arrowhead of blue steel, the vessel in front of them looked for all the world like the old, wooden pirate ships you have seen in pictures. It had cannon ports along the sides, large cabin windows on the back, and fifteen wide, square sails. Unlike a regular pirate ship, however, dozens of tall, metal poles with propellers sprang up from the deck like dandelions in a garden.

Kolonius pounded a fist on the bridge console. "We've got him this time." He grabbed the intercom microphone. "This is it, everyone! The chance you've all been waiting for! Today we put an end to that pirate and settle the score he owes each and every one of you!"

An angry cheer went up from all corners of the ship, and Gwendolyn had to cover her ears.

"Today we make a stand for all of Tohk! Make ready! Battle positions!"

"Battle positions?" Sparrow glanced around. "Does this ship *have* weapons?"

Brunswick gave an amused grunt. "Just you watch, sprout."

The crew exploded into a flurry of practiced activity. Kolonius continued shouting. "Stow the sails! Drop wheel and raise action stations! Open the bridge! Raise the canons! Today Drekk pays for your homes! For your families! For Tohk!"

The ship transformed around them. The sails retracted into the masts, which lowered into the ship. The wheel helm sank into the floor. The whole front wall of the bridge split open, and the control deck telescoped outward into the open air, offering an unobstructed view of the sky around them.

Two large chairs rose out of the deck. They were surrounded by a golden framework of wheels, levers, switches, dials, and other controls. Torin and Ching jumped into the chairs, and they swiveled and turned in all directions, calibrating.

Other chairs rose up on the sides of the decks and the wings, each with long-barreled cannons mounted on their sides.

The *Lucrative Endeavour* was girded for war, its finery tucked away, its fangs bared. Raiding parties stood ready, guns and blades drawn.

"Wasp crews! Hangar deck!" Brunswick shouted. "You two, Cap'n says yer to come wit' me."

They looked at Kolonius, who nodded. "You know the plan." He gave Sparrow a firm handshake. "I wanted to say, those beasts back at the Coves? Well done. I might just forget that little radio stunt of yours. Take care of her." He nodded toward Gwendolyn. "Watch each other's backs. I'll see you when it's over. Bring that sister of yours back in one piece."

Sparrow gave the older boy a serious nod. "I will."

Kolonius turned to Gwendolyn. "Now then, Sparky, you keep that book of mine safe, do you hear? I don't want to find out it's been used for lining birdcages."

"No, sir." She saluted and patted her bag where she had stowed her copy of *Kolonius Thrash and the Perilous Pirates*.

He returned the salute playfully. "Good luck, Gwendolyn."

She smiled and rolled her eyes. "*Now* you remember my name."

Brunswick led them down to the hangar bay. "Can't say I'm too fond o' this plan. Barreling in, guns blazing. We're liable to lose a lot of good people."

"What choice do we have?" Sparrow said. "We've got to save Starling, and get the pistol back, or that shadow monster will destroy everything."

"Aye, lad, but it's rash. Not sure Cap'n's worked it all the way through. He ain't thinkin' straight, on account o' that sister of yers and seein' as how he's had a bit too much experience losin' those he cares about."

"So why didn't you say something?" Gwendolyn said.

Brunswick waved dismissively. "Ach, there's no talkin' to him when he gets like this, 'specially with Drekk. At his age, he's likely to charge in just to spite me if I said anything against it. And, well, it's not like I've got a better idea. Just a bad feelin' is all."

They reached the hangar and he said no more on the subject. The bay doors were open to the rising red sun. The crew was busy making adjustments to a fleet of large metal contraptions.

"What are those?" Gwendolyn asked.

"Those? Those are Wasps," Brunswick said.

They approached one, and Gwendolyn thought it looked like a reclined bicycle with a sail attached. There was a seat, and two control pedals stuck out in front. A metal wing-strut extended to each side, with gyroscoping propellers at the end. Behind the seat was a thin mast with a long triangular sail. A long-barreled weapon gave the craft a vicious point at the front, from which Gwendolyn guessed it got its name. Sparrow touched it in awe.

"Careful of the stinger, there, mate. It's loaded," warned Brunswick.

"We're supposed to fly in *that?*" Gwendolyn exclaimed. The whole thing was made of metal tubing thinner than her wrist.

"They're light, they're nimble, and those stingers can do some right damage."

"Shouldn't we have two?" Gwendolyn asked.

"Ye shouldn't even have one! Right couple o' babes ye are, but time's tight, and Cap'n says we don't have much choice. So don't go crashin', and don't try anythin' fancy."

Sparrow cracked his knuckles. "We birds were made to fly."

"Oh, no you don't," Gwendolyn said. "I don't fancy myself splattered across the Spiced Seas. I'm flying."

Sparrow balked. "What? No, I'm flying."

"We both know your sister would agree with me. End of discussion."

He crossed his arms. "Totally unfair."

Brunswick laughed and gave Gwendolyn a quick flying lesson, including how to use the pedals to turn the propellers, control the sail, and fire the stinger. It seemed surprisingly easy. Gwendolyn worried about that. Things that seem easier than they should usually turn out to be disastrously difficult.

"A'right, saddle up, and good luck to ya." And he hobbled away.

"Brunswick!" Gwendolyn chased after him, leaving a puzzled Sparrow to find a way to attach himself to the single-seat vehicle.

Brunswick turned. "What is it, sprout?"

Gwendolyn bit her lip. "Back at the Coves, Drekk said something about Kolonius being his cabin boy. None of that was in my book, and I was wondering . . ."

Brunswick's jaw tightened. "Ye caught that, did ye? Yes, Kolonius *was* Drekk's cabin boy. Forced to, ye see? Kept captive. They've got history, those two."

"What history?"

"Well, it ain't my story to tell."

"Brunswick, we need to know what we're getting into. Please?"

"Fine," he said. "I really must be a softie." He took a deep breath, dragging up old memories. "Kolonius was just a boy when Drekk raided his village. Wiped the whole place out. But Kolonius, small as he was, fought back. Managed to kill Drekk's cabin boy in the process. Drekk always liked that sort o' spirit, so he took Kolonius as a slave to replace him."

"How did he escape?" Gwendolyn asked.

"Hmph." Brunswick grunted a laugh. "He stole a ship, didn't he?"

"What? What ship?"

"Why, this 'un, of course! Stole the *Lucrative Endeavour* right out from under Drekk's nose! Took off with it one day when Drekk was out on a raid. Been flyin' it ever since, upgradin' it as he went. Swiped that fancy spinning sword, too."

Gwendolyn looked around at the crew. "So this is *Drekk's* ship? And, all these people?"

"Kytain's beard, no! Mostly they're just regular folk what Drekk's done some harm to. Left their homes to get some justice. 'Course, after he was done with 'em, most didn't have much home left to leave. But we took 'em in, and they've turned into a right bunch of air dogs. So today's personal, you see?"

"I think so. What about you, Brunswick? Something tells me Kolonius couldn't steal this ship all on his own. Didn't Kolonius mention something about you being a pirate?"

Brunswick stroked his orange mustache, his thoughts miles and years away. "Err, that's complicated, that is. But enough storytellin'! Best see to yer mission." He left before she could say a word.

Gwendolyn walked back across the deck. Sparrow was sitting on a wing-strut, tied to the frame with his yellow scarf, clearly dubious about the safety it would provide.

She climbed in the pilot's chair and buckled in. "Okay. That's that. Comfortable?"

"Hardly," Sparrow said, ducking his head to avoid the pivoting sail.

She couldn't blame him. But Starling wouldn't be afraid, so she wouldn't be either. "Excellent. Then let's be off before the shooting starts, if you please." Gwendolyn pulled out Starling's goggles and strapped them on.

Sparrow grinned at that. "We could really use some of her parabrellas right now, huh?"

Gwendolyn shot a nervous smile back. "Actually, I was quite hoping we *won't* be needing them."

She flicked a switch and started the propellers. She grabbed the control stick, tapped the pedals, and the propellers swiveled and lifted them into the air. The Wasp wobbled a bit at first, but steadied as they drifted forward.

"There. That's not so ha—" Gwendolyn was interrupted by a screech of grinding metal as the nose of the Wasp dropped and carved a long gouge in the hangar floor. They scraped and squealed across the deck for an endless cringing moment, and then fell into the crimson sky. There was a sickening moment of free-fall, but then the propellers caught their weight and they puttered into the clouds.

"Good one," Sparrow groaned. He held a hand to his mouth, trying not to vomit.

Gwendolyn pivoted the sail to catch the wind. She steered them away from the two ships and into a patch of reddish-orange clouds. "Well, that's it then. Nothing to do but wait."

The *Lucrative Endeavour*'s blue metal hull sparkled in the sunlight. The large, wooden *Swift Retribution* slowed to turn, just as Kolonius had said it would. According to him, the *Retribution* had only minimal rear armaments, and would have to turn to get its main side cannons to bear.

Gwendolyn set the Wasp to hover and watched as the two ships drew closer.

Suddenly, as if the ships had crossed some invisible line in the sky, they opened fire. The *Swift Retribution* let loose a violent blast, a startling series of explosions and smoke, peppering the *Lucrative Endeavour* with whatever weapons it could. But as Kolonius had predicted, it wasn't many, as the pirate ship still hadn't turned enough to use its main cannons. Kolonius's crew opened up with the gunnery chairs, firing two bright lines of bullets from each one.

"Now?" asked Sparrow.

"Not yet," said Gwendolyn. "Remember the plan."

Kolonius stood on the open flight deck, barking orders. "Blow starboard vents, all pressure!"

"Aye, sir!" called Torin. He cranked a wheel and swiveled his chair to the right. Jets of steam erupted from the side of the ship, creating a new cloud in the early morning sky. The force of the vents pushed the *Endeavour* into a sideways slide, pivoting to stay directly behind the *Retribution.*

"Fire anchor cables!" Kolonius shouted. The *Endeavour* fired harpoons which buried themselves in the back side of the larger ship. One of the harpoons shattered the large cabin windows.

"Now?" repeated Sparrow.

"Not *yet,*" insisted Gwendolyn.

The two ships were now close enough that some on deck were sniping with long-barreled rifles. "Draw blades!" Kolonius called. "Prepare for shipboard combat! Make those pirates pay!"

Before the crew could obey, pirates in the riggings of the *Retribution* fired pneumo cables down at the *Endeavour.* The pirates zipped across, whooping battle cries as they landed on the deck of Kolonius's ship.

Kolonius raced into action. He leapt from the flight deck and sprinted toward the invading pirates. He drew his spiral longsword and cut pneumo lines as he passed. Pirates found their lines going slack in mid-slide and fell into the clouds, flailing and screaming.

The air was full of the clash of steel, the crack of rifle shot, and the smell of gunpowder. The ragtag crew of the *Endeavour* fought hard, each driven by some personal pain. Kolonius fought harder than anyone, his jeweled sword flashing as the handsome boy took on three pirates at a time, his dreadlocks whirling as he twirled.

The other Wasps took flight and harassed the decks of the *Retribution* like the swarm they were named for. But the pirates launched their own Wasps. Theirs didn't fire but soared high over the *Endeavour,* and pirates dropped from the wings.

Gwendolyn's jaw dropped as well. The jumping pirates tucked their limbs and shot forward like bullets. At the last moment, they flared their arms and exposed fin-like webbing between their arms and legs, gliding softly down. Then they pounced on unsuspecting crewman. Each drew two swords from their back and leapt into battle, and they seemed more skilled than the other pirates, jumping and flipping as they fought.

One of the sky-jumpers slammed into Wilhelm, and he fell overboard with a wild scream. Gwendolyn gasped, but the young sailor caught himself on a harpoon cable connecting the ships.

Carsair was amongst the pirates like a rampaging giant, swinging her hammer left and right as the nimble sky pirates danced around her. She caught one of them full in the chest, and he went flying over the side, but was not as fortunate as Wilhelm was.

Chaos reigned, smoke and steam filled the air, and Gwendolyn couldn't tell which side was winning.

"Now," she whispered.

Their Wasp slid out of the clouds, whirring and clicking. Everything was going according to plan.

"This still seems risky to me," Sparrow said. "Drekk said he'd kill Starling the second he spotted us."

"Kolonius knows what he's doing. He said Drekk would never throw away a valuable hostage without something to show for it. He'll be holding her as a backup plan, in case we decide to attack. Which means he'll keep her safe at the start of the battle, until he can benefit from a hostage exchange or something."

"Doesn't sound terribly safe. Seems like we're taking a lot of risks with my sister's life."

"Hence the rescuing. Get ready." Gwendolyn piloted the Wasp low toward the pirate ship, being careful to skirt the battle.

"Those big windows on the back, that's Drekk's quarters, yeah?" Sparrow said. "We could fly right up to them."

"We can't," Gwendolyn said. "With everyone zipping overhead, we'd be spotted, or squashed between the ships. We need to go under it, fly to the other end where the fighting is thinnest, sneak onboard, then down through the underside of the ship."

Around them, Drekk's Wasps engaged Kolonius's. One of Kolonius's crew was blasted out of the sky, followed by two of Drekk's. Gwendolyn lost sight of them in the clouds. She wondered how many people would die today to fix her mistakes.

They dove under the battle. The Wasp bucked in the wind, but she kept it under control. Flying seemed almost second nature. It was nice to be good at something for once, besides drawing and causing trouble. She felt the thrill of flight and battle alike run through her, almost washing away her fear.

They managed to sneak the Wasp to the far end of the ship. Using Sparrow's scarf, they lashed the Wasp to the deck rail and climbed onto the main deck.

On the other end of the ship, the battle raged. Gun smoke drifted across the deck. Gwendolyn could feel grit between her teeth and clinging to her skin. She heard Kolonius shouting somewhere. Then they opened a creaky hatch and climbed down.

It was a bit dark below decks, and it took their eyes a moment to adjust. "Which way, Gwendolyn?" Sparrow asked.

"That way," she whispered, remembering Kolonius's directions. They slunk through the corridors, which were grimy and filthy compared to the gleaming metal corridors of the *Endeavour*. The smell of a hundred armpits seemed to ooze from the walls. The muffled sounds of battle overhead frazzled Gwendolyn's nerves, and she jumped with every thump and clang.

"Wait!" Sparrow said. "I hear someone."

Gwendolyn listened. She could hear it as well: two deep voices, coming around the next corner. She and Sparrow hugged the wall and listened.

"Why are we stuck down here, guardin' the cap'n's lousy cabin, when there's a whole load of violence right above us? It's a criminal injustice, restraining our natural impulses like this. I signed up to smash heads, not to protect a pile of fancy bedsheets."

"I don't know nothin' about all that. All I knows is that Cap'n says to me, he says, 'Muffins. Bucket. You two stay 'ere and guard me cabin. Don't let no one in.' And I says, 'Even you?' And he makes that grumpy face he makes, and he says, 'No, you jabbery ninky-poop,' or sum fancy word o' his, 'you let me in, but not nobody else.' And the cap'n, he gets awful violent hisself, so here's I sit. Now do you have any threes, or don'choo?"

"Go fish. Well, the cap'n's right about one thing. You are a jabbery ninky-poop."

"Shut up, Muffins, 'fore I thump you."

Gwendolyn and Sparrow had to cover their mouths to keep from laughing. When they settled down, Sparrow whispered to her, "I'll distract them while you sneak into the cabin and grab the Pistola Luminant. I'll ditch these losers, then meet you back at the hatch."

"Are you sure you'll be all right?"

He smiled his wolfish grin. "Come on. If I can't outsmart *them,* I deserve to be caught." Sparrow reached into his coat and pulled out a battered paperback book: *Dr. Colluphid's 1001 Obtusely Bawdy Puns, Jibes, and Jeers.*

"What's that?" she whispered.

"Starling picked it up for me in the marketplace." He flipped through the pages. "Ah, perfect. That will do nicely."

Gwendolyn crouched in a doorway, out of sight, and gave him a thumbs-up. Sparrow tipped his cap, then leapt around the corner, reading from the book.

"Hey, you pusillanimous twits, you . . . fetid corpuscles. You haven't the brains god gave a cow, but you've certainly got the looks. Roust yourselves and come for a real fight, you ragged blister bottoms!" He turned and sprinted back down the hallway. "Your mothers were of questionable parentage!"

Two large, disgusting men barreled after him, one fat and one weasel-thin. "He called us names! Get 'im!"

"I 'ave no idea what you just said, but I'ma wring your neck for it, you li'l brat!"

When they had passed, Gwendolyn snuck around the corner, giggling quietly. She stepped over scattered playing cards and pushed open the large double doors. *Thank you, Dr. Colluphid,* she thought, and she went inside.

CHAPTER TWENTY-FOUR

Swift Retribution

Entering Drekk's cabin, Gwendolyn thought it made the one on the *Endeavour* look small. The rest of the pirate ship was dirty and grimy, but this was spotless except for the glass and wood debris scattered everywhere from the harpoon that had smashed through the enormous bank of curved windows. The harpoon was now embedded in the wall, stringing a foot-thick steel cable across the room.

There was a desk in the middle, twice the size of Kolonius's, and a gigantic four-poster bed behind that. A staircase led to a soaring walkway that ran along the windows, over shelves laden with books and trinkets. Lush, blue carpets squished pleasantly under Gwendolyn's tired feet. Drekk had clearly spared no expense when upgrading his new ship, and now she understood the unusual finery of Kolonius's cabin.

The sunlight colored the room in shades of fire and blood. Clouds of dust and the sounds of battle floated in through the broken window, reminding her to work quickly.

Gwendolyn looked around. No Starling. "Blast it, Kolonius," she grumbled. He'd sworn she'd be in the captain's quarters, the most secure location, under guard and away from the fighting. Looks like he didn't know everything.

"The pistol, then. Why would those guards have been out there unless there was something to guard?"

Checking the bookshelves turned up nothing, as did her search of the bed. She glanced around for any safes, strongboxes, or locked doors, but found none.

She plopped down in the comfortable desk chair, trying to think, but worry ate away at her thoughts. Every second she wasted down here, someone was getting hurt above. Not to mention Sparrow, who couldn't outrun those pirates forever. And any minute, Drekk could decide that Starling was more trouble than she was worth.

I must stay calm, she told herself. *If anyone can wonder their way out of this mess, it's me.* She took a deep breath, and put her head down on the desk to think.

Then she noticed something odd. The floor under the desk was covered in the same dust as the rest of the room, but there were strange tracks in it, which must have happened after the battle started. It looked like something had been slid across the floor. Or someone. She got down on the floor herself, sliding until she was under the desk, and looked up.

There, on the underside of the big sliding drawer, was a tiny, golden switch. There was no way to reach it unless you had been lying in this exact spot. Gwendolyn grinned.

She pressed the switch, and heard a click from across the

room. She slid out and saw a panel had opened in the wall. She ran over to it, took out a large velvet box, and flipped the clasp.

Inside was the Pistola Luminant, glowing softly.

"Brilliant. At least something went right for a change." She raced to the door and peeked out. The coast was still clear. Sparrow had done his job well. She touched the goggles on her head, hoping their owner would be all right, hoping Sparrow had managed to find her.

She crept back through the dark underbelly of the ship. The fighting above seemed to have intensified. Eventually she reached the ladder and hatchway to the deck above and paused, taking a deep breath to steady her nerves. She clambered out into the crimson sunlight, and the sound of battle roared up around her. The light was blinding after the darkness below.

Before she could get her bearings, a voice slid up behind her, dangerous, cold, and smooth, like black ice on a winding road. "It would seem that my ship is infested with rats. Or children, but really, what's the difference?"

Gwendolyn whipped around to see Tylerium Drekk in his red coat and feathered hat. At his side was Starling, arms tied behind her back, handkerchief tied between her teeth. The very picture of a damsel in distress, which Gwendolyn knew Starling would hate. Her pockets had all been sliced open, and her tool belts were gone. Drekk held her by the hair in one hand and held a long, jeweled pistol in the other. She grunted and struggled, but to no avail.

"Do you know what we do with rats on my ship? We exterminate them."

Fear surged through Gwendolyn like a shock of crystal lightning. She had brought up this very possibility the night before, during their planning.

"What about Drekk?" she'd said. "Won't he see all this coming?" she'd said.

But Kolonius had only snorted. "Drekk's too arrogant for his own good. He won't be able to resist getting up close and personal with me. He'd never expect that the pistol could be stolen from under his nose by a couple of *little girls,*" Kolonius mimicked Drekk's voice, though not as well as Starling. "Trust me. You'll be in and out before he even knows you're there," he had said with the utmost confidence.

Now, Drekk stood sneering across the deck at Gwendolyn, and she did not find the irony the least bit amusing.

"Come now," he said. "A full frontal attack from Kolonius Thrash? The boy was bound to have some ill-conceived plan to steal the pistol, but teenagers don't know the meaning of the word 'subtle.' Still, I may be a ruthless unethical murderer, but sending little girls to do your dirty work is just plain *unfashionable.* And they call *me* a pirate."

While he talked, Gwendolyn's hand crept toward the clasp on the velvet box.

"Ah-ah-ah, girlie." Drekk pressed his pistol to Starling's head. "If you so much as twitch, then so will I. Put it down, or this pretty friend of yours will quickly become a lot less pretty. And also dead."

Starling managed to spit out the handkerchief. "Gwendolyn,

go! Don't worry, I've got him right where I want hi—Ow!" she cried as Drekk whacked her with the pistol.

"Quiet, girl. I like my hostages silent, or in pieces. Now then, other girl, just like before. Slide it over."

Gwendolyn frantically tried to imagine a way out, but the only image she could bring to mind was Drekk's pistol and the dimple it was making in Starling's temple. Her heart beat faster. Clouds gathered in the sky above.

Sometimes, there are no good choices, she remembered. Slowly, she placed the box on the deck and slid it over.

It went wide, sliding off to Drekk's left.

He rolled his eyes and stepped over to it. "Oh, please. Someone thinks they're clever. Honestly, I can shoot her just as easily from over here—"

Bullets riddled the deck and cut a neat line in the wood between Drekk and the box.

Sparrow soared out of the sky on the Wasp, whooping loudly, his scarf streaming. He pulled hard on the sail and came around again.

Drekk never hesitated. He shoved Starling away, dove, and rolled, already running as he sprang to his feet. He sprinted across the deck without looking back as Sparrow swooped in, firing the stinger, but the shots went wide.

Drekk whirled, planted his feet, and fired one deliberate shot. The Wasp's right propeller exploded. Shrapnel shredded the sail. The Wasp dropped. Sparrow crashed into the deck and slid, screeching to a stop a foot away from Tylerium Drekk. The

Wasp was a mess of twisted metal and leaking fluids. Sparrow looked up groggily. "Okay, maybe I shouldn't be allowed to fly . . ."

"Look," Drekk crooned. "Another child to add to my collection. I may have to hire a nanny." He cocked his pistol and pointed it at Sparrow. "Oh well. The more he sends, the more I get to kill."

Gwendolyn's mind whirled. She thought back to the plan, thinking what to do next. But there had been no next. According to the plan, they should be back safe on the *Endeavour*, sipping cocoa and readying to fight the Abscess. And things were definitely not going according to plan.

A shot rang out, and the pirate's pistol shattered.

"Drekk!" Kolonius Thrash strode across the deck, tossing aside his own spent pistol. His one good eye burned with anger, and his ebony skin glistened with sweat. His spiral blade whirred and spun.

Tylerium Drekk's lip curled into a vicious sneer. "Thrash." He drew his rapier, jewels sparkling in the thin blade. "This time I'll take more than just your eye, boy, and kill you properly. Then you can see your family again, eh? I do love reunions."

They sized each other up for a tense moment, and Gwendolyn noticed the extra foot of height Drekk had on the younger captain. Then they leapt at each other.

The red-tinted sky began to grow dark.

The two captains battled furiously. Back and forth across the deck they went, the boy and the pirate, swords clashing. Drekk whipped his hat off and twirled it, drawing the eye from his sword, golden curls blowing in the wind. He drew Kolonius off guard and scored a piercing hit to the boy's shoulder.

Kolonius grimaced, but stood fast. He slashed the hat in two and pressed the attack.

Drekk had the reach, but Kolonius was younger and faster. Drekk's rapier had trouble blocking the heavier spiral blade. Kolonius battered through Drekk's defense, then came in with a thrust that nearly skewered the pirate.

The point of Drekk's rapier darted like a seamstress's needle as he changed tactics. "You know, I'm not sure I even want the *Endeavour* back anymore. I'd never rid it of the smell. We'll just have to scuttle it." He took a stab at the boy's wrist, but Kolonius countered, drew a short dagger with his free hand, and pushed Drekk back farther.

"Enough talk, Drekk. Fight or die. Hopefully both." Dark clouds crept across the sky.

Sparrow staggered to his feet and over to Gwendolyn, and the two of them began to untie Starling when they noticed blood on the deck.

"Starling, you're hurt!" Gwendolyn said.

"What? Again? No, I'm fine, I—" but as she tried to stand, she collapsed with a cry of pain. She looked at her leg. "Oh. I am not fine." A jagged piece of the Wasp was sticking out of her calf. "Heh," she said deliriously. "It stings. Get it?"

"Don't touch it. Here." Gwendolyn took her old school skirt from her satchel, cut a strip using her dagger, and bandaged the wound as best she could, wrapping carefully around the shard. She grabbed the box with the pistol and they helped Starling hobble to the pneumos, but the going was slow.

Kolonius pinned Drekk against the railing with one slash after another, sword and knife a blur. Drekk feigned a thrust and threw a spinning kick at the boy's legs, then jumped and climbed up the rigging. Soon he had gained enough height to escape the boy's sword, and Kolonius was forced to sheathe his dagger and climb as well.

"Running, Drekk? It won't help. Even vermin like you run out of holes sometime."

"Boy, you're too young to understand the difference between running and retreating. Didn't your parents ever teach you these things? Oh, that's right. I killed them."

Up they went, climbing through the forest of ropes and sails. With each cut, another rope went slack, but they climbed higher still.

Storm clouds blotted out the red sun.

Gwendolyn, Sparrow, and Starling made it to the aft deck of the *Swift Retribution*. The fighting had died down here, as Kolonius's crew had gained the upper hand and secured the pneumos. The pirates had been pushed back from the *Lucrative Endeavour* to their own ship and were out on the *Retribution*'s main deck, fighting tooth and nail as their captains dueled above them.

They got Starling onto a pneumo, despite her protests about Kolonius.

"You're in no shape to help anyone," said Gwendolyn. They extended the stirrup, helped her get her uninjured leg in place, then sent her zipping toward the *Lucrative Endeavour*. Gwendolyn insisted that Sparrow go next. She guarded the spot, dagger in hand, until he was safely across. Thunder rumbled, and Gwendolyn was startled to see that the sky was now a solid wall of black clouds.

She sheathed the dagger on her braided gold belt and zipped over, clutching the Pistola Luminant. She landed on the *Endeavour's* metal deck and turned to look at the *Retribution,* squinting for any sign of Kolonius.

The two swordsmen stood on the spar of the mainsail, balancing on the narrow wooden beam, propellers whirling around them. The wind howled. Lightning flashed, casting the duelists in silhouette against the black sky.

Brunswick ran past her. "What did I tell ye? Disaster. Least ye got the pistol. I'll get Kolonius." The burly man zipped to the other ship and hauled his way up the rigging.

The two captains moved back and forth across the beam, high above the deck, swinging on ropes that hung from the crow's nest. Their hair and clothes whipped around them, and if they said anything to each other, called out oaths or taunts, the words were lost to the wind.

They battled, neither giving an inch, back and forth, blade upon blade. All style had gone, each relying on sheer strength of hate as they battered each other with savage blows.

Drekk leaned in, twisted around Kolonius's spiral sword, and stabbed him through the forearm. Kolonius screamed in pain. His sword went flying into the clouds. The pirate reared back for a final blow—

And thick black tentacles erupted from the clouds and snapped the *Swift Retribution* in half.

CHAPTER TWENTY-FIVE

Falling Action

Gwendolyn gasped in speechless horror.

"No!" Starling shrieked, but she was drowned out by the sounds of snapping wood and tearing metal. The pirate ship split like an overripe melon, men and debris falling into the sky, its splintered halves held aloft by the massive tentacles.

The crew of the *Endeavor* scrambled to cast off the anchor cables that connected them to the pieces of Drekk's ship.

The Abscess gripped the remains of the *Swift Retribution,* and it began to feed. The wood faded to white and crumbled into dust, which was sucked greedily upward into the shadow.

Tentacles the size of skyscrapers sprouted smaller feelers that whipped about and snatched every piece of falling material, every scrap of cargo, every crewman who tumbled through the air. Gwendolyn caught a glimpse of Brunswick struggling in the grip of a tentacle as he disappeared into the shadows.

In seconds, it was over. There was not a single trace of the *Swift Retribution*, Tylerium Drekk, or Kolonius Thrash.

Starling was beside herself. "Kolonius!" she screamed, her voice hoarse and eyes red. Her only answer was a blood-curdling squeal from the Abscess.

Someone must have gotten to one of the control chairs, because the ship moved away from the black monstrosity. The rail guns pounded the Abscess, but with little effect. More tentacles surrounded the ship, dangling like jungle vines, slowing its progress.

"Gwendolyn! The pistol! We went to all the trouble to get that thing, so *use it!*" Sparrow said.

"Right!" She fumbled with the clasp on the velvet box and pointed the heavy, golden pistol at the tentacles which were now reaching toward them. She pulled the trigger and averted her eyes, flinching from whatever was going to happen—

Which was nothing.

She opened her eyes, pulled the trigger again, and again, getting only a dull click each time. *No, no, no!*

The tentacles wrapped around the pointed prow of the *Endeavour.*

"Gwendolyn, do something! Hurry!" Sparrow shouted.

"I'm trying! It's not working!" She kept pulling the trigger, but it might as well have been a golden paperweight.

She gazed out at the shadows that loomed so impossibly large. She was so small, and there was nothing she could do, and the darkness was rising inside of her as well. She had failed again.

"Come on," Starling said, checking her wrist device. "We've got to find a way to get out of here!"

"What?" said Sparrow.

"This is out of control! We'll grab one of those little plane things, find the nearest portal, and get off this world."

"We can't!" Gwendolyn said.

"Look around!" Starling said, wind whipping her hair into her face. "The pistol doesn't work! The whole plan was a failure, and Kolonius is gone! I'm not losing you, too. Either of you."

"No," Gwendolyn said. "This is my fault, I can't leave!"

"If she's staying, I'm staying!" Sparrow said. "And you're not going to get very far with that leg." He turned to Gwendolyn. "You have to try again. Focus. Kytain made this weapon, remember? Think about what those metal men said. Kytain had the spark, and you've got it too. Use it!"

She tried. She squeezed the trigger again, but nothing happened.

"I don't know! It isn't–"

And then, in the midst of all the noise and smoke and chaos, she saw something. Something so small that only Gwendolyn would notice.

A tiny, emerald leaf floated through the storm.

She stared at it, time seeming to stop, and then she felt a sudden surge of energy.

The three glass tubes on top of the pistol began to glow. They shone brighter and brighter until Gwendolyn could no longer look at them. She managed to aim the pistol just in time, as a beam of golden light exploded from the tip with a deafening thunderclap.

Her aim was high, and the bolt struck the clouds, tearing

a hole through the storm. A patch of red sky peered at them through the gap.

"It worked!" she shouted, but her joy was crushed as more tentacles emerged, thicker than tree trunks. Gwendolyn focused her mind, steeled her nerves, and *imagined.* She pictured the lightning shattering the Abscess into a thousand pieces, and the pistol fired. This blast met its mark, vaporizing a tentacle that wrapped around the prow.

She ran forward for a better shot, pushing past harried sailors. She pulled down Starling's goggles to protect against the rain as the wind tugged at her green dress.

A weapon of purest light that could defeat even the blackest evil, she thought, and pulled the trigger. The Pistola Luminant fired, living up to its name and reputation, again and again. It felt like an extension of Gwendolyn's arm. She felt the feeling of racing thoughts, new ideas spinning so fast she couldn't keep up with them, all that energy flowing down her arm like an electric tingle.

Each time, she poured herself into the weapon, and each time, she was rewarded with a mighty thunderbolt. She blasted the tentacles that reached down to block their path.

The *Endeavour* flew, one small girl perched on its prow like a figurehead, lighting the way in the darkness. The clouds stretched to the horizon, and tentacles were emerging on all sides. Gwendolyn didn't know who was flying, but they were pulling off fantastic swoops and turns with the large vessel. They dodged shadows that looked like giant groping hands, others that looked like clawed talons.

It's my nightmare, Gwendolyn thought. She remembered the wasteland, the childish voice of the Collector, the clouds reaching out for her.

The ship veered, and Gwendolyn was thrown against the railing. She started to fall over the side, but Sparrow was there, hugging her to the rail.

She squeezed her eyes shut, waiting for the ship to level, and an idea struck her. "Come on! Where's Starling?"

Sparrow pointed to where she sat in one of the gun turrets, shooting at the shadows with an angry fire in her eyes. Starling peppered the clouds with gunfire, her blue and black hair whipping against her face.

"I strapped her in and told her to do something useful. She didn't like it, but she's not in a position to argue," Sparrow shouted.

"All right!" Gwendolyn yelled. "We have to get to the flight deck!"

Sparrow nodded, and they clawed their way along. Sparrow clung to Gwendolyn, and she clung to the pistol, struggling to maintain their footing as the *Endeavour* itself struggled to evade the Abscess's grip.

Finally, they reached the control chairs on the flight deck. Ching and Torin were whirling madly in them.

"Torin!" Gwendolyn yelled, struggling to be heard above the wind.

"I'm a bit busy, girl!" He swung the ship to starboard to avoid another tentacle.

"Where are we headed?" yelled Sparrow.

"Away! This storm can't go on forever," answered Ching.

"But you can't keep *flying* like this forever!" Gwendolyn said.

"Who's she again?" Ching yelled to Torin.

"I'm the one who got us into this mess," Gwendolyn said. "And I'm about to get us out!"

"I'm open to suggestions!" Torin said.

"Fly up! Get above the storm. Right through the gap in the clouds."

"What gap?" he shouted back.

"This one," she pointed the pistol at the sky and took a deep breath. She willed it to fire, and a beam of light blasted a hole in the clouds above, revealing the crimson sky above.

Torin glanced at Ching, who nodded. They leaned their chairs back, and the ship shot up toward the hole, climbing for the safety of open sky.

Suffocating clouds rushed to engulf them. The noxious chemical scent of the Abscess was overpowering, burning Gwendolyn's nose and throat.

Ahead, the tiny window of sky was almost gone. Gwendolyn gritted her teeth and fired another bolt. The clouds were blasted open once more, and the ship burst into clean, open air.

They breathed a sigh of relief as the *Lucrative Endeavour* rose above an ocean of black clouds. The crimson sky was shockingly peaceful in contrast to the storm below. A cheer went up from the ragged remnants of the crew.

"You did it!" Sparrow yelled, and hugged her tight. Gwendolyn closed her eyes and squeezed him back.

Then a voice came from behind them—one that sent ice

water down Gwendolyn's spine. "This commotion is all terribly pointless, isn't it, Mister Five?"

"A most futile effort indeed, Mister Six."

Gwendolyn spun to see the two Faceless Gentlemen standing on the deck in dapper grey suits and bowler hats. Gwendolyn did not know she could be more scared than she already was, but the sight of the Faceless Gentlemen proved otherwise.

"We will have you, Ms. Gray. You will not escape."

"No indeed. The Whyte Proposal must be enforced. All must be cleansed to prevent another Fall."

Sparrow flicked open his collapsible sword and slashed through one of the men. Right through. His sword met no resistance, and Sparrow almost lost his balance.

Mister Five and Mister Six rippled like a reflection on a pond.

"They're not really here!" Gwendolyn shouted.

"That didn't stop them last time," Sparrow said.

"Nor shall it stop us this time." Mister Five reached for Sparrow, just as he had in the marketplace.

"No!" Gwendolyn shouted. She lunged forward and grabbed Mister Five's wrist . . . and caught it, solid under her fingers.

Mister Five reeled backward in shock, but Gwendolyn held fast. "If I can bring my imagination to life in the City, then I can bring the City to life in my imagination." She grabbed Mister Six as well, and managed to catch hold of his upper arm. For once it was the two men that seemed frozen in place. She focused on pulling, not with her arms, but with her mind, picturing the two men becoming real.

There was a *crack* of displaced air, and the two men stopped flickering and became completely solid.

"Finally!" Sparrow said. "Something I can hit!" He swung his sword at the one on the left.

The Faceless Gentleman caught the blade between his thumb and middle finger, with no more effort than grasping a falling leaf. "Forced physical manifestation, Mister Six," said Mister Five.

"The girl proves ever more surprising, Mister Five," said Mister Six. "The Collector may not wish to merely erase her after all."

Mister Five snapped his fingers, and the sword blade snapped in half. "No matter, Mister Six. I can still put my hand through the boy's head. It will merely be much *juicier* this time."

Gwendolyn was sick of them. Sick of their threats. Sick of running. At that moment, she could feel Cecilia Forthright's spit dribbling down her cheek again, and her insides blazed with fury. Yes, she was done running.

She raised the Pistola Luminant.

"Why don't you add this to your collection."

The bulbs glowed and the pistol fired.

The lightning struck the two men, and their skin seemed to glow for a moment. Then they exploded into a thousand fragments of light, like the shattering bulb in the laboratory. But as the fragments flew outward, they darkened, slowed, and reversed direction. Pieces of blackness sucked together like a miniature black hole, forming a sphere of dark energy. Then the sphere collapsed, and disappeared with a loud *pop*.

There was a maddened screech from the storm below, and

tentacles burst from the tops of the clouds. Hundreds of vines twisted together into one gigantic hand, which grabbed the *Lucrative Endeavour* by its rear propeller. The ship jolted to a halt, and the engines whined with the strain. The giant arm pulled the ship down. The clouds formed a fanged mouth to swallow them whole.

Gwendolyn leaned over the side, trying to get a clear shot, but the hull of the ship blocked her view. She fired into the clouds, but the ship was jerked farther downward. She leaned out more, but the sound of screaming made her turn.

The shadows had sprouted clouds of black insects, which swarmed over the terrified crewmen. They screamed and flailed, but to no avail. One by one they dissolved into piles of grey dust.

Sparrow cried out as a thin, black cord wrapped around his ankle and pulled. He slammed into the deck. The tentacle dragged him toward the edge. "No, no! Gwendolyn!" he shouted.

Gwendolyn turned, but the ship lurched and she slipped. She hit the deck hard, and the pistol spun away to her left, far out of reach. On her right, Sparrow was being dragged toward the edge. She looked at the pistol. She looked at Sparrow.

Sometimes there are no good choices, but this one was no choice at all. She dove to her right and grabbed Sparrow's hand in both of hers. It did little good; they were both pulled to the edge of the deck.

"Gwendolyn, no!" he screamed at her. "Get the pistol!"

"I will! But I'm getting you first!" There was a bang from the engines and the ship lurched violently. Cracks splintered the deck. The Pistola Luminant slid farther away from them.

Gwendolyn moved toward it, but Sparrow started slipping and she grabbed him again. The pistol caught in one of the cracks and stuck fast, fifteen feet down the railing from them. Fifteen feet too many.

The curl of smoke pulled Sparrow completely through the metal rails, but he grabbed one with his free hand. Gwendolyn helped him grab on with his other hand as well. Rail guns on the wings broke free, falling into the gaping mouth. Gwendolyn hoped Starling had not been on one of them.

Then she had an idea. "Don't move!" she yelled. She pulled off his scarf and tied his hands to the railing, but there was no way the scarf would hold long enough for her to get the pistol. Instead, she climbed over the rail and leaned out, holding onto the thin metal bar with one hand, drawing her dagger with the other.

She stared at the churning black ocean. She could see the aft end of the ship now, shadows spread across it like a web of coral. Her knees shook with fear, but she had no time for that now.

"Gwendolyn, leave me, grab the pistol!"

"No!" she yelled. She leaned out until she could hack at the shadow that clutched Sparrow's ankle. Once, twice, thrice she struck, and the shadow parted.

"Hurry!" She reached down to untie his hands. "Climb back up!"

"I will, now–"

There was an explosion from the engines and the ship lurched again. Gwendolyn slipped and fell. She twisted and managed to grab Sparrow's leg. She slammed into the side of the ship, barely managing to hold on.

She saw the tentacles tear into the *Endeavour*, saw crew members fall, flailing. They looked like little specks of color that vanished into the darkness.

There was another bang, and the Pistola Luminant came loose. Gwendolyn watched it, and time slowed for her again, magnifying every agonizing detail as the pistol tumbled off the edge of the ship.

She looked up at Sparrow, who was still dangling by his yellow scarf. For an endless moment, his brown eyes met her green ones. He seemed to read her mind, and shook his head at her, his mouth forming the word *no*, though she could not hear him over the sound of the ship tearing apart.

But again, she had no choice. Gwendolyn let go. Sparrow hung helpless, a look of shock and horror spreading across his face, but in moments he was just a blurry speck.

The wind tore at her clothes. She might have been screaming, she couldn't tell through the roar of the wind. Her stomach was in her throat, her mouth tasted like acid, and the noxious stench of the storm invaded her nose. And still she fell.

She looked for the golden pistol, and spotted it spinning toward the clouds below. She tucked her arms to her side as she'd seen the Wasp-jumping pirates do, and she shot forward. The glittering pistol came closer, just out of reach.

Her hair whipped painfully at her face. She grabbed for the pistol, but her finger only brushed the nozzle, sending it tumbling away. She reached, stretching, straining, and managed to grab the pearl grip.

Another loud *bang* made her look back. Above her, the *Lucrative Endeavour* struggled against the monstrous black hand. There was an explosion from the propellers, and the shadows tore off its enormous wings. The entire ship broke apart and was ripped to pieces by clawed tentacles, shredding crew and wreckage alike.

As Gwendolyn's only two friends vanished in a puff of dust, she felt her heart crumble as well.

Below, the clouds rushed to meet her, waving eager tentacles. The fanged mouth opened in a grin that stretched for miles. She gritted her teeth and pointed the Pistola Luminant down its throat.

She forced herself to block out the sounds, the rushing wind, the pain inside. She took a deep breath, gathering the storm of thoughts within her, channeling them, sending them into the magical weapon. She imagined that fanged mouth splitting open, shattering into a thousand shards of black glass like the Faceless Gentlemen.

She shouted into the wind. "Once upon a time, there was a girl named Gwendolyn!" The wind tore her words away, but she persisted. "And she was tired of always making things worse! And losing everything that mattered! And she would not let anyone else get hurt! And then one day, she fired her magical pistol, and she saved the world!"

A bolt of light erupted from the pistol, the force of it throwing her back and slowing her fall. She held the trigger, ignoring the pain in her arms as the pistol bucked and kicked. The beam of light tore into the fanged mouth, right down its shadowy gullet, cutting a swath of white in the blackness. Gwendolyn held on, riding the beam straight into the heart of the Abscess.

Then there was nothing but black smoke and rushing wind. She felt the sensation of being drained, as she had the day she'd met the Faceless Gentlemen, but now she gave of herself willingly. She poured herself into the pistol, and the beam poured into the clouds.

Then, cracks of white appeared. They surrounded her on all sides, growing and splintering. Cracks in the clouds, cracks in the shadow, cracks in the world. The universe itself was splitting open, the black clouds vanishing into the pure white light of day.

The white replaced the black, and she fell into the nothingness of the In-Between, her mind going as blank as her surroundings. Only one thought echoed inside her.

I'm all alone again.

Her vision dimmed, but she thought she could see a man standing in the nothingness. A dark man, tall and terrible. He reached for her. Then, there was a flash of blue, a swirl of hair, a rustle of leaves. She heard a scuffle, a woman cried out, and the dark man boomed like thunder.

And then, all was silent. Gwendolyn was no longer falling, but floating, suspended in an endless world of warm, white light, shimmering with colors just beyond her vision. The In-Between. She felt a gentle hand caress her hair. An unfamiliar voice whispered in her ear, a woman's voice, sweet and gentle.

"Well done, Gwendolyn. Well done."

CHAPTER TWENTY-SIX

A Most Unpleasant Homecoming

Tick . . . tick . . . tick . . .

After an eternity of silence, ticking filled her ears. Something soft and cool pressed against her back. The white world faded to a pale grey.

Gwendolyn realized that she was staring at her ceiling. She was in her bed, light streaming through her window, bedside clock ticking softly.

"Oh, no." She rolled over. "No, no, no!" She pounded her pillow with each word, as if it was responsible for bringing her here. She was in the City, in her own bedroom. But it might as well be a prison cell.

She wondered for a moment if the whole thing had been a dream, as most of us would when we wake up in our bed after a strange and terrible adventure. But when she threw back the covers, she saw her tattered green dress, smeared with the dirt and grime of another world. Her hands went to her head and found a pair of goggles nestled in the tangles. So, not a dream at all.

Her friends. They needed her. Or were they already gone? She had come home like she wanted, but it was *not* like she wanted, not like this. We might say that the grass is always greener on the other side, if the "grass" in this situation was really "people who needed Gwendolyn's help." Always out of reach.

She saw her bag leaning against the nightstand, and felt a burst of hope. She snatched it up and shook it out. Onto the bed fell a red book and a blue gem the size of her fist. Her eyes widened with surprise.

"You're no dream," she said as she lifted the Figment. The two capital *G's* shimmered back at her. How had it gotten in her bag? Had she recovered it somehow, in the In-Between?

She opened *Kolonius Thrash*, looking for some clue or explanation, but the sight that met her eyes was like ice in her veins. Every page was blank, even the cover. Not one spot of ink.

She had been too late.

She rushed to her desk and flipped open her sketchbook, to the picture of Sparrow and Starling. Or where the picture should have been. But there was only a blank page. The Abscess had taken them as well.

Your fault, stupid girl, she remembered, wincing to think how Sparrow would scold her for saying it. *It was all up to me, and I failed.* "Sparrow and Starling, darrow and darling," she sang in a soft, empty voice.

The shock of loss affects everyone differently. But the initial feeling is usually one of numbness. Gwendolyn sat on the bed, her insides as blank as her book. That worried her. *I've killed my friends,* she thought. *Shouldn't I feel something? Or do all murderers feel cold and empty?* She looked deep inside, but it was as though her heart had touched one of the crystals at the Coves.

She flung the sketchbook across the room. That was something, at least. Anger was better than nothing. Rage leapt like a wild animal in her chest. She wanted to jump, to stomp, to scream. She had destroyed the Abscess, blasted the Mister Men to pieces, and there was no one left for her to be mad *at.* She looked at the blank book, wanted to tear the pages out, rip them into tiny shreds and eat the pieces.

She had to see it for herself. She'd take the Figment to the Hall of Records, she'd claw at the walls until her fingers bled if she had to—

"Gwendolyn?"

She shrieked in surprise. Mother stood at the door, smartly dressed in a cream-colored blouse and black skirt, busily putting her hair in its bun.

"Oh. Sorry to startle you," Mother said through a mouth full of hairpins. "You'd better—what have you been into? You're filthy! And what are you wearing?"

Gwendolyn looked down at her green self. "Uh, it's a dress." How long had she been gone? Had they noticed her missing?

Mother rolled her eyes, and Gwendolyn thought she saw a flash of blue in them, brighter than their natural blue. "I can see that, but where did you get it? It's lovely, it's so . . . colorful. Why haven't I ever thought to buy you something colorful before?"

she murmured. She swept in and examined it, running the hem through her fingers, feeling the embroidered lilies. "Where did you find this?"

"The Mainspring Marketplace. A woman gave it to me." Saying it out loud nearly made her burst into tears.

Mother looked at her with a twinkle of amusement. "Ah. Another one of your imaginings. Well, you can tell me the whole thing on the way to the School. You'll have to hurry or we'll be late.

"W-what?" she stammered. "School?" The word seemed an alien thing in her mouth.

"Yes, Gwendolyn, the School. You *are* going, and I have neither time nor energy for this argument again. I don't suppose you have time to clean yourself up proper either. Dreadful, but there's nothing to be done. Be downstairs in five minutes. At least do something about your hair. I don't have time to braid it today." She tossed a headband onto Gwendolyn's bed and breezed out of the room, closing the door behind her.

Gwendolyn moved automatically, routine taking over while her mind whirled in pain and sadness and confusion, barely registering how strange Mother was acting. Or rather, how normal, in the face of everything. She felt herself strip off the faithful dress that had seen her through her adventures in Tohk, reaching for her starched and pressed school uniform. Then she stopped.

Something red in the closet broke through the fog of emotion. The dress she had transformed–how many nights ago had it been?—the same color as Sparrow's apple. She put that on instead, and the School would just have to deal with it.

Some part of her finished dressing and packing her bag, and she took a moment to collect her treasures, the blank book, and the Figment. She realized that she'd lost the Pistola Luminant, and even her small dagger. She'd lost everything. She grabbed her sketchbook with the now-blank picture of Sparrow and Starling. She couldn't leave them, even if they were already gone.

Especially if they were already gone.

Her body followed well-remembered patterns, not waiting for any conscious command, while her mind skittered about in search of something to grab hold of. School today. She was getting dizzy just trying to process everything, but she could focus on that much.

She looked at her hair in the mirror, an absolute terror of wild curls. She reluctantly took off Starling's goggles, snorted at the headband her mother had left, and stormed out.

~~~

"Look at you now," Mother said admiringly as she came downstairs. She was puttering around the living room, and Father was in his chair with his paper and coffee. "Is this another mysterious dress from the, the Mainland Market? Or did you get it from your badger friend, the one you wanted to have tea with?"

Father chuckled. "Tea with a badger? Well, I never."

Gwendolyn gaped at her. "What?"

"Oh, you were going on about it before you ran into that awful woman yesterday. Or was it the day before?"
~~~

Gwendolyn remembered, but she was utterly gobsmacked that her mother did. As her mother's gaze grew distant, Gwendolyn saw it again, for sure this time: a sparkle of blue. And she wondered how much her mother remembered of the time she'd been gone.

"Perhaps this is like the time she wore her shoes on her hands and declared it was the first annual Upside-Downy Day," said Father.

Gwendolyn actually blushed a little at that. She had been only eight, after all. She had grown at least several years over the past few days. "Well, I uh, didn't have any clean uniforms."

Mother gave her a sideways look. "Well, if they weren't all wadded up on the floor of your closet, and in the laundry like they were *supposed* to be . . ."

Father turned the page on his paper. "You look lovely, Bless. I daresay that stuffy old School could use a bit of a shake-up. Hasn't changed a whit since I was there, and lord knows there was enough that needed changing even back then. It'll give Mr. Percival a fit, that's for sure."

"Come along," Mother said. "You can tell me all about your new wardrobe on the way." And out they went.

~~~

Mother took her down the street, but there were no further questions as they walked, for which Gwendolyn was grateful. And they hadn't even seemed to notice that Gwendolyn had been missing at all, which Gwendolyn herself was *certainly* not going to mention.
~~~

The City seemed to mock her with its dullness, its identical grey skyscrapers the complete opposite of the colorful towers of Copernium. No more Sparrow and Starling, only Cecilia Forthright and Tommy Ungeroot. The thought turned her stomach.

But the day felt lighter, somehow. Perhaps the clouds weren't as thick. There seemed to be fewer people on the street, and the ones she saw seemed lost, directionless. Not the normal determined hustle of the morning commute.

"Here we are. Go on now." Mother gave her a nudge.

Gwendolyn looked up in shock. They were at the School already. She felt something snap inside, surprised she had anything left to break.

Suddenly, she hugged her mother, like she was a little girl again, though after all her adventures one could hardly have called her "little." She had never wanted to grow up, but adventure and loss seemed to have left her little choice in the matter. Still, mothers should be given proper hugs at any age, and Gwendolyn made the most of this one.

She had the urge to tell her mother everything, every last unbelievable detail. *I've been to another world, seen marvelous people and places. I tried to save them all, but I failed so completely.*

All that came out was a weak "I love you."

Mother was surprised by the embrace; that sort of thing simply was not done in the City, especially not in public. But she relaxed, and smiled. "I love you too, Bless. Sorry I'm not myself. Since you broke the Lambent yesterday . . . Or was it the day before? Strange." And there was that odd flicker of blue in her eyes again. "I've just been feeling . . . off. Oh well. Go on now, I'll pick you up after school and we'll find a new one. Don't think acting sweet will get you off the hook for smashing it." Her words were firm, but her tone was gentle, and she stroked Gwendolyn's filthy hair, some motherly part of her sensing her daughter's pain.

Gwendolyn nodded and broke away, trudging up the steps and through the doors of the School. Mother waved the whole time.

And for the first time in Gwendolyn's life in the City, something was different. At least, something that wasn't her. The hallways were not the usual silent, echoing corridors. They were a riot of noise and chaos. All the children were shouting and running in the halls, making the average school day misbehavior seem like mere child's play compared to this mayhem.

Gwendolyn felt a surge of terror. Something awful must be happening, like the way everyone had run screaming when she'd transformed poor Missy. Were the Faceless Gentlemen here? She had destroyed them!

But then she heard laughter, saw smiles on their faces, and knew something was *definitely* wrong, but it could not have been the Mister Men. For a moment, she forgot about the things she had lost, and ran up twelve flights of stairs crammed with crazed children to room 1253.

The classroom was a war zone, and the children had clearly been the winners. Some were standing on desks, some throwing paper across the room, some just sitting and talking. Mr. Percival looked to have completely surrendered, slumped over his desk with his arms over his head, cowering from the juvenile rioters.

She sighed. Whatever this was, she did not have the energy to deal with it right now. She tried to sneak through the adolescent jungle without attracting attention. But she hadn't taken two steps when Cecilia Forthright, tall, blonde, and horrible as ever, planted a palm squarely in her chest. "Uh-uh. Who said you could come in here, freak? This is *our* room now. And—oh my god, what are you wearing?" Her gang stood behind her, blocking Gwendolyn's path.

Gwendolyn looked Cecilia dead in the eye, her emerald ones boring into the older girl's pale blue. And instead of annoyance or anger, Gwendolyn found herself overwhelmed with a profound sense of could-not-possibly-care-less. She had fought pirates, ravenous beasts, and horrifying monsters, been threatened and shot at and flung to her death. There was not one thing that Cecilia-flipping-Forthright could do to bother her. Not even the slightest bit.

And Cecilia knew it.

Cecilia saw something in Gwendolyn's eyes. Something that scared her. She never in a thousand years could have told you what it was, but it rocked her back on her heels. It was the faraway look of someone who has been places and seen things. Cecilia, of course, did not even know there were places to see, and so it terrified her all the more.

Like all bullies, Cecilia picked on everyone to feel powerful, because she secretly worried that she was small and weak. When Cecilia saw the infinite gulf of the In-Between in Gwendolyn's eyes, and exactly how small she truly was, she saw a reflection of how small she felt inside herself. And that sort of truth can cut more deeply than a thousand words.

Gwendolyn only needed a single one. "Move."

Try as she might, Cecilia could not hold this red-headed witch's gaze. Her head dropped, and to her horror, her feet did as they were commanded and stepped aside.

And with that, Cecilia Forthright's power was broken as thoroughly as if Gwendolyn had charged in with sword drawn and lions roaring. Cecilia plopped down in her seat. The other Centrals had no idea what had just happened, but they could feel it, as children are pack animals and can detect such changes by instinct. They moved aside as well.

There was a time when such a victory would have thrilled Gwendolyn beyond words. But she found that she could not even care about this. Which, of course, is why it had worked.

Gwendolyn walked back to her seat, untouched by the raging chaos of the other children.

She sat down, whispered a soft hello to her desk, and sat quietly while she tried to figure out what was going on. The only other person in the room not going bonkers was Tommy Ungeroot. Like Gwendolyn, he sat at his desk quietly, which was unusual, and alone, which was not unusual.

"Tommy," Gwendolyn whispered.

He turned around. "Oh. You're back." He didn't sound entirely unpleased.

"Yes, I suppose I am. What in the world is happening?"

He grinned a gap-toothed grin. "Didn't you hear? It's the Lambents."

A drumbeat of dread started up in her. "What about the Lambents?"

"They ain't working." He held up the clear bead. "See? Nuffink." And nothing was what she saw. It might as well have been a large marble. "They all stopped yesterday, right in the middle of the afternoon. Teachers sent us home early, called it a 'technical difficulty.' They're outta their heads, don't know what to do with us now. The whole place has gone nuts. No one's listenin,' just doin' whatever they like."

"Then why are you all back here today?" Gwendolyn asked.

He grinned again. "Well, they ain't workin' at home, ain't they? Parents don't know what to do, neither. They don't want to deal with all this." He gestured to the class, which resembled a monkey exhibit at the zoo much more than it usually did. "So they sent us anyway. Get us out of their hair. Teachers are none too happy, but what are they gonna do? We've got 'em outnumbered."

The Lambents weren't working. Something stirred within her, under the layers of sadness and pain that had built up. Something that was almost like hope. It couldn't be a coincidence, right? She blasts the Mister Men, and the Abscess, or the Collector, or whatever they called it. And now the Lambents had gone dark.

"Tommy," she said, "I'm going to ask you something that will seem strange, but just humor me. Exactly how long have I been gone?"

He stared at her, puzzled. "How lo–" but something in Gwendolyn's stare must have stopped him. "Um, well, you weren't here yesterday, but nobody really noticed after all the mess with the Lambents. But you were here the day before that, when we got let out early. Wait. We got out early twice, didn't we? The Lambents yesterday, and before that it was because . . . er . . ."

"Because of Missy," Gwendolyn prompted.

"Right. Wait. Who?"

Gwendolyn sighed. "Never mind. Thank you." She leaned back in her chair to think.

One day. She'd only been gone one day, and her parents didn't remember it. But she had spent *three* in Tohk. Time must move differently between the worlds, she reasoned. Yesterday afternoon for them must have been when she had blown the Abscess apart with the Pistola Luminant. That must have been when the Lambents stopped working.

She had done it. The Lambents were dark. The Mister Men were gone, the Abscess destroyed. Stopping them in Tohk must have stopped them here as well. The Mister Men would never allow this sort of thing, all these changes, the School in chaos.

No more Lambents, all over the City. No more draining or erasing. Everyone was safe. Everyone was free.

She pulled the crimson book out of her bag. Well, not everyone, she thought.

At the front of the room, pencils were flying through the air, and one of them struck Mr. Percival squarely on his bald head. He shot up. "All right!" he roared in his reedy voice. "That is enough! Everyone, sit down!"

The class did not sit, but it did freeze. He'd never yelled like *that* before.

"No more, I tell you! We will sit down, and do this the old fashioned way! We will pull out our lists, and we will memorize them, and we will recite them, and we will have some order until the Lambents are working again, and everything will go back to normal!"

Gwendolyn looked at the small glass beads on some of the other desks. She looked down at the book, blank in her hands. And she had another idea.

Gwendolyn Gray said, "No."

"Is there a problem, Ms. Gray?" Mr. Percival said in a tone that indicated there most certainly should not be. Students turned to look at her.

Gwendolyn said it louder. "No, we won't. We aren't going to go back to normal. Normal is awful. What we need is something different."

From the two girls next to her, she heard a snort and a very unladylike comment about her hair. She whirled on them with a withering glare, and the two fell silent immediately.

Gwendolyn stood. "Why do you all do this?" she roared. She grabbed the Lambent from Tommy and strode around the room. "These things are horrible, and empty! And that's what it makes you! Empty!" She smashed the Lambent on the floor and knocked over Vivian Coleridge's desk for good measure. The students gasped.

Mr. Percival was turning red, seeing his fragile control slipping away again. "Ms. Gray! Sit down! This kind of behavior—"

"Is exactly what we need! Time to wake up, children!" She went back to her seat, reached into her bag, climbed on top of her desk, and held the Figment up for all to see. "You spend all day staring at those worthless things and mocking anyone who has the slightest idea of their own. But there is so much more. There are whole other worlds out there, and you're wasting the one we have. The City doesn't have to be grey and dull and boring. It can be wonderful!" she said.

The Figment flared to life and washed the room in blue, shining like a star.

She stood tall and proud on top of her desk, Figment thrust in the air like the sword of a mighty warrior, a mythical heroine commanding her troops. *For Kolonius,* she thought. *For Starling. For Sparrow.*

And then, something truly marvelous happened. Every Lambent in the room lit up. But not the cold and empty light of the Mister Men—they shone a bright, gorgeous blue. Gwendolyn remembered Professor Zangetsky and his Clockwork Phantasmagoria.

The classroom shimmered, and vanished.

CHAPTER TWENTY-SEVEN

. . . Must Always End

The students cried out in surprise. Walls and desks were gone, and the class was soaring over a lavender sea topped with patches of yellow spice. Two suns loomed on the horizon, painting the sky with a rainbow of colors.

Gwendolyn held the Figment aloft, guiding them through the image, clearer and more real than the ones from the professor's simple projector. She could smell the spices, feel the ocean breeze on her face. She poured herself into the images, willing them to life. It was exhausting, but she kept going. She would not let the Abscess have the last word. Because she realized something: The Faceless Gentlemen had never said they were erasing Tohk. They were *collecting* it. And all Gwendolyn needed to do was bring it back.

She changed the scene. They left the ocean, and soared over the Violet Veldt, Tohk's purple grasslands, hopping with field mites. She took them to the Coves, dark and foreboding, covered in spectacular glowing crystals. To the Marauder's Mouth, with its rickety walkways strung like tangled Christmas lights in the massive cave. And she flew them to Copernium itself, soaring over its proud towers, domes, gardens. People bustled along its streets, zipped on pneumos, and flew ships of all kinds.

The class was silent, floating along beside her. Most of them gaped in amazement, but some looked utterly terrified. Gwendolyn tried to make the images as real as possible. The Abscess was the Collector, after all, and she tried to pull the city back from its collection the way she had pulled the Mister Men into Tohk. And unlike Tohk, where she felt that strange emptiness when she tried to create something new, here she felt full, flush with all the power that no one was using, and she poured every last ounce of it into bringing Tohk back. And even still, it might not have been enough.

But it was. And it didn't stop there. She took the class to the land of Baroom, where the gum-trees grew, and a furry, orange Falderal was cavorting with its dark-furred brethren through brightly colored lands of sugar and sweet. She took them to a forest filled with rabbits and foxes. She flew them to a flowery field of her own invention, and they landed in a meadow of eye-wateringly beautiful blossoms. A bright-blue sky hung above, with a brilliant yellow sun shining cheerfully. The meadow stretched for miles, and the forest was just visible on the horizon, surrounding the enormous clearing. In the center of the field was a small hill, on top of which grew a large tree, branches green and leafy in all the splendor of summer.

The students stared at the sun in wonder, feeling its warmth for the first time. Some knelt down and ran their hands through the neon petals that carpeted what used to be the classroom floor, struggling to believe their eyes. Others huddled together in fear, or tried to hide under desks they could no longer see.

It's working. They're seeing it!

And Gwendolyn Gray had another idea. She tried to focus, to will her thoughts through the Figment as she had the Pistola Luminant. She didn't have much energy left, but she gave up the last of it, felt that sense of draining again but gave freely of herself. It was taking more of her, she was growing weaker, she wouldn't be able to do it.

Then there was a blinding blue flash, a blaze of white, and all the Lambents burst in a shower of harmless sparkling fragments. All over the City, in fact. Every Lambent simultaneously exploded. But all Gwendolyn saw was white.

Gwendolyn's vision cleared. The meadow was gone. The Figment was dark. And all the Lambents lay in pieces on the classroom floor, just like the one she had smashed at her house.

And in the middle of the room stood Missy Cartblatt, pale and trembling as always, but whole, and real, and completely rabbit ear-less.

The students erupted again, with a volcanic intensity, roaring and cheering and shouting. "Children! Children, stop it, this instant!" Mr. Percival banged on his desk for attention. "This is completely unacceptable! I-I-I don't know what is happening, but I-I-I will not tolerate this, this . . . insanity! Out to the schoolyard, all of you! Out!"

They scrambled out to the hard-packed dirt of the schoolyard, joining other students who were already there and wandering about in absence of any adult authority.

A crowd surrounded Missy. Some wanted to know where she had been. Others seemed unaware she'd been missing at all. All of them remembered her. Missy, shy at the best of times, cringed from the attention. She said she didn't know what they were talking about. But she met Gwendolyn's eyes for a moment. They shared a look, and Missy gave her a small but grateful nod. Then she was swept away by the crowd.

Gwendolyn had her own crowd to deal with. They patted her on the back and shouted questions at her. Ian Haldrake gave her a thumbs-up. "That was amazing! Never seen anything like *that* in the Lambents before! Keep it up, Gwenny. Guys, you'll never guess what Gwendolyn did to the Lambents!" He ran off to tell students in other classes. It would be all over the School like wildfire. Who knew, by the end of the day, she could be more popular than Cecilia Forthright.

Great. Just what she always never wanted.

Others looked at her more warily. "What was that? How did she do that?" they whispered.

She didn't want the attention any more than Missy, and she was too tired to give answers. Eventually the students got bored of not getting any and separated into their usual groups, and Gwendolyn was able to sneak away. There was something she had to see.

She wandered to the single, scraggly tree that grew in the corner, its branches permanently bare, where she ate her lonely lunch each day. For once, she didn't mind the solitude. She felt drained. She had brought her imagination to life—she had controlled it, shared it. She had even brought Missy back somehow. She supposed that wasn't too much different than bringing Criminy to life, though it had been a lot more difficult. But hopefully that wasn't all.

She pulled *Kolonius Thrash* out of her bag. Her fingers trembled as they opened it. But the sight that met her eyes nearly made her dance with joy. Words were flowing across its pages. Faster and faster, paragraphs, pages, chapters, all flooding back at once. Kolonius, Brunswick, Torin, Carsair! She followed the racing text to the back of the book. The map of Tohk was complete and whole once more, and she spotted the cog-shaped dot of Copernium. She looked at the cover where fresh gold letters glinted at her.

Kolonius Thrash and the Perilous Pirates

by Stanley Kirby

She opened her sketchbook as well and found a picture of two colorful children. They were back. It was all back. She did it! Her tired heart gave a leap. She smiled and brushed her fingers against the picture. *Sparrow and Starling, darrow and darling.*

Her grin froze. She had to get back to Tohk. She had to find them. All she had to do was take the Figment to the Hall of Records after school, use it to open the portal . . .

A shadow fell over her book. "What *was* that?" asked Tommy Ungeroot.

Gwendolyn blinked up at him. "What?"

"Those things you showed us, all that stuff. Where did it come from?"

Gwendolyn shrugged, and held up the book.

"And that is?"

"Well, what do you think?" she asked, not unkindly, but with genuine curiosity.

"Looks like a book, but I've never seen one like that a'fore. It's all," he cocked his head, "shiny. Mind if I sit here? That is, uh, if your tree don't mind."

Gwendolyn couldn't help but grin. "I'd ask him, but he probably wouldn't answer. I'm sure it's fine."

Tommy sat next to her. "So, um, what's in there, anyway? The book, I mean."

Her grin widened. He seemed so nervous. She handed it to him. "Take a look. But be careful. It's my very favorite."

He took the book with reverent awe and started flipping through it, seeming most interested in the illustrations. Gwendolyn just leaned back and looked up at the sky through the bare branches. She had never felt so tired. A soft breeze caressed her cheek, and she listened to the tree's waving branches and Tommy's rustling pages.

She couldn't stay here. No matter how tired she was, Sparrow and Starling were out there somewhere. She needed to use the Figment to get through the portal in the Hall of Records to find them.

But as she looked into the Figment, she saw that it was nearly empty now, just a fist-sized piece of clear crystal. The world did not shift colors like it had before. It looked disappointingly normal. She looked deeper, trying to find any spark of power, and saw a flicker of blue.

The blue grew and grew until she felt as if she'd fallen into it, tumbling down a deep pool of water. The tumbling stopped, and she found herself on warm, green grass underneath the sheltering leaves of a magnificent tree. Birds chirped. Sunlight dappled the ground in leafy patterns. And standing in front of her were the two people she wanted to see most in the world.

"Sparrow! Starling!" She leapt up and threw herself at them, and the three shared a long, huddled embrace.

"Hey there, girlie," Sparrow whispered.

"You did it," said Starling.

When they pulled apart, Gwendolyn glanced around. "What happened? Where are we? Where did you go?"

They were in her meadow of neon flowers, standing under the tree on the hill. At the horizon, Gwendolyn could see the line of trees forming a circle around them. The blue sky had turned a rich, warm gold, and the yellow sun was dipping low in the west.

Starling looked around. "Well, if we're anywhere, I suppose we're in your imagination."

Gwendolyn frowned. "So, this isn't real?"

Sparrow laughed, but it seemed oddly forced. "Ha! Who's to say what's real? But we're *here*. Hey, look over there, I think that's the forest where we first met."

She frowned. "No it isn't, you found me on the Edge, remember? You pushed me off a building."

He and Starling exchanged glances. "You chased us first," he said.

"But what happened on the ship?" Gwendolyn asked. "I fell

into the In-Between, and I heard this woman's voice, and I woke up at home, and Tohk was gone! How did I get back home? What happened?"

"You happened," Starling replied. "I don't know anything about any voice. After you jumped off the ship, everything went black. But you must have hurt the Abscess. It was weak enough that you were able to stop it while you were in the City and bring back Tohk from wherever the Collector took it. And the next thing we knew, we were here." She sounded surprisingly glum about that fact.

"Yes, but *then* what happened? How did I bring it all back, and why are we here? I still don't understand."

"Yes you do," said Sparrow, gently. "You just don't think you do."

Gwendolyn slapped his arm playfully, trying to lighten their moods. "What does that mean? Why are you both acting so sad? We won, didn't we? Now we can have all the adventures we wish. I've got the Figment! We can travel the worlds together! I'll come back through this afternoon and . . ." she trailed off, noticing their expressions.

Sparrow opened his mouth to speak, but nothing came out. His eyes were red.

Starling stepped in to help. "I'm afraid you can't, Gwendolyn. It doesn't work that way."

"What doesn't work what way? Quit hiding things and just tell me for once!" But she feared she didn't want the answer.

"Imagination," Sparrow choked out. "It's different now. Or you're different now, anyway."

Before Gwendolyn could respond, Starling hugged her tight. Gwendolyn was surprised at the show of affection from the girl who was always so careful and calculating.

"You were so brave. You rescued me, you stopped the Abscess, you saved the world. Both worlds, maybe." Starling held her at arm's length. "But it took a massive amount of energy. The pistol, the Figment. It drained you. You used up your power blasting the Mister Men, wounding the Abscess, tearing a literal hole in the universe, then bringing back Copernium and Missy and everything else. You don't have the power to imagine us into the City anymore. We can't stay."

"But if we use the portal, then—"

"You can't steer without the Figment, Gwendolyn," Sparrow said. "You may have used its power to somehow imagine where you wanted to go, but now it's drained as well. Even if you found a portal, you'd never find us or your home again. You'd be just another Castaway, tossed from one random world to the next."

"But you're here now! You found me when I needed you, and I still need you!"

"No, Gwendolyn," Sparrow said. "When you needed us, you *created* us. We came from you. And now, we're going. The Figment is already fading."

Sure enough, the sky was darkening. Gwendolyn stopped for a long, incredulous moment, studying the pair as if seeing them for the first time. Which, in a way, she was. "No, you told me where you come from, you got lost and couldn't find your way back."

Starling looked at her, the older girl's eyes sparkling with tears. “That’s the story you imagined for us, Gwendolyn, and it’s as true a story as Kolonius’s or any other. But we’re only here because you wished us to be.”

“No, no, no, I don’t believe it! You’re real, you’re not just something I made up, like Criminy! Or the Neyora! You’re here, you’re alive!”

Starling nodded. “Like Professor Zangetsky said. Ideas are wild things, and if you’re not careful, they take on a life of their own and run away from you. Just like Kolonius’s book was written by that Stanley Kirby person. It didn’t make Kolonius any less real.”

“You come from another world, that’s all! I would know, otherwise.”

“You *do* know otherwise,” Sparrow said, frustration breaking through the sadness. “We’re a part of you. You know everything we know. And you know that this is the truth.” His battered yellow scarf fluttered in the floral-scented breeze.

Gwendolyn felt as if her heart were going to tear into thirds. Or perhaps already had. “But you showed me so much. The things we’ve done, I could never have done on my own. I would have been lost without you. I *was* lost without you.” She could not bear the thought of losing them again, not now, not after everything.

Sparrow pushed past his sister and took Gwendolyn’s hand in both of his. “You are stronger than you think. Everything we know, we know because *you* were clever enough to know it. Everything we did was because *you* were brave enough to do it. But now you have to be brave enough for this last part. To walk out of here on your own.”

She sniffed. "So . . . so you're not real, then."

Starling shrugged. "Who gets to say what's real and what isn't?"

"I don't care, just don't go!"

"Gwendolyn, we're not even here right now," Sparrow choked. "Only in your mind. You don't have enough energy to create things anymore. You used it all bringing back Missy, not to mention an entire world. That takes a lot of strength. So no more Criminys, no more bunny ears. No more us. A small sacrifice for saving two worlds."

A sudden tumble forward, and her arms were around his neck.

"I don't want you to go," she sobbed into his wavy hair. "I . . . I love you."

She had said the words to her parents hundreds of times before, but now they felt strange and unfamiliar in her mouth.

Sparrow hugged her back. "Of course you do, Gwendolyn. I'm literally the boy of your dreams." He leaned in closer. "But you know what? I love you too," he whispered, his lips brushing her ear. It tickled, and Gwendolyn giggled a little in spite of herself.

And then he kissed her. Long and warm and wonderful. Gwendolyn had never felt something so utterly fantastic, soft and fluttering and all sorts of things she had no name for. He wrapped her tightly in his arms, and they were together. For once, time was kind, and the moment seemed to stretch on forever. Gwendolyn dearly wished it would.

Starling took a sudden and intense interest in the bark on the tree.

"I don't want to go either," he whispered, pulling away. "But we'll never really be gone. I *did* promise. You created us, and we will always be with you." He tapped two fingers against her heart and smiled as a tear rolled down his cheek. "Right here."

"That is the corniest nonsense I've ever heard, and it really doesn't make me feel any better." Gwendolyn brushed away a tear of her own but couldn't keep from smiling back. It *did* help. A little. "Can't we find a way to go back to how it was? On the ship, looking for pirates and adventure?"

Starling put a hand on her shoulder. "You can never go back, Gwendolyn. All we can ever do is choose how we move forward. We're sorry we didn't tell you. You weren't ready to know until now, and so *we* didn't know until now either. But it's time for us to go."

"I, um, I have your goggles," she added lamely. "I didn't exactly bring them with me."

Starling smiled. "Keep 'em. I'll make some more." She leaned forward, planted a soft kiss on Gwendolyn's brow, and brushed a lock of fiery hair away from her face.

Gwendolyn was trying to be strong, but she could bear it no more, and warm tears ran down her cheeks. "Goodbye, Starling. Goodbye, Sparrow. I—" But her voice gave out in a ragged squeak.

Sparrow took her by the hand. "It's all right. We know. Here, I want to show you something." He pointed over her shoulder. "Look there. Toward the sun."

She turned and saw it setting over the distant forest, all orange and yellow and swollen.

"I see it. It's very pretty. What about it?" She turned back, but the two of them were gone, and Gwendolyn was alone, with nothing but the tree for company.

There was a flutter of movement, and she looked up to see two small birds winging their way toward the sunset. She heard a brief burst of birdsong on the wind.

Sparrow and Starling, darrow and darling, she thought. *Fly home, little birds.*

She stood under that tree for a long time. She didn't know what to do. She didn't want to do anything. So she simply stared at the golden sky.

And as she stared, the sky seemed to pull away from her, shrinking and fading until she found herself looking at grey clouds through bare, spindly branches. She looked down. The Figment was completely dark now, nothing but clear glass. Even her initials had faded.

She felt lost, adrift at sea. She wanted to cry again, but if she started she might never ever stop. She refused. She would not let her classmates see her cry, not here.

After all, she was not a little girl anymore.

What now? Mother would pick her up at the end of the day, take her home. She'd probably go straight to bed, where she'd cry herself to sleep, only to do it all again the next day. And the next. Maybe it would get easier. Probably not.

And then there was the City. No more Lambents. She had destroyed them, all of them, she suspected. What would that do in the long run? More questions sprang to mind. The Wall—what lay on the other side? And those two she had seen when she fell from the ship—the dark man, and the woman with the gentle voice. And there was still the whole mystery of the Collector to solve. She had hurt him, Starling said, but who was he, and what did he want? Was he gone for good? One way or another, Gwendolyn Gray knew that her troubles were far from over.

"Gwendolyn?" Tommy said.

She jerked and sat up. She had completely forgotten he was there. "Err, yes?" She rubbed her eyes, which were wet.

"I, um . . . your dress. It's pretty. Same color as this book."

She looked down. It was indeed. She focused on the dress, thinking of the brilliant blue of the Figment, and *willed* the dress to change color, but it remained as stubbornly unchanged as her shoes had in the marketplace. Even such a simple thing was beyond her now. She was empty.

"What's a *pie-rate?*" Tommy pointed to the book.

She snorted, and couldn't stop the smile that spread across her face. It hurt a little. "A *pirate* is sort of like a robber, someone who steals things, only on ships, you know, boats, and they sail around and . . ." She stopped. "I tell you what, why don't you just start reading from the beginning, and I'll explain as we go."

"Oh, all right then." He turned back to the first page. "Ko . . . Ko-lo-nye-oos . . ."

"*Ko-lo-nee-uhss,*" she corrected.

He squinted. "You sure?"

She grinned. "Yes, fairly sure."

"Kolonius. Thrash. And the peri . . . peri-loose . . ."

"*Perilous*. It means dangerous."

"*Kolonius Thrash and the Perilous Pirates*. Robber-people, right? *By Stanley Kirby. Chapter One.*"

Gwendolyn lay back in the dirt, arms behind her head, helping every now and then. She was only half paying attention.

Her friends were gone. She couldn't get back to Tohk, and they probably wouldn't be there in any case. She was all alone again.

Then she looked over at Tommy, struggling to read the thick, red book.

No. Perhaps not quite as alone as all that.

And she felt, at least for the moment, a little better. She had won, after all. Hadn't she? She had saved Tohk, and the City. Incited riots in the School. She smiled again. Rebellious Rioting Gwendolyn.

"Hey, Gwen?"

"Yes, Tommy?"

"What's this?"

She turned. Tommy was pointing at the inside of the back cover. The cover lining was a swirl of shades of red, but in the center was an embossed golden stamp of some kind.

"I don't know. I've never noticed it before." She leaned in closer.

Kolonius Thrash and the Perilous Pirates

By Stanley Kirby

328A5H

If found, please return to

The Library of All Wonder

"What's a *lib-erry*?" Tommy asked.

Gwendolyn frowned in thought. "I don't know." She looked

down at the Figment, but it was cold and unhelpful. She was much too tired to worry about it now. "Just keep reading."

She lay back again and looked into the branches of the scraggly tree, hoping to see her two little birds, the red one with a yellow stripe at its throat, the larger one with bits of shimmering blue and orange. But the branches were as empty and barren as they had always been.

No, wait, not quite. Something caught her eye. Something small, so high up in the tree that anyone else would have missed it. But Gwendolyn, after all, was a clever noticer.

There, on the very tip of the highest branch, grew a single, impossible, emerald leaf.

And So Ends

The Marvelous Adventures of

GWENDOLYN GRAY

ACKNOWLEDGMENTS AND APOLOGIES

Special thanks to my wonderful wife, Kori. I love you, Kitty. Sorry for waking you up at ungodly hours with my clacking. And to Theodore, who makes every day so much more fun. We'll have to have that badger tea party soon. Sorry you're probably still too young to read this.

To Mom and Dad and Grammy, who always said I'd do something like this. Sorry it took so long.

To the Amazing Caroline, Editor of My Dreams (now her official title), who understands my little girl better than anybody else. Thank you for plucking her out of obscurity and helping me polish her off. Sorry I'm a glutton for notes. To the rest of the awesome team at Jolly Fish Press and North Star Editions for making this a real thing I can hold in my hands and wave at people like a crazy person.

To all my students, who've had to hear me blabber about this for years and whose enraptured faces kept me going when I wanted to quit. You all asked if you could be in the book, so here you are. Thanks to YOUR NAME HERE. Sorry for making some of you cry in class; it must have been terribly embarrassing. To those who had to listen when they were too cool to care: sorry, not sorry. And a special thanks to my very *favorite* student. (You know who you are.)

To Matt, for having my back from day one. To Andy at Scheer Hoffman Creative, for always listening to my stories and for his excellent photographs of me (one of which is probably on the next page or something—flip around, you'll find it). And to Nate, for his amazing illustrations back when this wasn't a book. Sorry for talking your ears off about my made-up nonsense.

To the #5amwritersclub, whose coffee-fueled Twitter rants remind me that I'm not the only maniac in the world. Sorry none of the donuts were real. And an outsized, major thanks to the Pitch Crit Crew, particularly my very first writing friend, Danielle; the amazing Aften; and the world's best cheerleader and critique partner, Jueneke. Sorry I can't do better than some acknowledgments, but you all live really far away.

And lastly, I'm sorry for the lies I just told, since I'm not really sorry at all.

ABOUT THE AUTHOR

B. A. Williamson is the overly caffeinated writer of *The Marvelous Adventures of Gwendolyn Gray*. When not doing battle with the demons in the typewriter, he can be found wandering Indianapolis with his family, singing in a tuxedo, or taming middle schoolers. He is a winner of the Eli Lilly Teacher Creativity Fellowship. Please direct all complaints and darkest secrets to @BAWrites on social media, or visit gwendolyngray.com.

DISCARDED BY
FREEPORT
MEMORIAL LIBRARY